Wormwood

T. A. Welton

Dedication

This book is dedicated to all those who believe in miracles.

About the Author

T. A. Welton lives in Oregon with her husband, children, and three fur babies. She has an MBA from Ana Maria College of Paxton, Massachusetts, and has worked as a CFO for many years in the advertising industry. She has always been a storyteller.

Chapter 1

It was hot and sticky inside the Wormwood House of God Church as Pastor Ezra Collins began to talk about the third angel. Jordy Hart was shifting in his seat, hoping to catch any breeze coming in through the window. His wife, Amelia, was using a little hand fan to stir the thick air, but it did little. Their youngest, Laura, or Petunia as they called her, was getting restless, trying to snatch a fly out of the air. Her older brother, Brian, looked on with annoyance. Jordy reached over to still Petunia's hands from swatting at the fly. Around him, he could hear other parents, trying to wrangle their restless children, just as they were.

"The third angel sounded his mighty trumpet," the pastor said, in a strong, steady voice that echoed through the rafters of the church. "A great star streaked through the night sky like a mighty torch passing over a third of the rivers and springs, turning the water bitter. Many people who drank from the bitter waters died. The star was called Wormwood. This is the prophecy. So, my good people, we end service today before our children melt. God Bless."

Outside on the steps, Pastor Ezra Collins greeted the departing congregation. When it was Jordy's turn, he nodded to the pastor, "That was a good sermon today, Pastor."

"A bit long for the little ones in this heat, I think." He laughed, chucking Petunia under the chin good-naturedly.

"Please come over to the house for Sunday dinner," Amelia offered. "We are having chicken with all the trimmings."

"I would be pleased to do so. Thank you, Amelia." He made a slight bow.

Jordy and his family walked down the stairs, giving other people in line a chance to see the pastor. Ever since the pastor lost his wife last year, everyone in Wormwood invited the pastor to come and eat on Sunday and Wednesday after services. It was the Christian thing to do. Today, it was the Hart's turn, and they did it with a welcoming heart.

Wormwood was a small town of two hundred and thirty-one people. And in Jordy's opinion, they were the best people on earth. He was born here and had not traveled much in his life other than to deliver his crops in the fall to the Paxton weighing yard. So, his opinion, admittedly, was a bit one-sided. But his father always said that you can judge a man's true nature by his actions. And there was not a stinker in the whole town.

Jordy turned the truck onto the long dirt driveway, frowning at the dust trail rising from behind as the tires kicked up the dirt. It had been a hot, dry spring, and summer was promising to follow up with more of the same. Life as a farmer was always at the mercy of the weather. He looked up into the clear, blue sky, hoping the man upstairs would send him a little rain soon for his crops.

When they pulled into the yard, Walter, Petunia's pet pig, was rooting around near Amelia's prized garden. "What did I tell you, young lady, about making sure that pig is secured?" Amelia scolded.

"Aw, Mom, he gets lonely." Petunia pouted.

As soon as the truck stopped, Amelia was out of the truck, shooing away the persistent pig. "Go help your mother with Walter," Jordy said to both his children. "Brian, go on, help your sister before your mother wants to cook Walter in a pot."

Petunia's eyes grew large, and she scurried out of the truck to chase down her wayward pig. Brian followed with less enthusiasm. Jordy chuckled as he parked the truck by the barn before meeting Amelia on the steps of the house. He was followed onto the porch with a chorus of barking from the dogs that danced excitedly at his feet.

"I'm going to roast that pig if he steps one foot in my garden," Amelia blustered.

Jordy knew it was all talk. Walter was family. They had saved him after his mother died suddenly. He was just a tiny, helpless creature that bonded with Petunia. When it was time for the other piglets to go, Walter stayed behind. This was his home.

"I'm going in to start dinner," Amelia said, turning for the door.

Jordy was going to join her when they heard the roar of loud engines coming down the street, heading for town. Amelia paused at the door to wait and see what was happening. Four large trucks and several motorcycles came into view as they raced down the road, breaking the stillness in the air. Jordy watched as they approached from under the covered porch.

A familiar sensation washed over him—his mother had always called it "Jordy's Tempest." The last time he'd felt this way was five years ago, when a twister tore through his lower field. But this time, the feelings were more powerful than ever before. The tension grew inside him, coiling like a snake in his chest, as the trucks and motorcycles passed by the house. It became stronger and more pronounced. It filled him to his core, cutting off his oxygen, as he grabbed hold of the porch railing to steady himself. The hairs on the back of his neck raised as the dread settled into cold fear. Something bad was coming.

Chapter 2

"So, what do we know about them?" Jordy asked, as the pastor and his neighbor, Phil Miller, sat out on the porch after dinner.

"Jed Gilmore said, they are all held up at the Appleton's place."

Jordy frowned. "That place has been boarded up for, what, like five years now?"

"Yeah, Jed wanted to buy it as it borders his land. But after Gabe died, his family moved, and he couldn't get the kids to budge on settling on a reasonable price."

"We should take a ride over there and welcome the new people to town," Pastor Ezra suggested.

"I guess, we could do that," Jordy said, but he couldn't get past the spell that he had earlier. Something bad is coming, kept flickering in the back of his mind.

"They look like a rough crew," Phil said. "Lenny Dawson said that they came into his store as they were passing through and cleaned him out of beer and whiskey."

"They might be celebrating their good fortune in coming to live in Wormwood." Pastor Ezra smiled. "We should bring a welcome basket filled with food. Make them feel welcome and get off on the right footing with the strangers. Nothing makes a stranger into a friend better than being a good neighbor."

Jordy was of the opinion that they should gather torches and pitchforks to run their asses out of town. "I just wish we knew more about them. The Appleton place doesn't even have power or decent plumbing after being boarded up for five years. The roof is questionable and probably leaks. Are all those men going to live in that tiny farmhouse? There must be a couple dozen of them. It seems strange."

Pastor Ezra laughed. "Jordy, they may be simple folk that are not afraid of hard work. The barn on the Appleton place is spacious and in decent condition. Perhaps they are intending to live a simple life without creature comforts, while they fix up the place."

Jordy and Phil exchanged looks. "I guess that it wouldn't hurt to go over there and welcome them to town," Phil said. "We could all put something in the basket. At least we would have some idea of their intentions."

"Ok, let's go over there tomorrow," Jordy said, giving in under the pressure. "I'll have Amelia go around town and see who wants to contribute."

"I'm sure everyone will give something," Pastor Ezra said with a smile. "We can go tomorrow afternoon."

"Alright. I'll see if Bree will whip up a pie." Phil smiled.

"One taste of Bree's pie, and we will never get rid of them," Jordy said, laughing. He was warming to the idea.

"Well, it's time for me to head along home," Pastor Ezra said, as he gingerly rose from his chair. It was clear that the pastor was in pain as he stood holding on to the arm of the chair to steady himself. "My old bones are not what they used to be."

Jordy had noticed over the last year the pastor's limp was more pronounced and he shuffled his feet more when he walked. "I'll give you a ride home."

"No, I can give him a ride," Phil said. "I was planning to stop off at Finn's for a drink and see what the others in town are saying about the new people. Did you want to come, Jordy?"

Jordy shook his head. "Not tonight. I have work in the fields first thing tomorrow."

"It will be an interesting day tomorrow," Pastor Ezra said, taking one step at a time as he was leaving.

Jordy agreed with him on that. He still felt the gnawing doubt nibbling in the back of his mind. "See you tomorrow."

Chapter 3

Jordy met Cesar Sanchez in his field right after breakfast the next morning. Cesar's son, Laz, was already walking the rows, with a hoe in his hand, yanking out weeds. Cesar was leaning on his hoe, looking down the rows with a critical eye.

"I know that look," Jordy said, coming up to stand next to him.

Cesar turned and glanced at Jordy with a faint smile curving his lips. "Laz is not happy. I had hoped that he would adjust. I was hoping to have him back to help me with the farm, but I think that he will re-enlist."

"He's got a taste of the world away from Wormwood."

"Yeah, small-town life must seem even smaller after spreading your wings and seeing the world where you can use a cell phone without it dropping your calls or go out to eat and have anything that strikes your fancy, instead of settling for the daily specials at Finns. You can walk the street, and blend into a sea of strangers instead of everyone knowing your name. I see the attraction."

Jordy nodded. "Give him time to sort it out."

Cesar sighed and looked around the field. "We need some rain. The crop is behind in growth by a couple of weeks." Reaching down, he picked up a handful of dirt and let it sift through his fingers. "So dry. It's stunting the growth."

"I know. Even with irrigation, it is only just getting by."

"Are you going to go drop off the welcome basket this afternoon?"

From the hooded eyes and Cesar's mouth set in a thin, flat line, Jordy knew that Cesar's feelings for the new people were the same as his. When you work shoulder-to-shoulder with a man every day, you understand his heart. "Yeah, I'm going."

"Me, too," Cesar grunted. "I don't have a good feeling about it."

"I know what you mean."

Cesar arched one bushy eyebrow. "What does your early warning system say?"

Cesar was one of the only people outside of his family that knew about Jordy's tempest. They had been working in the lower field, five years ago, when Jordy felt the ominous pull of one of his spells. He'd gone frantic, insisting they leave immediately. Cesar thought Jordy had snapped his cookie but followed him. They had barely escaped the field when the twister touched down. After that, Jordy had confided in Cesar about the spells, knowing his secret was safe.

"Nothing good will come of this."

"Hmm, agreed."

They worked until noon and quit to go clean up before heading to town. When Jordy got back to the house, Amelia was just finishing up the large gift basket going to the new people. "That looks good," Jordy said, placing a gentle kiss on her cheek,

"You stink, take a shower," she said wrinkling her nose, cringing away from him.

Jordy laughed, reaching for her, but Amelia laughed, avoiding his outstretched arms. "You are just no fun," Jordy pouted.

"I'm plenty of fun with a clean man." Amelia tossed back.

Jordy turned and reached for Petunia, sitting on the stool near the kitchen table. Petunia squealed and raced off the stool around the table to stand, laughing with her mother. "All the women in this house are no fun," he said, looking forlorn.

Jordy chuckled and walked off to the bathroom to shower. In twenty minutes, he returned to the kitchen and was rewarded with a hug from his wife. "Better?" he asked.

"Yes, totally kissable."

His son, Brian, was rolling his eyes, "You guys need to get a room."

"Yeah," Petunia agreed, placing her small hands on her hips, but then frowned. "Isn't the kitchen a room?"

They all laughed, and Jordy reached down to ruffle her hair. "Yes, sweetheart, the kitchen is a room."

"So, are you going over to see the new people?" Brian asked. "I heard they are weird."

"Who told you that?" Jordy asked, picking up the basket.

"All the kids at school say so." Brian shrugged.

"We should not judge people that we have yet to meet, Brian." Amelia pointed out.

"Yes, we need to give them a chance," Jordy said, but internally he agreed. The new people were weird.

Jordy put the basket in the backseat of the pickup and drove into town. Everyone was gathered by the fountain of the third angel at the center of town. Jordy parked next to Jed Gilmore's big truck and got out, taking the gift basket with him. Jed was in a serious conversation with Phil Miller when Jordy walked up. Jed's farmland bordered that of the new people. Jordy wondered if the conversation had to do with them.

"What's happening?" Jordy asked, reading the tense expressions on their faces.

"Jed was just saying how he found one of his fences cut, and he has one of his calves missing," Phil said, turning to Jordy.

"I repaired the fence, but Margie's calf is missing," Jed said, pushing back the visor of his ball cap.

"Maybe it wandered off," Jordy suggested.

Jed's face scrunched into a grimace. "And maybe it had help."

Pastor Ezra and Cesar walked up, interrupting them. "I see we have a lovely gift basket there. The town has done well to welcome the new people into our community." Pastor Ezra was pleased.

"Should we get this clambake over with?" Jed said. "I have work to do."

"Yes, of course," Pastor Ezra agreed.

Jed and Phil got into Jed's truck after helping Pastor Ezra, along with the gift basket into the backseat. Jordy and Cesar climbed into the back bed of the truck to take a seat up by the cab. Jordy got a feeling as they drove that this was not going to go as the good pastor hoped. In fact, there was a fluttering in his gut, that forewarned him of trouble.

Chapter 4

They turned off the road onto the Appleton farm's long, gravel driveway. The fields had long ago gone to seed and grew a tangled mix of grass and weeds behind the pasture fences. Jordy remembered when this was one of the nicer farms in town. The sky had grown dark and turbulent, almost a forewarning of what was to come. In the distance, Jordy heard a motorcycle revving its engine. Other than that, it was quiet, with only the sound of the gravel crunching under their tires. When the truck stopped halfway up the drive, Jordy and Cesar exchanged glances as they both frowned.

Jordy got to his feet and looked over the cab. "It appears the new people have put up a fence across the driveway."

Cesar joined Jordy looking over the cab of the truck. "Looks like they don't like company."

"Oh, I was hoping it was to keep them inside," Jordy said with an uneasy smile.

"Those men at the fence are armed," Cesar pointed out.

It was then that Jordy spotted the holstered guns on each of the hips of the two men standing at the gate. They looked tough, their eyes cold and fixed on him. Phil stepped out of the truck and walked toward them. Jordy couldn't make out the conversation, but he noticed one of the men resting his hand on the grip of his gun. The other man pulled out what appeared to be a two-way radio, speaking into it. Moments later, the distant rumble of motorcycles grew steadily louder.

Four motorcycle riders rode up to the gate and stopped. Phil was joined by Pastor Ezra still separated by the closed gate. Jordy and Cesar climbed out of the back of the truck. Jordy noticed that Jed stayed behind inside the truck. As they walked up to the gate, Jordy reached into the truck and retrieved the gift basket. There was a tense silence at the gate as the men all stared at one another. Jordy had the feeling the new people were sizing them up. Looking for weakness.

"I'm Pastor Ezra. We have come here to welcome you to our community." The pastor smiled and looked at Jordy.

"Yes, we brought you a gift basket." Jordy held the basket out to them.

The new people looked at each other, and then one of them, the tall man in the middle with the shrewd blue eyes, laughed, and the others followed, laughing with him. Jordy decided that the big man in the middle with the blue eyes was the leader.

The Bible says the devil will be disguised as a beautiful angel of light, and only when the mask drops away will the monster be revealed. For Jordy, he knew that he was looking at the devil with blue eyes or something remarkably close.

"I'm Evander. Thank you for the reception and gift basket." He gestured to one of his men to take the basket.

"We were hoping to come in and sit down," Pastor Ezra said. "We could talk and get to know each other."

"Sorry, Padre, not happening." Evander never got off his bike. "Now get in your truck and run along. I'll see you in town from time to time."

For his part, Pastor Ezra was not put off. "I understand, you are busy moving in and fixing the place up. Some other time, perhaps?"

Evander laughed. "Sure, like I said, I'll see you around town." He started his bike, and the others followed. The roar of the engines made it impossible to talk any further.

As they walked back to the truck, he saw the men helping themselves to the basket, stuffing pastries into their faces while pushing each other aside. It reminded Jordy of hungry dogs around a single bowl of food. As the truck pulled away, Jordy saw them pointing and laughing at them. To the new people, they were a joke.

"Well," Cesar said, "That went about the way that I thought it would."

"I was hoping for better, but it could have gone worse."

"I have a feeling worse is coming."

"Yeah, me too."

Chapter 5

The rain finally came, breaking the heatwave. Jordy sat outside beneath the covered porch, enjoying the smell of the rain and the gentle cool breeze. Amelia sat beside him, knitting a pink sweater for Petunia. "Are you going to tell me how it went with the new people today?" Amelia looked up at him.

Jordy shrugged. "There is not much to tell."

"Did they like the gift basket?" She put her knitting aside and turned to face him.

"They never let us pass through the gate that they erected. They enjoyed the basket, though." He remembered them ripping into it like wild, hungry dogs.

"Did they say anything? Where are they from? What are they planning?"

Jordy shook his head. "They took the basket and sent us on our way. We never made it passed the gate."

"Well, that was rude."

"We were not welcome there. They made it quite clear. The leader's name is Evander. Now you know as much as I do." Except they were armed. He left that part out.

"So now what?"

"Now we wait and see what they will do. I rather hope that they stay where they are. If I never see them again, I'd be fine with that."

"Still, it's odd. I saw a couple of women in town from their group. It was the same, they did not want anything to do with us, either. Bree said hi to them and they ignored her. There was a toughness about them, too. They pushed their carts down the aisle, shoving past anyone in their way, tossing things in the cart with no care at all. Strange."

"I guess we will see them in town from time to time. It's unavoidable. Let's just stick to ourselves and see what happens." This was just the beginning, Jordy thought. It will get worse. He felt it.

Chapter 6

J ordy was gassing up his truck when a small caravan with a truck and two SUVs passed through town. They were strangers. Hard looking men with dark eyes that seemed to look right through him. The truck was a small, unmarked box truck. A black GMC SUV with heavily tinted windows led the way with another following up from the rear. They were headed out of town, driving towards the new people's place.

Jed was standing by a pump, watching them, too. "There they go again. That is the third time this week."

Jordy glanced over at him. "What do you suppose they are carrying?"

"Something that takes armed guards."

"How do you know that they have armed guards?"

"I've been watching them. They drive up to the gate and they get out of the Jimmy's and talk to the guards at the gate. Then, they get back in their cars and drive up to the barn. They load the truck and then leave. Wash and repeat."

Jordy had just paid for the gas and was about to leave when he heard yelling. It was the Morrison girl, one of the new people was harassing her. Sheriff Clancy was already on his way over. As soon as he arrived, the guy turned on him, pulling a knife. Without hesitation, Jordy and Jed sprinted across the road. Jordy had no plan, but he was ready to jump in. Seeing he was outnumbered, the guy quickly dropped the knife, raising his hands in surrender.

The town had one jail cell in the back of the Sheriff's office. Sheriff Clancy nodded to Jed and Jordy as he cuffed the man. "What's your name, son?" Sheriff Clancy said as he seated him down on the curve.

"Conrad, and you would be smart to just let me go," he said, as his eyes ran hotly over Kelly Morrison.

Kelly stood trembling on the sidewalk. She was sixteen, and before today, had never witnessed anything like this. And neither had the town of Wormwood.

"Kelly, go along home," Jordy said softly, gently patting her on the shoulder.

Kelly nodded, still looking shaken. She walked away, not taking her eyes from Conrad out of fear that he would escape and come after her.

"Do you want to explain to me what was going on today?" Sheriff Clancy asked.

Conrad was in his early twenties with long dark hair and even darker eyes. He glared up at the sheriff. "None of your fucking business," he spat. "Now, this is going to go one of two ways, you are either going to let me go, and we call this a misunderstanding, or my boys are going to ride into town and stir up some shit. You want to be a hero, Sheriff?"

Sheriff Clancy smiled down at him. "I guess, I'll let you decide that while you cool your heels in jail."

"You are making a mistake." Conrad's stare was direct and steady.

"That may be so, young fella." Sheriff Clancy pulled Conrad to his feet and noticed the shoulder holster tucked under his leather jacket. "What do we have here?"

Conrad didn't answer, he just stared at Sheriff Clancy with unspent fury. When the sheriff reached inside his jacket to disarm him, Conrad turned with unexpected skill and kicked Sheriff Clancy in the face, knocking him backward. Jed didn't hesitate, he punched Conrad in the face, sending him to his knees. Jordy went over to steady the sheriff.

Things were happening so fast that Jordy was trying to make sense of it. Jed and Jordy helped the sheriff escort Conrad to jail. All the way there, Conrad sent them promising glances filled with contempt as a slight trickle of blood coming from his nose dripped down his face. The town's people were gathering, watching as they walked to the Sheriff's office. In their faces, Jordy could read the fear and concern that matched his own. Jordy knew this was the beginning of something bigger. It was the catalyst that would uncork the bottle and let the evil spread.

Chapter 7

Jordy was sitting out on his porch the next night, having a glass of iced tea after working in the fields all day. It was a beautiful night with a full moon rising and the crickets serenading him from the tall grass at the edge of the driveway. His muscles were sore, and he was tired, but the knowledge that it was due from laboring on his crops eased his mind. There was something about putting in a long day working on what you loved. It was satisfying.

He spotted Phil walking up the driveway. Jordy frowned. It was late for a visit. It was true what they said about farmers being early to bed and early to rise. Most folks around here did the same. So, Phil coming up his driveway at nine o'clock was unusual.

"Hey, Jordy, I was hoping to find you out here. Can we talk?" Phil looked troubled.

"Sure, have a seat. Do you want an iced tea?" Jordy got the first stirrings of uneasiness.

Phil climbed the steps and sat down in a chair beside him. "No, I'm good."

"What's on your mind, Phil?"

"I was in town today standing outside of Winslow's Coffee Shop. Jed was telling us about what happened with Sheriff Clancy and Kelly Morrison.'

"Yes, I know, I was there."

"Jed said that this guy, Conrad. He was after Kelly, and there was a fight." Phil was looking at him.

"Yes, the guy pulled a knife and got into it with the sheriff."

"Yeah, and then Jed cleaned his clock by punching the punk in the nose."

"Yes, that is all true." Jordy was wondering where this was going. Was Phil trying to confirm what Jed told him?

Phil nodded. "So, we were standing there at Winslow's, drinking coffee, when Evander and two of his goons rode up on their bikes. They go inside the sheriff's office."

"I anticipated that would happen." Jordy sat up straighter, feeling this was going someplace that he was not going to like.

"Well, they come out with Conrad twenty minutes later. They were laughing when they came out. Conrad turns to Jed and points at him, cocking his thumb up like he was shooting a gun." Phil copied the gesture. "It was a threat."

"Then what happened?" Jordy felt the uneasiness increase in his gut.

"They rode out of town whooping and hollering. Jed was pissed. We went over to the Sheriff's office to ask what the hell had just happened. Why did he freaking let that little weasel go? This Conrad should see jail time for what he pulled."

"What did he say?" This wasn't good. None of it.

"Sheriff Clancy gave us some lame shit about Conrad being young and impulsive and that Evander promised to reign him in and keep him on the straight and narrow. Do you believe that?"

"We told him about how Conrad had threatened Jed not even a minute after his release. Do you know what he said?"

"I'm guessing it was nothing that you wanted to hear."

"You guessed right. He said that boys would be boys and dismissed us. He lectured us about having more tolerance for the new people."

"That sounds like a bucket load of shit." Jordy knew that tolerance and a dollar would just buy more shit.

"We want to have a meeting of the men in town and see what we can do. If the sheriff won't keep the peace, then we need to do it." Phil was fired up.

"Now hold on, Phil. It was just one incidence. I'm not siding with the sheriff, but we need to approach this cautiously." This was a powder keg looking to explode.

Phil sighed, running his fingers through his hair in frustration. "Maybe you are right. But I don't have a good feeling about this."

"Neither do I."

Chapter 8

Jordy and Cesar were sitting at Finn's, having a beer and playing a game of dominos with a few of the guys. Laz was beating them. "Is that any way to treat your father?" Cesar grumbled.

"All is fair in dominos," Laz said with a grin.

It was the first night that they had gone out since planting season. When they heard the roar of the motorcycles outside, they paused the game. "I think that we should wrap this up," Cesar said, looking over his shoulder at the door.

"Yeah, I need to be up early tomorrow to start the lower field," Jordy agreed.

"One more game," Laz said. "I'm winning."

Reluctantly, Cesar said. "Ok, one more game."

Six of the newcomers entered the tavern, settling into the seats along the wall by the windows. Jordy immediately recognized Evander and two of the others from their meeting at the gate during the gift basket exchange. As Evander broke away from the group and headed toward their table, a knot formed in Jordy's stomach.

Evander took the seat next to Jordy. "Dominos. Do you mind if I play?"

Jordy exchanged glances with Laz and Cesar. "Sure, you can play."

Evander smiled. "You know my name. Who are you?"

Jordy had a feeling that he knew who they were already. "I'm Jordy. And this is Cesar and Laz."

Evander nodded. "So, Jordy, you own that spread just outside of town?"

"Yes, that's right."

"And Cesar and Laz are your neighbors?" Evander was considering them. His cool blue eyes ran over them, almost akin to a snake's.

"Right again," Cesar said with an unreadable expression.

So, Jordy was right. Evander had done his homework, learning about the town. He would bet that he knew everyone. "So, you know that we are farmers. What do you do?"

Evander chuckled. "I'm a businessman. Just like you are."

Good, no answer, Jordy thought. "Why Wormwood?"

"I like it here. It's quiet." Evander shrugged his powerful shoulders.

The server came over to their table. "Can I get you another drink, Jordy?"

Evander answered before Jordy could. "I'd like to buy a round for everyone."

The server did not hide her surprise. "Yes, sir, coming up."

When the server left, Jordy said, "That is very generous of you, thank you."

"I'm a generous man to my friends." Evander tipped his head. "The food that was in the basket was very good. I was wondering if I could talk some of the ladies in town into doing some cooking for us. I would pay for everything, including a fair wage."

Dangling that in front of people in town would go a long way in mending fences, Jordy thought. "I would imagine that people would appreciate the offer. What are you looking for?"

"What do your wives cook for you? I'm a simple man, and I'm sure whatever they make, would make me happy."

"Well, I'm sure Esmae would love a little extra money doing what she loves to do most," Cesar said. "I will ask my wife."

Evander nodded and smiled. "What about you, Jordy? Do you think your wife would agree?"

"I would have to ask her." Jordy knew better than to agree without asking. Emilia wouldn't have it any other way.

"Good." When the drinks came, Evander placed his hand on Jordy's shoulder. "Jordy, can I have a word with you outside?"

Jordy resisted the urge to knock his hand away. There was something about Evander that didn't sit right with him. "Yes, of course."

Jordy followed Evander outside in the fading moonlight. Evander took a seat in one of the chairs at the end of the building meant for the lunch crowd. Jordy sat across from him. "What can I help you with?" Jordy got right to the point, not wishing to stay out here alone with him any longer than necessary.

"You are a simple man, Jordy?"

Jordy frowned. "I guess." Where was this going?

"An honest man."

"I like to think so." Evander was watching him with a stare that was almost unsettling.

"A man that would do anything for his friends and family."

Jordy nodded. "Yes."

"I would like us to become friends."

Not likely, Jordy thought. "Why?"

"I'm a stranger here. I think that I could use a friend here that I could trust. A man that can help me adjust to Wormwood."

Use was the word that stood out the most to Jordy. "Why me?"

"Because I value honesty above all else. I am a very good judge of character. I sense you are a good man."

There were a lot of things Jordy wanted to say but didn't. "Let's get to the point. What is it that you want?"

Evander threw back his head and laughed. "I see that you are not a man that values any pretense. All right, I want your guidance to keep the peace between my people and the town's people. We got off to a rocky start with the brush-up with Conrad."

"That is an understatement. Conrad was out of control. Are you able to control your people?"

There was a flare of anger in his eyes before it was extinguished. "About as well as you can control the town's people."

Beneath the biker façade and leather, there was a calculating, intelligent mind, Jordy thought. "Good point," Jordy conceded.

"So, this is my proposal, we spend a little time getting to know each other so that you can see that I am not such a bad guy."

"And in return for this friendship?" Jordy was suspicious. His gut was still winding as his tempest flared.

"You tell me if there is a problem."

"I'll think about it." Jordy was not going to just commit to it. He needed to think about it more.

"Good," Zander said, rising from his chair. "I'll swing by your place tomorrow and talk to you and Cesar about cooking for me. At the same time, I would like to meet the wives and see how they feel about it. I really hope they agree. I can't take much more of what my guys make, and the daily specials here are subpar at best."

The idea of him coming to his home and meeting his family was repulsive. "All right. I'm done in the fields by four o'clock most days."

"Then let's say around five."

Without waiting for a response, he turned and walked back into Finn's, leaving Jordy to trail behind. But any dread Jordy had about enduring more of his company vanished when Evander rounded up his group of misfits and headed for the door. Moments later, there was the roar of motorcycles, and they were gone, racing down Main Street.

People inside Finn's were talking amongst themselves as Jordy sat down beside Cesar. "So, what was that?" Cesar asked.

"He is coming to my house tomorrow at five to see about his food offer. He wants to meet our wives." Jordy finished his drink in one large gulp.

Cesar chuckled. "I'm not going to lie; it would be nice to have a little extra money."

"Yeah, but I don't trust him."

"Take his money," Laz said. "Besides, you can keep tabs on him with this."

That was true. Jordy didn't mention the whole friendship offer. It was still too repulsive to say aloud.

Chapter 9

Normally, an offer of a side hustle like Evander was offering would be welcomed. Emilia and Esmae were inside, cooking food for their guests, that would arrive soon. But as Jordy sat under his covered porch with Laz and Cesar, his gut was tied into a knot. His tempest was brewing, warning of imminent danger.

"I hope he likes the food," Cesar said, sipping his iced tea. Esmae is excited, spending the money before we even have it.

Laz shrugged. "What choice does he have? Emilia and Mom are the best cooks in town. Bree works at the school, so she is out of the running. And Peggy Burrows can't cook a decent meal unless he wants to live on only bread and fried eggs."

Cesar chuckled. "I always sidestep her offerings at the Fourth of July festival. Besides, there is always great barbeque and chili there." Cesar turned to Jordy. "You are quiet tonight, my friend."

"I'm just thinking." It was not a lie. His mind was consumed with all the what-ifs.

"You think too much. Relax. Be more like me. Wait and see."

Jordy knew that Cesar was right, but he couldn't help it. Evander made him uneasy. "I'm working on it," He smiled.

The jeep pulled up the driveway in a slow crawl. Inside was Evander and three leather-clad men riding with him. Their sharp eyes were scanning their surroundings as the jeep rolled up the gravel driveway. They were like sentinels watching to protect their evil master, Jordy mused. The knot in his gut twisted tighter. When they parked, Evander hopped out with his men, waving to them with a grin splitting his face.

"So, the big man arrives," Laz whispered.

"I hope he brought his checkbook," Cesar said with a deep chuckle.

"As long as that is all he brings," Jordy grumbled.

The three men stayed by the jeep as Evander bounded up the steps. "You guys look chill. Any chance of getting a glass of whatever you are having?"

Jordy rose to his feet and gestured to the picnic table on the lawn by the barn. "We have the picnic table all set up for you. The wives have been cooking up a storm. I'll run inside and see when the food is coming out. I'll grab you an iced tea while I'm checking."

Evander rocked back on the heels of his leather boots. "That sounds amazing. I didn't anticipate dinner. Wonderful."

Jordy did not say anything more but went into the house. He wondered what Evander expected. With such an offer, of course, the women would want to win the prize. It felt like manipulation. Jordy took down a tall glass and filled it with ice. "How much longer? Evander is outside on the porch." Jordy poured the tea over the ice.

Amelia snuck over to the window and peeked outside. "Wow, he's taller than I thought," she said, scurrying back to the tray that she and Esmae were loading with food. "Three minutes. Take our guests over to the picnic table."

Jordy nodded, heading back to the door, glass in hand. When he got outside, Evander was casually leaning against the railing. When Evander reached for the glass, their fingers touched, and Jordy restrained from flinching. What was it about this man that had him so on edge? He's dealt with assholes in the past, but this guy just had all his senses heightened. It was like he was a poisonous snake.

Jordy gestured to the picnic table. "The ladies are ready to bring out the food. Why don't you and your friends join us at the picnic table."

They started walking to the table. "Oh, they won't be eating," Evander said, looking at the men standing by the jeep.

They sat down. Laz's attention was still on the men by the jeep. "They work for you?"

Evander nodded, taking a seat across from Jordy, Cesar, and Laz. "They work as security, among other things. You look fit. Ever think about working security?"

Laz shook his head. "I'm a farmer like my father."

Cesar looked at his son, the pride shining in his eyes. "We have been farmers for generations."

"It is an honorable craft." Evander picked up his drink, still studying Laz from over the rim of his glass.

"Where are you from originally?" Jordy asked.

Evander's attention shifted to Jordy. "Here and there. I lived abroad for a time. Now I'm here."

Jordy couldn't help but notice that the question had never truly been answered. Before he could press further, Amilia and Esmae appeared with two trays piled high with food. Jordy and Cesar met them halfway, relieving them of the heavy loads. One tray held roast chicken, potatoes, collard greens, and sweet rolls. The other was packed with Esmae's empanadas, enchiladas, tamales, and guacamole with all the fixings. Amilia followed with a chocolate cake. It was a feast.

Evander was not shy, helping himself to a little of everything. "This looks amazing, and I bet it tastes even better."

"I feel bad for your men having to stand there while we eat," Amelia said, looking over at them. "Can I make them up each a plate?"

Evander smiled in understanding. "I'm sure that they would appreciate it."

Amelia and Esmae rose from their chairs and fixed each man a plate of food. But before they could bring it to them, Evander motioned for his men to come to the table. "This is Oscar, Aiden, and Ethan. The ladies have decided you need to eat."

Each man nodded and said, "Thank you, Ma'am." As they took their plates.

There was a formality about it that was in stark contrast to the biker persona. Jordy watched, keeping a bland expression on his face. Something about this did not add up. Once the men walked back to the jeep, they stood there eating, but their eyes were trained on their surroundings. One man stood facing to the right, and the other was looking off to the left; the man in the middle watched Evander and occasionally glanced over his shoulder.

Evander pushed away his plate, rubbing his flat stomach. "Well, ladies, you have outdone yourselves. I'm assuming that some of this will go home with me?"

"Yes, we planned to send some of it back with you." Amelia chuckled.

Evander grinned. "Good, I have set up an account at the store so that you can pick up everything that you need there. Would a delivery twice a week be doable?"

Amelia and Esmae exchanged glances and nodded. "Yes, I think that we can manage that."

"Good," Evander said, reaching into his pocket, and taking out two envelopes. One for each. He slid it across the table to Esmae and Amelia.

Amelia looked up at him after opening the envelope. "This is too much…" she started to say.

Evander interrupted her, holding up his hand. "I pay for what people are worth. So, if we could pack this up, I really need to be going. Can you make sure some of that cake is in there? Wow, that was good."

Jordy was dying to know what was in the envelope, but judging by Amelia's face, it was a lot. Cesar and Jordy helped bring the trays to the house so they could pack up the food into the baskets. Amelia whispered into his ear. "Two thousand dollars."

Two thousand dollars for each Amelia and Esmae to cook a few meals seemed over the top. Not that Amelia wasn't worth it, she was. But for a stranger to pay that kind of money was crazy. Jordy thought Evander would pay no more than five hundred. That seemed more than a reasonable price. It bothered him. He felt like Evander was paying them off. For what, he didn't know.

Jordy, Cesar, and Laz sat on the porch after Evander left. "Those guys with Evander are ex-military," Laz said.

"How do you know?" Jordy asked, looking at him.

Laz snorted. "The holsters inside their jacket were unsnapped. Their posture is straight and alert. I've been around enough military personnel to recognize it. Did you notice the way they never stopped running surveillance on the areas? Those men are locked and loaded, ready to go."

"Now, why would a man living out here need to bring that much heat?" Cesar asked.

"That is a very good question," Jordy said. "It was the same as when we met Evander that first time at the gate. Those guys were armed guards, too."

"Evander seems like a nice enough fella, though," Cesar said.

Jordy shrugged. "I don't trust him."

"I guess that we will see in time," Cesar said.

Chapter 10

Cesar and Jordy had gone into town after working the fields to pick up replacement parts for their irrigation system. The rain had been a blessing, but it was not something they could count on to continue. Soon, it will become less and less frequent, and they will be dependent on the irrigation system or risk losing their crops.

They pulled into Hadley's Feed and Grain store. As they parked, Cesar turned to Jordy from the passenger seat. "I wonder what is happening over there?" He gestured to the Sheriff's office.

There was a small crowd gathered outside on the street in front of the Sheriff's office. "I don't know," Jordy said, feeling the first stirrings of uneasiness.

They parked in front of the store and went inside. Hadley's Feed and Grain catered to the farmers around town. It had everything from seeds to screwdrivers and everything in between. Jack Hadley was looking out the window at the crowd across the street. His face was screwed up into a frown before he turned to greet them. "What can I do for you?" He said with an easy smile.

"We need some parts." Jordy held up the parts that he was looking for.

"I need a couple of new sprinkler heads, too," Cesar added.

Jack glanced out the window one last time before coming around the counter. "I have everything you need back here."

"What is going on across the street?" Jordy asked as they followed behind.

Jack turned to them, his face creasing into another frown. "Kelly Morrison did not make it to school this morning. Her parents are worried sick. They are gathering up some people to go out looking for her. I'm planning to go after I close today. Dan Howard is bringing his dogs to search."

"Maybe she is just ditching school," Cesar said. "You know how teenagers can be."

Jack shook his head. "Maybe, but they found her backpack and bike by the side of the street. It doesn't look good. If she was ditching, why leave your bike and backpack behind?"

"Yeah, that sounds sketchy," Jordy agreed. He thought about his kids. If that happened, he would know it meant trouble.

"I hope we find her before dark. On your way out of town, can you look for her?" Jack was gathering the parts for them from the back.

"Will do," Jordy said. "I'll look around my place, too."

Cesar nodded solemnly. "Yeah, me too. I hope they find her."

Jordy's thoughts jumped to Conrad. He couldn't shake the suspicion that Conrad might be involved. The way he had looked at Kelly that day in town still gnawed at him—it wasn't just a glance; it felt like a silent promise that he'd be back for her.

Chapter 11

Amelia and Jordy sat on the porch having a glass of iced tea as they watched Petunia playing with Walter, her pet pig. Petunia was chasing him, and the little pig scampered across the yard with Petunia hot on his heels. Jordy and Amelia turned and looked at each other, laughing. His son, Brian, was sitting at the end of the porch, strumming his guitar, when he stopped and looked at his parents.

"Do you think that they will find Kelly?" Brian asked.

There was a sadness in his son's eyes that Jordy had never seen before. He looked so mature, sitting there with his guitar balanced on his knee. "I hope so, son," Jordy said.

He and Cesar had looked for Kelly on their way home. After he got home, he took out the ATV and roamed his property with his dogs, but there was no sign of her. He hoped the people from the town were having better luck.

"There are a bunch of us from school that are going searching for her tomorrow," Brian said.

"Hopefully, she turns up before then," Amelia said.

Brian nodded. "I hope so, too. Pastor Ezra and Phil are putting the search together. Are you going to come?"

Brian rarely asked for much. He was a good boy who worked hard on the farm and to keep his grades up at school. "You said after school tomorrow? Yeah, I can come if she hasn't turned up by then."

"Some kids at school think the new people are to blame." Brian looked between his mother and father.

Jordy had the same feeling. "We don't know anything about what happened to her. This could be nothing more than just a misunderstanding that she is having with her parents."

"I don't think Evander would have anything to do with something like this," Amelia said.

Jordy wasn't so sure. He refused to defend Evander. "I heard Dan Howard was going to use his dogs to track her. Hopefully, they find her and return Kelly home."

"Tomorrow, Ezmae and I are going to bring a casserole over to the Morrison's house. I can't imagine what they must be going through."

Jordy and Amelia traded glances. He could see that she was more worried than she let on. They didn't need to say it aloud but neither of them thought the outcome was going to be a good one. Every hour that slipped by was an hour lost. With a missing child, time was the enemy. The person who has them could be miles away by now. The trail would grow cold, and the missing become lost behind the miles of time that forever marches forward. The longer Kelly was gone, the less likely she would come home alive.

Jordy glanced at his kids. Brian had gone back to serenading them with his guitar, and Petunia was giggling as she ran across the yard with her pig and the dogs. What would he do if something took one of them away from him? It was too painful to contemplate. A man has few things in life that mean more to him. His family is number one. Everything else can be replaced.

Chapter 12

They met in the school parking lot. Jordy, Cesar, and Laz came together to search for Kelly Morrison. Pastor Ezra and Phil were organizing the search, putting the kids into groups with some of the adults. The Morrisons looked tired and ragged from worry. Kelly's parents, Jean, and Paul, looked like they had aged ten years. It was hard to watch. This could happen to any of them, Jordy thought. Jean was walking around in a daze as people gathered to search. The one obvious person missing was Sheriff Clancy.

"I wonder why the Sheriff isn't here," Cesar said, looking around.

Phil scoffed. "He told the Morrisons that he thinks Kelly is a runaway."

"Look who's coming to search," Laz said under his breath.

"I almost expected this," Jordy said. The guilty always shows up at the crime scene in the movies. And in real life, too, he thought.

Evander pulled into the parking lot with two of his men. He parked next to Jordy's truck. "I brought refreshments for the people searching," Evander said. He got out of the jeep while his men pulled out three coolers from the back. One of the men with him was Conrad.

Pastor Ezra came over with a smile. "Thank you, that was very thoughtful."

"I hope she is found safe," Evander said, turning to Jordy. "Tomorrow, when you stop by, I would like to talk to you."

Jordy saw Phil perk up and move a little closer to hear the conversation. "Fine," Jordy said.

Jean Morrison headed for Evander, and from the look on her face, Jordy knew it was trouble. The pastor turned to walk over, trying to head her off, but Jean had her sights on Evander, and nothing was going to stop her.

"You," Jean shouted, pointing at Evander. "You tell me where my baby is."

Paul Morrison was trying to hold his wife back, but the momma bear was still coming straight for Evander. Jean shook off Paul and sidestepped Pastor Ezra. She was glaring at Evander. Paul grabbed her around the waist, lifting her off her feet as she kicked and bucked. "He knows where she is, I tell you. I know he does."

All eyes were on Jean Morrison and Evander. The crowd had fallen silent, watching and waiting to see what would unfold. Paul Morrison, cradling his wife in his arms, carried her toward a tent set up at the far end of the parking lot. Even after they disappeared inside, Jean's screams and sobs could still be heard.

Evander acted like he didn't notice Jean as people stood watching. Jordy saw darkness pass over Evander's face for just a couple of seconds before the impassive mask dropped back into place. "Very good, I'll leave you to your search," he said blandly. "I am still a stranger here and learning my way around. I'll leave the searching to the locals who know what they are doing." Evander nodded and climbed back into his jeep, going back the way he came.

Phil opened the coolers once Evander left. "Wow, I'll say this for him, he knows how to pack a cooler. There has to be every kind of drink in there known to man." He reached inside, pulling out a soda.

"Yeah, he likes to go big when spending money," Jordy said.

Phil was still looking at Jordy. "I wouldn't know."

"Something on your mind, Phil?" Jordy asked. Knowing that there was, from the looks, Phil was throwing his way.

"Just curious about Evander and what he wants." Phil was looking at Jordy suspiciously.

"Well, that makes two of us." Jordy didn't like Phil's implication.

"Make that three of us," Cesar added. He held up three fingers.

"Make it four," Laz said.

Phil nodded. "I need to go back to organizing the kids and check on Jean and Paul. I'll send Brian over with your search grid."

Jordy said nothing, watching him stalk away.

"What do you suppose Evander wants to talk about?" Cesar said.

"Who gives a shit?" Jordy didn't want to talk to Evander. Whatever it was, he didn't care.

Cesar nodded. "Yeah, I feel the same. I didn't like seeing Jean Morrison so upset. The Morrisons are good people. Evander acted like he didn't even notice her."

"Oh, he noticed and was none too happy," Jordy said.

"Neither were his men," Laz said. They reached down, unsnapping their holsters.

"For what?" Jordy asked. "Were they planning to shoot Jean right here in front of everyone?"

"His men seem to take this security seriously." Cesar frowned.

"They are hired guns," Laz said. "They are paid to take it seriously."

Brian came over with the search area for them. "Looks like we are heading off with the B team."

"Ok. Grab a few drinks and let's wait in the truck," Jordy said, forcing a smile, as he ruffled his boy's hair.

The last thing he wanted was for his son to think that he was unhappy about helping search. He had a bad feeling about it, though. His gut was twisting into a knot. Something bad was coming.

Chapter 13

They had been searching for four hours, working their way through the grid list. It was hot and painstakingly slow work, searching through the underbrush and thick ground cover. They had found nothing. Jordy pulled over onto the shoulder of Old Common Road and parked. This was the last place for them to search today. Dan Howard and his son pulled ahead of them to park ten feet away. Jed and his two sons pulled in ahead of Dan Howard. They would enter the woods and walk in a line, searching for Kelly.

When Jordy got out of the truck, he nearly keeled over as the tempest in his gut churned and tightened. He held on to the door of the truck for support, trying his best to hide it from the others. But Cesar was not easily fooled.

"Brian, why don't you walk with Laz," Cesar said, coming to stand next to Jordy. "Your early warning system going off?"

"Yeah, something bad is coming," Jordy said, panting.

"Let's take it slow and easy."

"Planning on it," Jordy said, straightening up.

They walked into the woods beneath a thick canopy of Cypress trees overhead. The rich, earthy smell of the woods greeted them. The air was still and thick. Jordy felt the knot in his gut tighten with every step he took. The danger was closer.

"Brian," Jordy called, leaning up against a tree. "Go up to the truck and wait for us there. It's hot, go have a drink."

"But dad," Brian whined.

"Go on now," Jordy urged.

Cesar was standing beside him. "She is here?" he whispered.

Jordy nodded. "I think so."

They walked in further. The air was heavy and humid, with dense underbrush making walking a challenge. The sun-dappled ground from the shafts of sunlight filtering down through the leaves overhead only added to the eeriness that surrounded them. Faraway, a bird shrieked making Jordy and Cesar both jump startled.

"It's creepy here," Laz said.

They had only walked another ten feet when they came to an abrupt stop. Beneath some brush, two bare legs were visible. Laz rushed over but froze just before reaching her. "I think she's dead," he whispered, his voice strained.

Jordy and Cesar caught up to him and stopped beside Laz. There were traces of blood on the legs that were discolored. There was a slight smell that only the dead left behind. If that was Kelly, she was no more.

"Let's call the others," Cesar said, averting his eyes.

"I'll go," Laz said. "Their boys don't need to see this."

Jordy and Cesar waited behind. Jordy's tempest eased, his gut unwinding now that the danger was revealed. Minutes later, Dan Howard and Laz came through the woods. For a moment, the four of them stood in silence. There was nothing they could do to help her. She was long past that. A heavy sadness filled Jordy's heart. Kelly was just a kid with her whole life ahead of her. The waste of it all was overwhelming. A precious life snuffed out long before its time.

"Jed is with the boys by the trucks," Dan said. "He is calling it into the Sheriff."

"So much for her running away," Cesar said grimly.

Jordy knew it was Conrad who did this. In his heart, he knew that Evander knew it, too. None of them were safe. This was only the beginning.

Chapter 14

Jordy sat on the tailgate of his truck, while the Sheriff was questioning Cesar and Laz. He had already questioned everyone else, saving Jordy for last. The naked body in the woods was Kelly. At least, that was the going theory. ID was going to take time. There was not much left of her head. Someone had shot her in the face with a shotgun, shattering her once beautiful face.

Doc Willows came and took away the body. Doc's brother, Ben, ran the only funeral home in town and served as both undertaker and coroner. It was eerie seeing them both on the scene. They worked in tandem, taking Kelly away with great care. One would perform the autopsy, and the other would make arrangements with the Morrisons to bury their daughter. Jordy supposed it was all part of the circle of life. Doc helped bring them into the world while his brother saw them to their final resting place.

Jordy just sat watching while his son sat with the other boys. After he talked to Brian, he was upset. This was not supposed to happen to someone they knew. Someone their age. All four boys were upset. Kelly was the first person to be killed that was close to their age. Youth have a protective barrier around them where nothing bad can happen…until it does. Only the old or sick are supposed to die. Today, they learned differently. The boys sat, huddled together in the back of Jed's truck, talking. Jordy understood. Sometimes, it's easier to deal with confusing emotions with your friends rather than with family.

Sheriff Clancy came over and sat on the tailgate next to Jordy. "Tough day," he said.

Jordy looked over at him. "Have you notified the Morrison's?"

"They know that we found a body. But not much more than that. Doc identified a beauty mark on the upper left shoulder of the body making it a positive ID for Kelly."

He had hoped by some miracle that it wasn't her. "That's too bad."

Sheriff Clancy nodded. "It is. I'm heading over to talk to the family after I talk to you. I'm still trying to figure out how to keep them from seeing her."

Jordy snorted. "Good luck with that. Nothing could keep me from going to my child. I don't care how bad it is to look at. It is still my child."

"Understandable. Tell me about coming here and finding her."

"There isn't much to tell. We were given a search grid. This was the last stop for the day. We walked into the woods. It was eerie. It wasn't long before we found two legs sticking out from beneath some underbrush. There was the smell of something dead in the air. We knew it was Kelly."

The sheriff nodded. "You sent Brian back to the truck before you found her?"

"Yes, it was hot in there. Humid. The air was dead, stagnant. I had a bad feeling. I sent him back to the truck to get a drink."

"I see. It was good that you did that. How do you think that she got there?"

Jordy shook his head. "She didn't walk in on her own in bare feet."

"No, I don't suppose that she did."

"She was murdered and dumped there," Jordy said flatly.

"It's under investigation. It could be an accident. A hunter might have shot her accidentally. We need to investigate it."

Accidental shooting? Is he for real? "She didn't look like she had on any clothes. What would she be doing in the woods naked?"

Sheriff Clancy shrugged. "You never know with kids today. Maybe she was getting in touch with nature. Who knows."

Jordy swung his legs, pointing to his boots. "I had a hard time walking in there with these on. That girl was barefoot."

Sheriff Clancy hopped off the tailgate. "Like I said, it's under investigation. You are free to leave. Give Amelia my best."

Jordy watched him walk away, anger simmering beneath the surface. This was bullshit, he thought. An accidental shooting by some random hunter? No way. What the hell was really going on here?

Chapter 15

Amelia was busy cooking when he got up the next morning. The house smelled of chicken and dumplings, fresh bread, and pastries. He helped himself to a cup of coffee and one of the pastries cooling on a tray.

"Is this all for the Morrisons or for Evander?" Jordy asked, biting into the warm blueberry turnover.

Amelia paused to take a sip from her coffee mug. "It's for both. Can you run Evander's food over to him? Esmae and I are going to bring some food over to the Morrisons this morning."

Jordy nodded. "Be happy to help."

"I just can't imagine what the Morrisons are going through." Amelia looked out the window checking on Petunia playing with Walter, the pig, in the yard.

Jordy followed her gaze. He knew what was going through her mind. Hold your children close because you just never know. "Where's Brian?"

"In his room. He's pretty upset still. I heard him get up last night, wandering around the house."

"Yeah, he took it pretty hard. I think that he had it in his head that we would find Kelly alive and bring her home."

"Yeah, death is complicated, especially when you are young. They canceled school today. Pastor Ezra is visiting everyone today to talk. He has been visiting with the Morrisons and talking to Jean. She is a mess."

"It's understandable." He reached for another turnover, and Amelia slapped his hand. "No more turnovers, I'm going to make breakfast."

He flashed her a guilty smile. "Are you sure? You look pretty busy."

"I'm positive. Besides, the kids need to eat. You can't work in the fields all day on a belly full of turnovers."

"I don't know, they are pretty tasty."

"Out of my kitchen." She chased him away from the pastries.

He chuckled and went down the hallway to Brian's room. Brian was sitting on his bed, reading. He looked up, pulling the earbuds from his ears, when he spotted his father. "Hi, Dad," he said, straightening up and putting the book aside.

"How are you? Your mother said that you were having trouble sleeping last night." Jordy took a chair that was near the bed.

"I'm ok," Brian said, frowning. "It's just that I saw Kelly riding her bike to school the morning that she disappeared. I feel guilty about it. I was in a hurry to get to school to play basketball with my friends before classes started. I just keep thinking that if I would have ridden along with her, she might still be here."

"Brian, there is no way that you could know this was coming. There are too many what-ifs to consider. What if she left ten minutes later? Would that have changed anything? What if she took a different way to school? What if, what if… Sometimes, things just happen that are beyond our control."

Brian nodded. "I guess."

"Get cleaned up. Mom is making breakfast."

"I'm not really hungry."

"Try to eat something. Your mother works hard. Her reward is seeing us eat the fruits of her labor. It makes her happy."

"Ok, thanks for talking to me, Dad." Brian looked up at him, looking much younger than his years.

"Anytime, son. You can always talk to me about anything." He was proud of his boy. One day, he would grow into a fine man.

Chapter 16

After breakfast, he loaded Evander's basket into the truck and headed out to pick up Cesar. He thought about his conversation with the sheriff yesterday. It still troubled him. How could he even consider that hunters caused Kelly's death? It was ridiculous. But then, maybe the Sheriff didn't want to believe that he had a murder on his hands. That would mean having to talk to Evander and his people. He wondered if the sheriff was afraid of them, and that is why he was so quick to rule out Kelly's death in an accident.

He pulled into the Sanchez driveway, spotting Cesar already waiting outside. When he spotted Jordy coming up the drive, he picked up the basket of food and started walking to the truck.

"Good morning," Cesar said, stowing the basket in the back next to Jordy's. "I see that we got more rain last night. The weather people must be on drugs, they keep saying we are heading for a drought."

"Oh, don't even utter the D word," Jordy moaned.

Cesar laughed. "Yeah, too early in the morning. Sorry."

Jordy turned onto the main road out of town, heading towards Evander's place. "Yesterday was quite the day."

"Yeah, Esmae was very upset. She has been cooking since yesterday. I feel so bad for the Morrisons."

"Me, too. What did the Sheriff talk to you about?" Jordy was curious if he was floating the same bullshit story to Cesar.

Cesar turned in his seat. "You know, I don't understand the sheriff. I've never known the man to be so unresponsive."

"He told me that he believes Kelly was killed by hunters."

"Hunters? Is he nuts? That girl was murdered up close and personal. Laz saw her when they pulled her out from under the brush. He said she took a point-blank shot in the face with what looked like a 12 gauge. It obliterated her face."

"I know, but that is what he is leaning towards."

"This makes no sense." Cesar was shaking his head.

Jordy pulled into Evander's long, gravel driveway. The pasturelands that were once lush were now a tangle of weeds and grass that pressed up against the fences that bordered the driveway. As the breeze pushed the grass, it flattened, shivering, almost looking like water rippling over the ground. In Jordy's opinion, it was a waste of good farmland left to waste away. When they came up to the gate with the guards standing like sentries, Jordy slowed to a stop.

To his surprise, the guards opened the fence, signaling for him to pull forward. He exchanged surprised glances with Cesar. "Looks like they are going to let us pass through," Jordy said.

"I'd rather just drop this thing off and be on our way."

"Me, too."

Jordy pulled forward and the guard, he recognized as Aiden, came up to his window. "Follow the road down to the house. The boss is waiting for you inside." Aiden pointed down the road.

Jordy nodded. "Ok, thank you."

"What do you suppose this is about?" Cesar said once they pulled away from the guards.

"No idea," Jordy said, chewing nervously on his bottom lip.

He followed the road, familiar with it from past visits to the Appleton's. Though the road was familiar, nothing else was. As they turned down the slight incline, the house and outbuildings came into view. He exchanged glances with Cesar.

"I almost want to ask, where the hell are we?" Cesar whispered, looking around.

The boarded-up, ramshackle house that once stood there, was now a striking manner house that was four times the size of the once tiny farmhouse. The barn remained, but beside it stood three long outbuildings that looked like Army barracks. There were at least a dozen jeeps and trucks parked along with the familiar motorcycles scattered around the driveway.

"How?" Jordy said, looking around after he parked close to the house.

"No idea," Cesar looked as shocked as Jordy.

Chapter 17

A man in a suit answered the door. Cesar took off his sweat-stained ball cap from his head as they were let inside. Jordy held the basket of food, feeling out of place. "You must be the farmers," he said, his hard, dark eyes sliding over them, landing on distaste. "I will see if the master is ready to see you."

The master? Jordy glanced at Cesar, who looked as confused as Jordy felt. "Strange."

"Like stepping into a time warp in a B movie."

The inside of the house was, if anything, even more impressive. Once, after marrying his wife, they had taken a honeymoon, staying in a fancy hotel. He remembered thinking that this was how the other half lived. But he was wrong. The hotel they had stayed in was a popup shack in comparison. From the gleaming hardwood floors to the sculptures, it was a miniature palace.

"Good, you have arrived," Evander said, dressed as he normally was in jeans and a tee shirt. The contrast between him and Simon was laughable. "Come inside, let's have a drink and talk."

A drink? "All right," Jordy said, still holding on to the basket of food.

"Simon, take the baskets into the kitchen," Evander instructed.

Simon walked over and retrieved the baskets. "I'll leave these by the door for when you leave." Simon turned on his heel and strolled away before Cesar or Jordy had time to say a word to him.

Evander was already walking off down the hallway. They followed, looking around as one room unfolded into the next, each as impressive as the last. Who is that man, Jordy wondered? Why is he here in Wormwood? He was obviously wealthy. Though Jordy loved Wormwood, he understood its shortcomings. Jordy was a small-town boy, born and raised. But Evander didn't even fall close to that. So, why was he here? What did he want?

Evander took them to a room that had a large desk placed near the windows. In front of the desk there were two leather couches that spread out across the room. There was a small bar to one side where Evander walked and poured himself a drink.

"Sit down," Evander said, gesturing to the couches. "What can I get you? Bourbon, Scotch, Gin?"

"It's a little early for me for that," Cesar said. "How about coffee?"

Evander turned with a glass of bourbon in his hand. "Coffee it is then. Jordy?"

"Coffee would be great."

Evander pulled out his cell phone. "Bring in two mugs of coffee for our guests. Simon will bring it shortly." Evander smiled, taking a seat across from them. "I heard about the girl being found. That is tough."

Jordy wondered if Evander heard this straight from the mouth of her killer. "Yes, it's very sad. She was just a kid."

Simon brought in the coffee on a silver tray along with cream and sugar. Once he set the tray down on the coffee table in front of them, he turned and looked at Evander. "Will there be anything else, sir?" he asked.

"No. Simon, that will be all." Evander picked up his glass and drained the contents getting up and pouring himself another.

Jordy and Cesar prepared their coffee, but Jordy's mind was racing with questions. Simon was clearly some sort of butler or assistant, but why was he paying the wives to cook for him? None of it added up.

Evander came back and sat across from them, his glass resting in his hand. "I wanted to talk to you about the town."

Jordy looked at him. "What about it?"

"I'm sensing an issue about the girl that died. Her mother was quite upset. Why was it directed a me?" Evander was frowning.

Cesar tipped his head at him. "It's a small town. A fly can't land on dog shit without the whole town knowing it. Conrad made quite an impression."

Evander scowled. "Yeah, that was stupid. I was not pleased with him. They blame Conrad for the girl's death, and that falls back on me?"

"Well, you are the face of this operation. He works for you?"

"Yes, he does. If I thought he did that, I would turn him in."

"You don't think that he is responsible?" Cesar asked, skeptically.

"I know how it looks," Evander admitted. "I need to fix this. How can I make this go away?"

Jordy and Cesar exchanged glances. "I don't know," Jordy said, being truthful. "People will draw their own conclusions. It will take time to change beliefs."

Evander focused on Cesar. "What about you? Any suggestions?"

"Appeal to the Morrisons and see if you can make peace with them. Make a gesture."

It was a good suggestion, Jordy thought, but what would Evander do? "It won't be easy where Jean is so destroyed. She clearly blames you for her daughter's death."

Evander threw his glass across the room chattering the glass against the wall. "Damn you, Conrad, for bringing down this shit on me."

Both Cesar and Jordy jumped, raising to their feet when the glass exploded upon hitting the wall.

"I apologize for losing my temper, please sit," Evander said, softly.

Jordy and Cesar sat uneasily back down. "Can I ask you something?" Jordy asked.

"Yes, anything," Evander said, sitting back on the couch.

Jordy was frowning, struggling to understand all of this. "Why does it matter what the town thinks? You live out here, independent from the town."

Evander looked at Jordy for what seemed like a long time. "I need the town to accept me. I have a business that travels through it. Traveling around the town to come here is a long and unnecessary detour. The people that I deal with will not take kindly to rumors or innuendo."

Jordy still didn't understand it. Who were these people that he was in business with? Why did it matter if the town hated him? "If that is all-important to you, then you need to convince the Morrisons that you had nothing to do with the death of their daughter."

Evander ran his fingers through his long, dark hair in frustration. "Ok, and you think if I patch it up with the Morrisons, the town will be satisfied?"

"It's a good start," Cesar said. "Small towns are slow to accept newcomers. So, there is that. Show up and get to know folks. Let them see who you are."

"Can't I just buy them all a pony or something?" Evander grumbled.

Jordy chuckled, shaking his head. "Trust can't be bought. You earn it."

Chapter 18

Jordy breathed a sigh of relief once they turned onto the road back to town. "I'm sure glad that is over with. That guy just rubs me the wrong way."

Cesar stretched out his legs, rubbing the back of his neck. "I know what you mean. I almost shit myself when he threw that glass across the room, shattering it against the wall. Dudes got a temper. I'm glad I'm not the focus of it."

"So, how the hell do you think that he got all that shit built in such a short period of time?"

"It had to come in from Corbet. No way did that crap come through town without people noticing." Cesar frowned. "There had to be massive loads of supplies and men to get that all done."

Jordy nodded, glancing over at Cesar. "What do you suppose is in all the outbuildings?"

"No idea, and I don't want to know. Whatever that guy has cooking can just remain his secret."

Jordy pulled into the gas station to fill up before heading back to the farm to tend his crops. Cesar got out and ran into the station to buy drinks. Jed and Phil were standing out in front of Winslow's having a coffee. Jordy waved to them when he got out to pump his gas. Phil and Jed waved and walked over to talk to him.

His last encounter with Phil was still bothering him. Phil was always looking for a conspiracy. If it wasn't the government planning something, then it was something else. Jordy was surprised that he didn't walk around wearing a tinfoil hat to keep away the radio waves coming from the mother ship.

"We were talking about Kelly," Phil said, leaning against Jordy's truck. "I guess the funeral will be on Saturday. Bree is going to watch the little kids at the church while we all attend the services."

"That's a real good idea," Jordy said.

"Do you think that any of Evander's people will come?" Jed asked.

Cesar put the water bottles in the truck and joined them. "I highly doubt it," he said.

"Yeah, I wonder if he feels any guilt," Jed said.

Jordy shrugged. "He told us that he is confused about why Jean blames him."

Phil snorted. "I blame him, too."

"We were just over at his place," Cesar said. "You would not recognize it."

Jed narrowed his eyes. "Yeah, there have been trucks going in and out of that place both night and day coming in from Corbet."

Jordy and Cesar exchanged glances. "We thought everything was coming in through Corbet."

"Why were you over there?" Phil asked, suspiciously.

Jordy shrugged, but he knew that expression on Phil's face. "We were dropping something off to Evander. To our surprise, he let us through the gate."

"What did he say?" Jed asked.

"He says he had nothing to do with it," Cesar said. "He wanted to know how to make it right."

"Well, short of resurrecting their daughter, nothing." Phil scoffed.

Cesar was looking at Jed, ignoring Phil. "I told him that he needed to make a gesture to them. Show people that he had nothing to do with it."

Jed shrugged. "That is a tall order. Everyone saw what his boy did. The only conclusion is that he had something to do with it. It was not a hunter, that is for sure."

"We need to get going. I've got fields to tend." Jordy would have liked to stay longer talking to Jed, but Phil was getting on his last nerve.

"I'll stop over later," Jed said, flashing a rare smile. "After I finish with the cows."

Jordy nodded. "You know where I'll be."

Jordy and Cesar watched them walk off. "Phil sure can be an ass sometimes," Cesar whispered.

"Yup, been that way since he was a kid. Even in school, he would be suspicious of everything."

"Yeah, but this time, I must agree with him. There is something strange about Evander and his crew."

"No argument there."

Chapter 19

Jordy was sitting out on his porch with Amelia when Jed's truck pulled into the driveway. "I'll go in and get you guys a beer," Amelia said.

"You don't have to go inside." Jordy looked at his pretty wife, wondering again how he got so lucky.

"I need to get Petunia into the bathtub before bed." She leaned down and kissed his cheek before going inside.

Jed came up the stairs and sat down next to Jordy. "Long day?"

"Yes, but the rain is helping. If it were not for battling the weeds, I would be a happy man."

Amelia stepped out with two frosty beers. "How are you, Jed?"

"Doing better now," he said, taking the beer from her.

"Well, good night." Amelia smiled. "I have a very dirty little girl that I need to tend to before bed."

Jed chuckled. "I'm guessing Diane is doing the same thing at home with my kids."

Amelia left them and Jordy was wondering what was on Jed's mind. His visits were rare. "Nice night," he said.

"It is." Jed turned to look at him. "You know Evander better than most. What's his story?"

Jordy shrugged. "I wish that I knew. His conversations with us are limited and to the point. Mostly small talk and nothing of substance."

"He must have a lot of money to do what he is doing."

"Yes, no argument there."

"So, why is he here? Why Wormwood?"

"That, my friend, is the one-million-dollar question." Jordy took a sip from his beer.

"Did he ever say what he does out there?"

"Nope. The only thing he did say was that it is important to him to have a good relationship with the town. The people that he works with want to see that."

"The guys in the black SUVs with the box trucks? Hmm, I wonder why that is?"

"No idea."

"My guess is that they are coming up from the south. The only way to the Appleton place is through the town unless they take a crazy long detour through Corbet. But what should it matter what the town thinks?"

"I asked him that. He said it matters."

"Weird," Jed said, frowning.

Jordy tapped his beer to Jed's. "I'll drink to that."

Chapter 20

The morning of the funeral dawned bright and sunny. After dropping off Petunia and Brian at the church, Jordy and Amelia parked, waiting for the funeral procession to begin. Cesar was in his truck behind them. The Morrisons were having a private service inside the Willow's Funeral Home with Pastor Ezra. Once that was finished, they would all follow the hearse to the Wormwood Cemetery for a public service.

"I'm sure glad that Bree decided to watch the kids in the church basement," Amelia said, checking her makeup in the visor mirror.

"Me, too." Jordy agreed. "There is plenty of time for children to experience death when they get older. I don't even want to be here, and I'm an adult."

"It's a sad day. Jean and Paul look years older under all that grief. Hopefully in time, it will get easier."

"Does it ever get easier, or do you just adapt?" Jordy looked into his wife's sad eyes.

She reached up and stroked his jaw. "I think you adjust to not seeing them. Life moves on, but we never stop missing them. We never stop wondering what they would have accomplished and are filled with sorrow at what they missed out on in life. Graduating, falling in love, and having a family of their own. Parents are not supposed to bury their children."

"Yeah, I can't even imagine."

"Me either."

The big double doors at Willow's Funeral Home opened, and six pallbearers carried out the walnut casket covered in red roses down the stairs to the waiting hearse. The Morrisons and Pastor Ezra followed behind it with their heads bent in sorrow. Paul supported Jean as she stumbled her way down the stairs, helping her into the back of Lenny Dawson's black Cadilac.

Jordy started his truck and filed into line behind the hearse, for Kelly's final trip through town. Sheriff Casey led the way in his cruiser, lights flashing. They drove in a somber procession the short distance to the cemetery, pulling to the shoulder. The grave was easy to spot. There were more flowers than Jordy had ever seen in one place. It was a funeral fit for a princess. There was even a stringed instrument quartet playing music off to the side of the grave.

Amelia looked at Jordy in surprise. "This had to cost a fortune," she whispered.

Evander did this, Jordy thought, but did not say it aloud. "Yes, it must have."

Jordy and Amelia took their places at the side of the grave with Cesar and Esmae. The pastor began his sermon. Jean quietly wept throughout the hour-long service, while Jordy kept his head bowed for most of it. When he finally looked up, his eyes locked on Evander, standing among the gravestones across the cemetery. Dressed in a black suit, his long hair tied back, and dark sunglasses hiding his eyes, Evander's presence was unmistakable. Yet Jordy could almost feel the intensity of those piercing blue eyes scanning the group. A chill crept down Jordy's spine, his gut tightening with unease. His inner storm surged. Evander gave him a nod, a faint smile curling his lips before he turned and disappeared into a sleek, black limousine. Jordy knew, deep down—something bad was on the horizon.

Chapter 21

They drove back into town, a long line of mourners coming from the cemetery. The plan was to meet over at Finn's for lunch before picking up the kids at the church. Then, tonight, they would all meet over at the Morrison's house, bringing food for the family and paying their respects. Making tribute was a tradition in Wormwood. Jordy remembered when his mother passed, it was the same. People would stop by dropping off food. At the end of the night, he had more food than they could eat in a month.

The cars stopped, and Jordy frowned. "I wonder why we are stopping," he said.

He glanced at Amelia. She sat frozen, her hands cupped over her mouth, her eyes wide with horror as she stared out of the windshield. "Oh my God," she whispered.

Jordy followed her frightened gaze. Hanging from a limb on the old oak tree was a body hanging by its neck, legs dangling in the breeze high above the road. "Oh, shit," Jordy muttered. "Stay here."

Amelia nodded, unable to speak.

Jordy got out of the truck and joined the other people gathering around the base of the tree. Cesar joined him. All of them looking up at the dead man with the swollen, bluish face, covered in bruises, that hung from the tree. He was barely recognizable, but Jordy knew him. It was Conrad.

"Is that who I think it is?" Cesar asked, breathlessly.

"It is," Jordy said. "Someone needs to call the sheriff and let him know what we have here."

"I'm on it," Phil said.

"We need to get him down before one of the kids sees it," Jed said.

"I'll cut him down," Laz volunteered. He climbed the tree, pulling a knife from his back pocket.

"Laz, wait for the sheriff," Jordy said. "It's a crime scene. We need to wait."

The sheriff's cruiser pulled up along the side of the cars, pulling over to the shoulder of the road. "Well, isn't this a fine piece of shit?" Sheriff Clancy muttered. "Today of all days."

"Can Laz cut him down?" Jordy asked.

"Yes, cut him down in the back of Jed's truck. We will take him to Doc Willows. Damn it."

Jordy stood to the side with Cesar. "Evander?" Cesar whispered.

Jordy nodded, averting his eyes from the scene. "Likely. Part of his grand gesture."

"But killing your own man?"

"As the saying goes, he who sows the wind, will reap the whirlwind. I don't think this will go the way Evander thinks it will."

"No, it's horrific." The body hit the back bed of Jed's truck with a sickening thump when Laz cut the rope. Cesar winced.

"Ok, let's get the body to Docs. Everyone, pick up your kids and go home." The Sheriff got into his cruiser, riding in front of Jed's truck with his lights flashing, heading to Doc Willow's place.

"I'll get the kids and stop by your place later on tonight," Cesar said.

"Yeah, we can make tribute together."

"Do you think people will still turn out for it?"

"They will. The Morrisons deserve it. People will make a tribute. Besides, we could all use a little what is normal."

Chapter 22

"I want to stay here and never leave the farm again," Amelia said, when Jordy asked her if she wanted to make tribute with him.

"I don't blame you," Jordy said, holding her a little closer, as they sat together on the porch. The farm had always been their refuge, even through the hardest of times.

"I don't understand what happened. Why would that man do that in such a public way?" She looked up at him with tears shining brightly in her eyes.

Jordy placed a kiss on the top of her head. Conrad didn't have much say in the matter, Jordy thought wryly. He was sure that Evander had him killed, making his own tribute to the Morrisons. "I don't know," he whispered.

When Cesar pulled into the driveway with Laz, Amelia got up from her chair. "I'm heading inside. There is no reason to let them see me so upset." Her smile was shaky. "The food for the Morisons is all packed up in a bag on the table."

Jordy nodded in understanding. "I won't be long."

Cesar and Laz climbed the steps and sat down in the chairs next to Jordy. "What a bizarre day," Cesar said. "Esmae is staying home with the kids."

"So is Amelia. She told me that she never wants to leave the farm again."

"Same as Esmae."

"For a small town, lately, we sure have our share of craziness." Laz looked between Cesar and Jordy.

"I just wish it was back to normal," Jordy said.

"I hear that," Cesar agreed.

"Shall we go?" Jordy gestured to the door.

"Yeah, I want to get back to Esmae and the kids." Cesar rubbed his hands over his face. "This simple farmer is tired."

Laz elbowed him in the ribs. "You are always tired."

Cesar snorted. "Hey, a funeral and a murder added some extra mileage."

Jordy chuckled. "A little thing like that?" Jordy rose from his chair. "Let me grab the food for the Morrisons, and then let's go."

They climbed into Cesar's truck and drove the short distance to the Morrisons. The street was lined with cars and trucks, packed with people coming to pay their respects. Cesar, Laz, and Jordy got out, each carrying bags of food as they made their way up to the house. In the yard, Paul Morrison sat among a group of about two dozen people, laughing and sipping what looked like bourbon from a water glass.

"Hey, my friends, join us," Paul called out as they walked across the front yard.

Jordy was shocked by the transformation from the man that he saw this morning at the funeral. Paul was laughing and enjoying himself. It was like he was celebrating a graduation instead of the funeral of his daughter. Cesar and Jordy exchanged glances. "Paul," Jordy said, nodding, holding up the bags of food.

"Oh, you can leave those on the steps by the front door." His eyes rested on Cesar. "Did Esmae send any of her quesadillas?"

Cesar shrugged holding out the bag to him. "I'm not sure."

Paul took the bag and opened it, dumping the contents of the bag onto the picnic table for everyone to help themselves. "Oh, yes, I'm starving," he said, laughing.

Jordy was not sure what to say to him. For the first time in his life, he was speechless as Paul dove into the food. Five men from the town joined him. "Well, give Jean our best," Jordy said, placing the bags of food by the stairs.

"Wait, before you leave, you have to make a toast with us," Paul said, unsteadily pouring bourbon into three Dixie cups.

Jordy, Laz, and Cesar hesitantly picked up the cups, waiting for the toast. Paul held up his water glass, slopping some of the bourbon over the edges. "May that bastard rot in hell. And may his master soon follow him there."

Jordy only made believe to take a drink. Something stirred from inside him, warning him. It was different than a warning signal from his tempest. This was like a nudge from above. It was a physical push from inside his brain, warning him not to drink it. He walked the cup to the trash and threw it away. Cesar and Laz did the same. They said good night and left.

"Did you feel that?" Laz said, amazed, as they walked back to the truck.

"It was like something told me not to drink it," Cesar said, looking around nervously as he made the sign of the cross.

"I felt it. That was strange." Jordy was still processing what had just happened.

Chapter 23

They said little on their way back to Jordy's. Each was caught up in their own thoughts. When they reached Jordy's farm, they got out of the truck and climbed the stairs to sit on the porch, looking out into the night. The rising full moon cast its silvery light on the fields, making them look haunted, as a balmy breeze caressed their faces. It was a beautiful night, except they could not enjoy it, still troubled about the strange feeling that had come over them at the Morrisons.

"What do you think it was?" Laz asked, breaking the silence.

"For me, it was like something was whispering inside of my mind. Don't drink it." Cesar looked from Jordy to Laz.

"It was the same for me. I got the feeling it was bad." Jordy felt a shiver run down his back.

Laz nodded. "Yes, it said it was bad. But more of a feeling, not in words."

"Yes, that is how I understood it, too." Cesar agreed.

"So, what was it?" Laz asked.

"Jordy, is this like your early warning system?" Cesar asked, looking nervously from Laz to Jordy.

"Early warning system?" Laz asked, frowning.

Jordy didn't blame Cesar for asking the question. After all, they had just shared. "No, this was different. When I get the feeling something bad is coming, it is more of a visceral reaction in my gut. No, this was something different."

"How long have you had that?" Laz asked.

Jordy sighed. "Since I was a child."

Laz leaned closer, his eyes scanning Jordy's face. "Does it always come true…when you get this feeling?"

"It does, but I don't always know what is coming until it is here. Where this was more direct and to the point. I knew the drink was bad. I knew to not drink it."

Cesar glanced at Jordy. "Do you think that whatever it was, came from you? You sent out a signal or something to us, telling us not to drink it?"

Jordy shook his head. "I don't think so."

Laz sighed. "What I'm wondering is why was the bourbon bad? What was wrong with it?"

Cesar shook his head. "No idea. The other men there were drinking it."

"Maybe it was not the drink as much as the toast that Paul made," Laz theorized.

"He didn't say anything other than what we were all thinking," Cesar said. "Conrad deserves to roast his nuts in hell for what he did to Kelly."

"Agreed. No, I think it was the drink itself that was bad for some reason. Though, I have no idea why." Jordy was still trying to recall what had happened by replaying it over in his mind. Were they missing something?

Cesar rose to his feet and stretched. "I need to get some sleep. The fields will be waiting in the morning."

"I think we should keep this thing a secret," Laz said, rising to his feet. "I have the feeling that whatever it was should stay between us."

"Agreed, besides, who would believe us?" Cesar said.

"I guess, welcome to the club," Jordy said with a chuckle and a shrug.

Both Laz and Cesar laughed. "Let's see what tomorrow will bring."

Chapter 24

Jordy worked the fields for most of the day, until the unexpected rain shower started at three o'clock in the afternoon. The weather forecast called for hot, dry weather, but any rain was welcomed. The crops had recovered nicely from the earlier dry weather of the Spring, promising to yield a strong harvest if they could keep up with the water and sunshine.

When Jordy arrived home, he found Phil sitting on the porch, sipping iced tea, with Bree and Amelia beside him. "Well, this is a nice surprise," Jordy said as he walked up the steps.

"Bree made us a pie," Amelia said, rising from her chair. "Here, sit down. I'll pour you a drink. Bree and I will finish getting dinner together."

Jordy nodded, taking a seat next to Phil. "I am starved," he said, gladly accepting the drink Amelia poured for him.

After Amelia and Bree went into the house, Phil turned to him. "Have you heard about Paul Morrison?"

"No, I've been working in the fields all day. What's happened?" Here it was, he thought. He had been waiting all day. Laz and Cesar were, too.

"We were at the Morrisons for tribute last night. Paul and a few guys were partying hard. They had rummaged through some of the bags of food, spilling more on the ground than eating it. So, I helped Jean take some of the food inside the house before I left around nine."

"Yeah, Paul was pretty lit when we stopped over there earlier." Jordy shrugged. "He went through a lot losing Kelly. I figured that he was just blowing off steam."

"Around eleven o'clock, Paul and some guys from town went to Finn's. Some of Evander's guys were there. Finn said Paul and the guys from town started picking a fight with Evander's crew. But the way Finn tells it, Paul and the other guys were on something. They were hallucinating and shit."

"Hallucinating?" Jordy frowned. Not good.

"Yeah, Finn said that they were howling like dogs as they went after Evander's guys. Paul got pretty banged up. Doc did what he could for those guys, but in the end, he sent them to the hospital in Camden. Finn said, it would have been worse if it were not for Evander's guys detaining them. They took them all down and held them there so that they didn't get hurt any worse."

The bourbon, Jordy thought. Something was in it. Drugs? "How is Paul?"

"He's got a lot of broken bones like the others. He's going to have a long recovery from what I hear. I was planning to go visit him when Jean said that he could receive visitors. I can't imagine what they got into."

"When I was there, he was drinking bourbon."

"I didn't see any bourbon when I was there. They were drinking vodka or rum, I think. Odd because Paul isn't a drinker."

"You said Evander's guys held them until what?" Jordy asked.

"Oh, Sheriff Clancy got there and cuffed them, taking them to Doc Willow's office. Finn said, they were like mad dogs, bucking and snarling. It was lucky Evander's guys were there to help."

"Yeah, real lucky." Jordy didn't think luck had anything to do with it. So, Evander's guys save the day? But who spiked the bourbon? And whose idea was it to go to Finn's?

Chapter 25

Evander was sitting on Jordy's porch the next morning when he came outside to head to the fields. "Good morning," he said, cheerfully.

Jordy thought it was, until he spotted him outside waiting. "Good morning. What brings you out so early?"

"I wanted to catch you before work." Evander rose to his feet and followed Jordy to his truck.

"Oh, what is so important?" He paused by the door of his truck.

"I was wondering what you have heard in town."

"Well, people are still upset about finding Conrad hanging from the old oak tree. It upset people."

Evander shrugged. "Well, he was a confused, young man that made mistakes. What else have you heard?"

Hmm, he was more than that, Jordy thought. He was a murderer and evil, just like his boss. "Then the thing with Paul Morrison at Finn's."

"Yes, it is funny what grief can do to a man's soul," Evander said.

"Is that why you paid for Kelly's funeral? Was that for the Morrisons or for the town to see?"

"It was the least that I could do."

"Yes, it was lucky your guys were at Finn's the other night, too."

Evander smiled. "Happy coincidence. I hear Paul will heal up just fine."

Jordy thought it was all bullshit. "What do you want, Evander?"

"That's the Jordy that I know and love. Right to the point." Evander rocked back on his heels and laughed. "Am I making progress with the town?"

Jordy still didn't understand his need for the town to accept him. "Yes, there are some that are changing their opinion."

"Excellent. Well, I'll let you go off to work. I'll be around later."

Jordy watched him walk to his car. This time, he drove a sleek, black Mercedes. Was it possible that Evander could be responsible for all of the things happening? Conrad was found dangling from a tree in front of the entire town. Drugging Paul and getting him to go to Finn's, only so that his men could rescue Paul from himself. Paul and Jean were the loudest among Eveander's critics. Now silenced. It was either, first, an amazing coincidence, or second, Evander was the most calculating man that he had ever known. He was betting on the latter.

Chapter 26

Jordy picked up Cesar and Laz to go to Finn's to play dominos. Cesar hopped in the passenger side of the truck, while Laz sat in the back behind his father. "I saw Phil today," Cesar said,

"What did he have to say?" Jordy said, pulling out of Cesar's driveway. Phil knew everything in town. If you wanted information on anything, Phil was the man to talk to.

"Paul was finally released from the hospital but still has a long way to go with his recovery."

Jordy nodded. It was understandable that Paul would need more time to heal all the broken bones he'd accumulated. "I'm sure Jean will be happy to have him home. Maybe their life can finally start to getting back to normal."

"The other guys have been released, too," Laz said. "Some of them will have injuries that will last a lifetime. Ralph White is thinking of selling the farm."

Jordy glanced up in the rearview at Laz in surprise. "Really?"

"Yes, if he sells, we should look to pick up some of his acreage," Cesar said.

Jordy nodded. "We could see what he is looking to do. He's got water rights to the stream. I would love to get my hands all over that."

"If we put in on it together, I think we could swing it." Cesar smiled.

"I would like to throw in on that," Laz said. "I have some money saved from when I served. It's not a lot, but I'd like to invest."

Cesar traded glances with Jordy and smiled. "So, you have decided to stay?"

Laz laughed. "I never said that I was leaving."

"Yeah, but I could see that you were not happy," Cesar said.

"I'm not unhappy, Pop. I just would like to have my own land. If this comes up, I will."

Jordy nodded in understanding. "There is something in knowing that the ground beneath your feet belongs to you. I get it."

"So, what do you think?" Cesar asked, turning to Jordy.

"Yeah, Let's see what Ralph decides."

Life returning to normal was good after all the chaos. Planning for the future is what people do. He had not seen Evander in a few weeks since he showed up at this house that last morning. When he dropped off the baskets of food, the guards took it and handed him and Cesar a check. That is the way that he wanted to keep it.

He pulled into Finn's, surprised at how few people were there for a Friday night. It was early, he thought. The late-night crowd may show up closer to nine. He parked near the door, having his choice of where to park.

They picked a table across the room and set up the dominos. Jordy ordered a round of beers, while Cesar ordered sandwiches. Jordy had been looking forward to this all afternoon. Amelia was having the ladies over to do whatever ladies do. She practically rushed his ass out of the house. He smiled.

"What's so funny?" Laz asked.

"I was just thinking how my wife couldn't wait to get rid of me tonight. Ladies night."

Cesar chuckled. "Esmae was the same. They are doing some sort of beauty crap at your house."

Jordy sat down, pulling his beer closer. "I'll stick to beer and dominos."

"Me, too, brother." Cesar sat back and sighed.

They were on their second round of beers. Finn's had filled up with people with more coming through the door. One of the Jeffery brothers had brought his guitar and was playing in the corner as he sang a Country and Western ballad. Some people were dancing while others were laughing and talking among themselves all around them. Some stopped by now and again to say hello.

At nine-thirty, the door opened, and Evander and his crew walked inside. The place got noticeably quieter. The air inside seemed to dull and grow heavy. Jordy wondered if it was his imagination, but one look and Cesar and Laz and he knew that they felt it too.

There was an Asian man with them wearing a short sleeve, white dress shirt and slacks. He seemed out of place here. The Wong brothers looked at him and left shortly after he arrived. From the tight expression on their faces, Tommy Wong and his brother, Simon, did not like what they saw. They were playing poker two tables over from them. Tommy and Simon folded their hands and left. It was odd because the Wong brothers were part of the late-night crowd at Finn's, always staying until the last call.

Jordy wondered if it was the colorful tattoos on the man's arms that caused the Wong brothers to leave. The man had intricate tattoos on both of his forearms. The tattoos also looked out of place on the man. Whatever it was, it made Jordy uneasy. He tried not to look up at their table. "We should call it a night after this game," Jordy said, as the tempest in his gut churned and rolled.

"The early warning system kicking in?" Laz whispered.

Jordy nodded. "It's letting me know that it is time to go."

Chapter 27

Jordy was just about ready to leave Finn's when the bartender, Tiny, brought over another round of drinks. But instead of three beers on the tray, there was an added glass of bourbon. Jordy looked up at him, puzzled. "We didn't order these," he explained.

Tiny nodded. "They did." He gestured to Evander's table.

The Asian man was already heading over to their table. Jordy's tempest flared to life. "We got incoming," Jordy whispered.

Laz looked over Jordy's shoulder. "Coming in hot."

The Asian man stopped beside Jordy's chair. "May I join you?" he asked in perfect English.

Jordy gave a curt nod. "Yes. I'm assuming we have you to thank for the drinks?"

He sat down in the chair beside Jordy. "It is nothing. May I play? It has been a long time, but I think that I will remember. I am Henry Lee, it is nice to meet you."

"I'm Jordy, and this is Cesar and Laz." Jordy gestured across the table. "We were getting ready to leave…" Jordy started.

"But you will stay now." Henry reached over, taking his glass from the tray.

Jordy had no doubt that it was a command. The man's eyes glittered cold and determined.

"Well, I guess we have time to play one more game," Cesar said, taking a beer from the tray.

Laz followed his father's lead, taking a beer, too. Jordy and Henry were still locked in a silent battle of wills. "Jordy, pass the salt," Laz said.

Jordy stole a glance at Laz, relieved to break the unsettling eye contact. His gut tightened with an intensifying tempest. This man was not good; if anything, he was more malevolent than Evander. Jordy noticed the tattoos on Henry Lee's arms—a dragon winding around a triangle with an eye peering out from its center. He had seen that triangle tattoo before, but he struggled to recall where.

"Salt?" Henry asked. "Why do you put salt in your beer?"

Laz shrugged. "It makes it taste sweeter."

Henry turned his attention back to Jordy. "Tell me about this town."

"It's like any small town," Jordy said. "People work hard and live a humble life."

"What do you do, Jordy Hart?" Henry asked.

Jordy had not told him what his last name was. So, Henry Lee already knew who he was. It did not surprise him. "I'm a farmer."

"What do you grow?" Henry was watching the game being played out on the table.

"Corn and wheat, mostly."

"My grandfather was a farmer. Farmers are the purest of men. Are you of pure heart, Jordy?"

It was a strange question. "I try to be good and honest."

"Yes, I can sense that about all three of you. I have a sense of these things. What do you sense about me?" Henry stared into his eyes.

Jordy looked away, not liking what he saw there. "I don't know you well enough to judge."

Henry chuckled humorlessly. "I think you know enough." Henry rose from his chair. "It was nice to meet you. Jordy. I'll be seeing you again." With a nod, Henry walked back to Evander's table.

"What the hell was that about?" Laz whispered.

"Beats me," Jordy said, uneasily.

"I think that we should go." Cesar was already boxing up the dominos. "The next time, let's go fishing."

Jordy glanced over his shoulder. Henry was still watching him, raising his glass in a salute. His tempest flared white-hot.

Chapter 28

Jordy, Cesar, and Laz came out of Finn's and hopped into the truck. It was a dark, moonless night, and the air smelled like rain. He backed out of the parking lot and headed for Cesar's farm. The tempest in his gut was still churning from an unseen danger that was yet to be named. Some of Evander's boys were standing outside of Finn's. The men watched them leave, and Jordy got the feeling that they were ordered to do it.

"So, what the hell was that?" Cesar growled. Dealing with his own tempest.

"Henry Lee? Who the fuck is he?" Laz was looking out the back window for anyone following them.

"I don't know," Jordy said, still troubled by the encounter. It was like seeing a venomous snake, resting on a rock in the sun. You didn't need to see its fangs to know it was dangerous. Henry Lee was dangerous.

When they turned the corner, the Wang brothers were parked over on the shoulder of the road. Jordy checked his rearview mirrors, making sure that they were not being followed before pulling over to park behind them. He saw Cesar looking at him in confusion.

"Why are we stopping?" Laz asked from the backseat.

"They know something," Jordy said. "I want to find out what they know."

Tommy Wong got out of his car and waited by his driver's door for Jordy. He gave a slight, hesitant wave. Tommy looked nervous.

Jordy got out of the truck. Laz got out, too, but waited by Jordy's truck, keeping watch. Jordy walked up to Tommy. "Good evening," Jordy said, stopping next to Tommy.

Tommy nodded, looking up at the darkening sky. "Looks like more rain."

Jordy leaned against the car. "It does." Jordy was going to cut to the point. "What do you know about Henry Lee?"

"Is that his name?" When Jordy nodded, Tommy continued. "I don't know him. But if I'm right, he is a bad mother fucker. You don't want to know him. If Evander is running with these dudes, the town is screwed. They will wipe out anything standing in their way."

"How do you know that?" Jordy's tempest flared.

"His kind have been around for centuries. Where they go, chaos follows. My grandfather brushed up against them in the old country. It didn't end well. We are going to leave Wormwood for a while and go see some family in Kansas. You should do the same if you can."

"This is my home," Jordy said, defiantly.

"Not anymore," Tommy said, shaking his head.

"Tell me more."

"I'll tell you this, if Evander is dealing with them, then drugs or something equally as bad is involved. They are marking their territory. Henry Lee is going to make sure of it."

"But why involve the town?" Jordy didn't understand.

"Wormwood is a good cover for them. A sleepy little town of farmers. What could be better? It is like hiding in plain sight. Once they take over the town, there is no threat. No one will dare to defy them. It's what they do. If they think that you are a threat, they will find a way to solve it."

"How would they do that?"

"I have already said too much. I'm out of here." Tommy opened his car door to leave.

"Thanks, Tommy, good luck."

"I will not need luck, Jordy. Save it for the people that stay here."

Chapter 29

Jordy didn't sleep well last night. By the looks of Laz and Cesar, it was the same for them. They were working in Cesar's upper field. The rain from last night had stopped. The morning gave birth to another beautiful, sunny day. There was a cooling breeze shivering the wheat across the field. On any other day, it would be serene.

"I can't get this out of my head," Cesar said, pushing up his ball cap to wipe the perspiration from his forehead.

"I know, I've thought of little else." Jordy agreed.

"It just seems that we are being played. They are tightening the knot, and there is nothing that we can do to stop it."

Jordy felt the same. "See, that's the frustrating part. What can we do to stop it besides resist."

Laz frowned. "What could they do if we all resisted?"

Cesar looked out over the field. "I could think of some obvious things. They could set fire to our fields. Or they could kill one of us like they did Kelly."

Jordy nodded in agreement. "These are men capable of doing anything. Tommy mentioned that this is what they do. They have had plenty of practice in taking what matters most."

"We could call in the law from outside to investigate," Laz suggested.

"But investigate what? We have no idea what goes on at Evander's place. And when they come here and find nothing, what happens then? That's the most troubling part."

"We just wait, then?" Cesar asked in frustration.

Jordy shrugged. "Look, I don't like this cat-and-mouse game any better than you do. But what choice do we have?"

Chapter 30

Two days later, Jordy was working in the field with Cesar and Laz when Phil ran up to them. It was the first time Jordy had ever seen Phil in his field. Right away, alarm bells went off in Jordy's head. Something had happened. Cesar exchanged uneasy glances with Jordy.

Phil was out of breath when he reached them. "They attacked some of Jed's cows."

"Take it easy, Phil. Tell us what happened. Who attacked Jed?" Jordy tried to calm Phil down.

Phil was panting. "Jed got up and went to feed his cows. Three were missing. He went and searched for them. He found two of them butchered. One is still missing."

"Butchered?" Laz asked.

"Yeah, throats slit, and pieces of them cut off and missing. They left them there like that for Jed to find." Phil was still panting but calmer.

"Where's Jed?" Cesar asked.

"He's at the sheriff's reporting it." Phil looked between Cesar and Jordy. "We need to go into town and see what happened."

Cesar and Jordy exchanged glances. "I guess we should go and see what this is about," Cesar said, uneasily.

"Yeah, let's finish up here and then go," Jordy agreed. So, this was the warning shot being fired over the bow.

"I get the feeling that this is only the beginning," Laz said.

Jordy nodded, turning to Phil. "Alright, we will meet you in an hour at Winslow's."

Phil sighed. "This is going to get worse if the sheriff doesn't act soon."

"Yeah, agreed." Jordy nodded reluctantly.

When Phil left, Cesar turned to Jordy. "How's that early warning system doing?"

"It's simmering."

"Good, as long as it doesn't come to a boil." Cesar laughed at Jordy's sour expression.

An hour later, Cesar, Laz, and Jordy rode into town. It was the busiest Jordy remembered seeing it. It was like when they all gathered to celebrate the Fourth of July. Cars and trucks were parked along the streets, and people were gathering at the fountain of the third angel. Wormwood was buzzing with anticipation. Jordy felt the knot in his gut tightening.

"People are really upset. I wonder how the sheriff will respond." Cesar leaned against the truck next to his son.

"We will see." But Jordy already knew that the sheriff would do nothing.

Pastor Ezra was walking around, trying to calm the crowd. Jordy was standing with Cesar and Laz in front of Winslow's having a coffee when Evander and Henry pulled up and stopped. Evander rolled down the window. Jordy could feel the eyes of the town on them.

"What's going on?" Evander asked, coolly.

"Someone butchered a couple of Jed's cows last night," Jordy said, not missing the slight smile that curled Henry's lips.

"Well, that is unfortunate," Evander said, smoothly.

Jordy wished that they would go on their way. "Yes, Jed is pretty upset."

"Well, Jed should watch who he messes with in the future," Henry said. "It's never a wise running your mouth when you don't know the players."

"What does that mean?" Jordy said, with his tempest coming to life in his gut.

"There is an old proverb in my country. Know your enemy as well as you know yourself, and you can fight a hundred battles without peril. If you are ignorant of the enemy and know only yourself, you will stand equal chances of winning and losing. If you know neither the enemy nor yourself, you are bound to be defeated in every battle. I would say that Jed falls into the last category."

Jordy never broke eye contact with him. "So, are you the enemy?"

Henry chuckled. "I'm but a messenger," he said with a thin smile.

"Well, I'd love to stay and see how this plays out, but we are having a barbeque," Evander said, with a large, toothy smile. "You should all stop by and have a steak."

Jordy shook his head. "I have fields to tend."

"You need to take time and relax, Jordy. You work too hard." Evander waved and put up his window before driving away.

"Steak?" Cesar said, grimacing.

"Yeah, two guesses where the meat came from," Laz said, growing uneasy.

Jordy looked around, people were gathering in front of the sheriff's office, waiting for Jed. "This is going to get bad."

"Yeah, the sheriff is not going to do anything," Laz said, echoing Jordy's thoughts.

"You can almost feel the tension in the air," Cesar said, narrowing his eyes on the crowd.

"It's like before we would be sent out on patrol," Laz said. "The enemy was close…waiting to spring their trap."

Jordy felt that the trap had already sprung, and they were caught inside of it. He thought about what Henry had said about knowing your enemy as well as you know yourself. That was the problem.

Evander had spent time getting to know them. But what did they really know about Eveander? Nothing. Evander knew just how to exploit their weaknesses. It made them all vulnerable.

Chapter 31

They waited for an hour and Jed never came out. People were getting restless, pacing outside the Sheriff's office. Jordy could feel the tension rising. Everyone knew that Jed loved those cows like family. They all had names, and Jed took exceptional care of them. The milk coming from Jed's farm was the best around. He said it was because it came from all the love poured into it.

Pastor Ezra wore a deep frown as he looked over his congregation. "What do you think could be taking so long?" he asked Jordy.

"I'm sure Jed must be pretty fired up," Jordy said, glancing at Cesar.

"Yes, Phil said that he was very upset," Cesar confirmed.

"I'm going to go inside and see what is holding this up," Pastor Ezra said.

"Do you want us to come with you, Pastor?" Jordy asked.

"Yes, Jordy, why don't you come with me? Any more than that, and it will look like we are storming the Sheriff's office." He chuckled. But there was an uncharacteristic uncertainty shining in his eyes.

Jordy nodded and followed the pastor to the door of the office. "We will go inside and check on Jed," the pastor called to the people milling about waiting.

When they tried the door, it was locked. "Well, that is strange," the pastor said, trying to twist the knob again.

"Here, let me try," Jordy said, knocking on the door. "Sheriff Clancy? It's Jordy and Pastor Ezra. Is everything ok?" Something was wrong. Why would he lock the door?

A few minutes passed with no response. Just as Jordy was about to try again, the door swung open. Sheriff Clancy stood in the doorway, looking hurried. "I'm busy right now," he said curtly, his eyes quickly scanning the faces of the crowd gathered outside.

"Sheriff, we are here to see about Jed." Pastor Ezra said, glancing uncertainly at Jordy.

"Come in," Sheriff Clancy said, stepping away from the door.

Once they were inside, the sheriff closed the door behind them, locking it. "Come in, gentlemen," Sheriff Clancy said, sitting behind his desk.

Pastor Ezra and Jordy looked around, but Jed was nowhere to be found. "Where is Jed?" Pastor Ezra asked in concern.

"Jed was very upset and was making threats, so I placed him on a twenty-four-hour hold. Apparently, an animal attacked his cows, and he is convinced it has to do with Evander."

"From the way that I heard it, the cows were left butchered in his field," Jordy said. "That does not sound like an animal to me."

"It's under investigation," Sheriff Clancy snapped defensively.

"Do you mean to say that you are locking Jed up in a cell?" Pastor Ezra looked at the Sheriff in disbelief.

"Yes, he was making threats. He needs time to cool off. Now, if that is all, I have work to do."

They were being dismissed. "Can I talk to him?" Jordy asked.

"No, he needs quiet time to reflect. I'm going to head out to his farm and take a look at the cows. I'll decide when I file a report. Now, if you will excuse me." The Sheriff rose from his chair and walked to the door.

He was showing them out. The pastor walked to the door with Jordy. Something was very wrong with all of this. Jordy paused at the door. "When you go to check out the cows, I'd like to go along with you."

"Why?" The sheriff was clearly not thrilled with his offer.

"Call it curiosity," Jordy said, walking out the door with the pastor.

"Suit yourself." Sheriff Clancy shrugged.

When they walked outside, people were waiting for them. "Where is Jed?" Phil asked, wearing his usual skeptical expression.

Pastor Ezra walked into the crowd. "The sheriff has decided to keep Jed until he calms down," he said. "Everything is fine. The good sheriff will investigate the matter."

The crowd grumbled. Jordy could hear them talking about their distrust of the sheriff. Jordy was in full agreement. Something wasn't right with any of this. Too many times, the sheriff had brushed aside the obvious, deciding on the obscure, instead. Was he compromised somehow?

Across the street, he saw Henry Lee, drinking a coffee in front of Winslow's. His dark eyes were following the pastor as he walked amongst the people restoring order and calming fears. When Henry noticed Jordy was watching, he raised his coffee cup in a salute before walking to a black SUV and hopping inside. Jordy did not like the way Henry was eyeing Pastor Ezra. It reminded him of a predator stalking its prey before it attacked. Jordy's tempest flared.

Chapter 32

Jordy and Cesar rode with Sheriff Clancy to check out the dead cows at Jed's farm. "Jed said they were in the lower field," Sheriff Clancy said, clearly not happy for the company.

They rode up to Jed's house in mostly silence. Diane, Jed's wife, was outside weeding the garden when they pulled into the yard. When she saw Sheriff Clancy, she rose to her feet. From her set expression, she was not happy to see him. "What do you want?" she asked from between gritted teeth.

"I need to see the cows, Diane." Sheriff Clancy ignored her tone.

She, in turn, playing it forward by ignoring the Sheriff, turning instead to Jordy. "Jed said that they are in the lower field."

"Have you seen them?" Jordy asked gently.

Diane shook her head. "Jed didn't want us to see it."

Jordy nodded in understanding. "Ok, I'm going to open the paddock gate and drive through the field."

"Jed said it wasn't pretty. I need to bury them once he releases my husband." Diane turned on her heel and went back to the garden.

Jed's sons, Bobby and David, watched from the porch with worried expressions. Jordy couldn't imagine what they must be thinking.

"Let's get this over with," Cesar said, not happy with the situation.

"I'm all for it," Sheriff Clancy agreed.

Jordy opened the paddock fence, and the sheriff drove inside the field. "Follow the fence line, and it will take you to the lower field," Jordy said, sitting in the passenger seat after closing the fence.

They drove along the fence, down a slight hill to where the grass was flattened and coated thick with blood. Flies buzzed around them when they got out of the car. But that was all there was to see. There were no carcasses of butchered cows on the ground. There were tire marks in the matted grass going up to the fence line. Jordy walked along it, noting that it looked like the fence had been recently repaired.

"This looks new," he gestured to the fence.

Sheriff Clancy shrugged. "What does that prove?"

"This does not make any sense," Cesar said, walking the scene. "From the amount of blood, clearly, the cows were killed here. Do you think someone drove in here and hauled away the carcasses?"

"It's an animal kill." Sheriff Clancy rolled his eyes.

"An animal killing?" Jordy asked in disbelief. "What animals do you know that can eat two cows whole?"

Cesar chuckled. "Last time I checked, anacondas hadn't grown legs, so they can walk into a field to devour cows."

"I'm telling you that this is the way that I see it." Sheriff Clancy stalked back to his car, leaving Jordy and Cesar to follow him.

When they got to the paddock gate, Jordy hopped out of the car to open the gate. "I'm going to let Diane know that the carcasses are gone," Jordy said.

"I'd rather you didn't do that," Sheriff Clancy said. "I'll call her and let her know. If Jed is calmer, I'll release him."

Jordy nodded, not looking to step on the Sheriff's toes any more than he already had. After all, Jordy had sort of invited himself into his investigation if it was an investigation. "Sure, however, you want to manage it."

Cesar exchanged a glance with Jordy, clearly on the same page. Jordy closed the gate and climbed back into the passenger seat. As they pulled out of the driveway, Sheriff Clancy turned to him. "I trust you both will keep what you saw to yourselves," he said, his tone more of a warning than a request.

Jordy glanced at him. "Why?"

"People in town are already tense, and going around telling them that we have vanishing cow carcasses is not going to help."

"I won't lie if asked." Jordy saw by the muscle working up and down Sheriff Clancy's jaw, that his answer was not what the sheriff wanted to hear.

"Fine, just don't go around offering it up. And for God's sake, don't tell Phil."

Jordy and Cesar smiled. "I won't go around offering it up." But if Phil asks…

Chapter 33

Jordy and Cesar met up with Laz when they got back. Most of the people that had gathered went back about their business. Phil was still standing with a small group near the fountain of the third angel, exchanging conspiracy theories. Though normally they were the far-fetched variety, Jordy wondered if they were on to something this time. Phil saw Jordy and Cesar hop out of Sheriff Clancy's car when they returned. It was sure to weave even more conspiracy theories.

Jordy didn't acknowledge Phil, rather content for now to pretend ignorance. He did not feel like fielding questions that he could not answer. He walked straight over to Laz. "Ready to go?" he asked.

"Sure," Laz said, tossing his coffee cup into the trash container at the side of Winslow's.

"Yeah, I'd like to get out of here," Cesar said, heading for Jordy's truck.

When Jordy got to the truck, Evander was waiting for him in his car. "Jordy?" he called.

The last thing that Jordy wanted or needed was to have a conversation with Evander. He turned slowly. Evander sat in the back seat of the black Mercedes with the window rolled down. The man driving was Aiden, one of his men. There was no sign of Henry.

Jordy walked up to the car, intending to tell him that he needed to get back to the farm. "Evander, what can I do for you?"

"Get in, let's take a ride." It was not a request.

Jordy nodded before turning to Cesar and tossing him the keys. "I'll meet you at your house."

Aiden got out of the car and opened the back door for him to get inside. Jordy went inside, sitting next to Evander. When the door closed, it felt like a trap snapping closed. He felt trapped. "What is this about?"

"Just a chat between friends." Evander nodded to Aiden, and they drove off towards Evander's place.

"What's on your mind?" Jordy watched him closely, not liking this at all.

"Jordy, you are special. I sense that. Henry senses it, too. I wanted to offer you a job."

Whatever Jordy was expecting, it was not this. When he got into the car, he thought this was going to be about Jed. Evander would try to gloss it over with some excuse, but the job offer came as a complete surprise. "A job?" Jordy asked flatly.

Evander nodded. "I can pay you handsomely. It would be enough so that you could hire a few men to work your land."

"Why? Doing what?"

"I recognize talent when I see it. It comes in many forms. I think that you have a gift. I would like to tap into that gift." Evander was looking at him. Jordy didn't like it.

"I have no idea what you are talking about. I'm just a simple farmer."

Evander laughed. "You are much more than that, my friend. Even now, I would bet you are feeling something warning you about me. Am I right?"

Oh, he was right on the money about that. His tempest had come to full life. But this time, he didn't have to wonder what danger was lurking in the shadows. It was sitting right there next to him. "I like my life the way that it is," he said, in all honesty.

"Life is about change, Jordy. Sometimes the change is for the good, and other times it is for…the not-so-good." Evander shifted his attention to Aiden. "Take us to Cesar's farm."

Jordy never took his eyes off Evander. When he turned his attention back on Jordy, he glimpsed something malevolent in Evander's icy blue eyes. "Think about my offer, Jordy," Evander said as the car came to a stop.

Jordy said nothing as he got out. Right now, he wanted to get as far away from Evander as he could. Whatever this was, he wanted nothing to do with it. Gift? What the hell was he talking about? Just more of Evander's tricks, he told himself.

Chapter 34

Cesar and Laz were sitting on the picnic bench in the backyard. Jordy took the seat across from them. "Glad that is over," he said, sighing.

"What did he want?" Cesar reached into the cooler, handing Jordy a beer.

"He offered me a job." Jordy popped the top on the can.

"What kind of job?" Laz asked.

"Beats the shit out of me," Jordy said, taking a long swallow.

"What did he say?" Cesar tipped his head at him.

"He said that he wanted to use my gift and offered to pay me." Jordy shrugged.

Cesar snorted. "Gift? Do you think he knows about your early warning system?"

"Who knows? Besides, what good is it to him? It's nothing that can be controlled."

"Somehow, he knows. But how?" Laz was frowning.

"I can't imagine. What good is it to him when he is the cause of it going off?"

"Damn, that is strange." Cesar was looking at Jordy with a puzzled look on his face.

"How did you end it with him?" Laz asked, reaching into the cooler for another beer.

"I told him that I would think about it. Though, that was a lie, I don't need to think about anything. The answer is no."

"So, what do we do now?" Cesar said. "Things are not heading in the right direction. I don't need your tempest to tell me that things in town are getting more complicated. This thing with the cows at Jed's place was a warning. Jed had stepped over a line with them, and they showed him what they can do if he does it again."

"Yeah, I see it that way too," Jordy agreed.

"I guess this is as good a time as any to tell you," Laz said, taking a big gulp of liquid courage.

Both Jordy and Cesar looked at him. "Tell us what?" Cesar asked.

"While you were off with the Sheriff, Phil told me that the Wong brothers were killed in a car crash, shortly after leaving town."

Jordy and Cesar winced. "They are dead?" Cesar asked in disbelief.

Laz nodded. "Phil said that they died instantly. The car smashed head-on into a tree and exploded on impact. The intensity of the flame left nothing but crispy critters."

Jordy remembered Tommy Wong telling him that he didn't need luck. He had thought leaving town would keep him safe, but clearly, that wasn't the case. "Where did Phil hear that?" he asked, his concern deepening.

"Jed told him," Laz said. "He was there in the Sheriff's office reporting that his fence was cut again, when the call came in."

"So much for leaving town to be safe," Cesar said.

"We are beginning to sound like Phil," Jordy said.

Cesar snorted. "Maybe Phil has a point this time."

"This is getting scary," Laz said, finishing his beer.

Chapter 35

Jordy was getting ready for church. Petunia was pouting, dressed in her Sunday best. She was told that she had to sit on the stool and wait so she didn't get dirty. Brian was making fun of her, and she stuck her tongue out at him. Jordy ruffled her hair as he walked by her. "There will be plenty of time to play with Walter when we get back."

"Yeah, no one wants to sit next to a pig girl at church," Brian said, laughing at Petunia's outraged expression.

"Walter doesn't smell, I washed him." She stuck out her tongue again.

Amelia shook her finger at Petunia. "If you use my soap again to wash that pig, I'm going to tan your hide."

Jordy chuckled. "You know that she does not even know what that means."

Amelia hid her smile. "It's all in the tone and delivery."

"It means that Mom is going to kick her ass." Brian tossed back.

Amelia spun around, pinning Brian with an icy glare. "Watch your mouth, young man. Or I'll take the soap that Petunia used to wash her pig and wash out your mouth with it."

Brian flinched. Petunia giggled. "Time to go," Jordy said, trying not to laugh.

Things had returned to near normal over the last week. With people still uneasy, Jordy hoped that Pastor Ezra had a good sermon planned. Today, after church, Pastor Ezra was coming over to share dinner with them. He was looking forward to a relaxing Sunday afternoon, sitting on the porch with a glass of iced tea.

They sat in their usual spot inside the church. They had made it here, and Petunia was still clean. So, miracles do exist, Jordy thought. He nodded to people as they passed by. Jed and his family sat where they normally did. Jed had been quiet, mostly keeping to himself on his farm since the incident. It was nice to see them out together as a family.

Pastor Ezra stood in front of the church. When everyone was seated, he began to speak, his voice filling the small church. "I want to begin by talking about forgiveness and understanding. I want to talk about welcoming strangers as Christ has welcomed you. Throughout the ages, hospitality has been important to God. Once, we were all strangers wandering the desert of life. God accepted us with open arms and an open heart. God welcomes the strangers to survive.

Now we have strangers in Wormwood. Instead of looking at them as a stranger, we should look at them as a new friend. Because they are different, we must not shun them. Instead, open your hearts and minds to them as God's people."

Jordy listened with his head bent. Pastor Ezra was asking a lot of his congregation, he thought. Forgiveness and understanding run along a two-way street, in his opinion. He doubted Evander would reciprocate. The sermon was as strong and powerful as all of Pastor Ezra's. In the end, it was about faith in God and man.

Pastor Ezra ended it the same as it began, asking his flock to try and be more understanding of strangers. He stood at the head of the church with a strength that was not only inspiring but instilled the healing power of God. Jordy looked around and people were responding to it. Even Jed nodded his head from time to time.

Outside, on the steps of the church, Pastor Ezra stood as people greeted him on their way outside. When it came time for Jordy, Pastor Ezra, took both of his hands into his. "What did you think of the sermon today?" he asked.

"It was uplifting as always."

"I'm so glad you are coming tonight for dinner. We are having a pot roast with peach cobbler for dessert." Amelia grinned at him.

"My favorite," Pastor Ezra said with a rare grin of his own.

"We will see you tonight, Pastor," Jordy said, walking down the stairs to make room for others in line.

As they walked to the truck, Jordy noticed Henry sitting in a car, parked across from the church. Once again, he was watching the Pastor. It made Jordy feel uneasy. He doubted Henry was a churchgoer, and the look on his face confirmed it. Contempt was the closest he could come to putting a name to it. He wondered why.

Chapter 36

Dinner had been enjoyable, and the conversation kept flowing. Pastor Ezra sat next to Petunia, listening to her tall tales about her pig. She was convinced that the little pig could understand every word she said to him. He was a super pig, according to Petunia. The pastor took it all in stride, telling her that Walter was truly a blessed pig. Jordy hid his smile behind his napkin.

They took their cobbler outside out on the porch, where it was cooler. Pastor Ezra sat beside Jordy, enjoying the cool breeze floating on the fragrant night air. But now, Pastor Ezra was quiet… pensive. Jordy wondered what was on his mind but waited for the pastor to ask him. He knew there was something coming.

"I had a visit from Henry Lee," Pastor Ezra said wistfully.

"Oh?" Jordy said, looking at the pastor as he stared out into the darkness.

"Do you know him?"

"Yes, we have met." Where was this going, Jordy wondered.

"He is a strange man. He asked me if what I was doing for the town was doing more harm than good." Pastor Ezra glanced at Jordy.

Jordy frowned. "Strange question to ask."

"He is of the belief that I am filling people with false hopes."

Jordy had seen the way that Henry watched the pastor. It troubled him. "Did he say why he thinks that?"

"He said that God is a fantasy made up by man to control people from their base urges. Henry is not a believer."

That did not surprise Jordy. "He is free to believe whatever he likes."

"He said that I sell God to feel important and support myself financially. I told him that what I sell is faith and love."

Jordy chuckled. "That must have fallen on deaf ears."

The pastor nodded in agreement. "I worry over Henry's salvation. His soul is in jeopardy."

In Jordy's opinion, that ship had already sailed. Henry had no soul. "Don't worry yourself over it too much. Henry has made his choice." But there was more, Jordy felt it.

"He told me that I should think about leaving town and set up someplace else."

"Did he?" Son of a bitch, Jordy fumed. His tempest was waking in his gut.

"He offered to build me a new church in Clayton. I think that he was serious."

"I see. What did you think about that?"

Pastor Ezra turned to face Jordy. "There is something not right about all of this. It felt more like a threat than an offer. Maybe Phil has a point in that some of the new people are not good."

"As the saying goes, even a broken clock is right at least twice a day."

Pastor Ezra looked troubled. "Yes, but it is still broken. I'm not ready to close my heart to the new people like some in town. But I think they bear watching. As I said in my sermon this morning, we must show them the light of God's people."

Or better yet, the business end of a gun, he thought. "I would agree," Jordy said, feeling uneasy.

"Henry was very interested in you, Jordy. He asked a lot of questions. Questions that I would not answer. He wanted to know if I ever saw your gift." The pastor was looking at Jordy intently. "I told him the truth, that I have never seen it."

"Gift?" Jordy decided to play dumb.

"Your mother, bless her soul, once came to me about it a long time ago when you were but a boy. At the time, I thought that she was being fanciful."

Jordy knew what was coming. "What did she say?"

"May told me that you had the ability to foresee bad things before they happened. I told her that God blesses people sometimes with sight that none of us have. She said that you knew that your father had passed before the sheriff even delivered the news. Is that true?"

It was true. He had been playing ball outside with his friends when his tempest flared. Jordy remembered as if it was yesterday. It had told him that his father was dead. At the time, he thought that he was losing his mind. He didn't know how, but he knew it was true, his father was either dead or dying. He had rushed home and told his mother. God, she had been so furious, thinking he was just trying to scare her. But twenty minutes later, the sheriff arrived with the news—his father had died in a car crash, driving the old farm truck. "It is true," he whispered.

"May said that there were other times too. You knew that a tree would fall in the park. You cleared everyone away that was sitting on the picnic bench just before it fell, crushing everything below."

Jordy nodded. "I did." It was like confessing to a sin.

"I told Henry none of this. But he is very interested in it." Pastor Ezra covered Jordy's hand with his. "A gift from God is coveted and must be protected, Jordy. Hold it close."

Chapter 37

Jordy was taking a break from working in the fields. The sun was hot today, floating in a clear blue sky above. Cesar, Laz, and Jordy sat under an old oak tree in the shade, sipping on some cool water while eating muffins, Amelia had packed for him. The conversation with Pastor Ezra still bothered him as he stared down the cornrows.

"What's on your mind, my friend?" Cesar asked.

Jordy swirled the water around in his cup. "Pastor Ezra was at the house last night for dinner. He told me that Henry told him that he should leave town. Henry even offered to build him a church in Clayton."

Cesar flinched. "Did he say why?"

Before Jordy answered, Laz said, "He wants to destroy all faith here."

Jordy glanced at Laz. "Why do you say that?"

Laz shrugged. "Where there is faith, there is hope. Where there is hope, there is a community. Where there is a community, there is a reason to fight for home and each other."

Yes, Jordy thought. As long as people were united, they would fight. "I never thought about that."

Cesar looked skeptical. "So, they want Pastor Ezra to leave to crush our faith?"

"Why else would they want Pastor Ezra to go? Henry said to the pastor that he fills our heads with fantasies and that God is nothing more than man's way to keep us from our base instincts."

"Like fear?" Laz snorted.

Jordy nodded. "Yes, maybe something like that. I have seen Henry watching the pastor. I saw him yesterday after service ended, sitting in a car watching him. The look on his face was nothing short of contempt."

Cesar snorted. "But that is freaking crazy. We have homes and family to hold us together. Getting rid of the pastor will not undo that."

"But it is a start," Laz said. "Look at what these assholes have already done. Everyone in town is afraid of them. They take away the law, and then they attack our faith. They are slowly taking over."

Cesar shook his head. "But why? Why not live and let live? No one is fighting them or standing against them."

Laz sighed. "In war, the towns have good infrastructure. They need the town. If there is no law or faith to hold the people together and the community suffers, then the enemy can rule unopposed."

"That's grim," Jordy said. His tempest swirled, tightening in his gut. Somewhere deep inside him, he knew it was true.

Laz looked deep in thought. "It makes sense. They want us to exist only to serve them."

Cesar snorted. "Jordy's early warning system is the fly in the ointment, as they say. It warns us when they are going to pull shit. That is why they want you to work for them. If this is all true, it's going to get worse. It would be nice to have a warning."

Jordy shook his head. "They will just have to live without my help. Besides, how would I be of any help to them?"

"By staying on the sidelines and not doing a thing," Laz answered, easily.

Jordy snorted. "It's not reliable enough to be of any use to anyone. Most of the time, when it goes off, I don't even know what it means until it happens. There isn't any time to react."

"I was thinking about that," Cesar said. "It has never really been tested, though. You have lived here your whole life where it is safe and predictable. Until now, there has been nothing to set it off and see what it can do. Do you remember the day of the twister?"

Jordy sighed, not really wanting to think about it. "Yes, I remember."

"We were down the backfield. The sky was dark, and the wind picked up. Lightning split the heavens, and the thunder cracked, splitting the air all around us. Do you remember what you said?"

"I said that we needed to leave." What was the point?

"Yes, you said we needed to leave and go to the woods. At the time, I thought that you were crazy." Cesar was looking at him intently. "You knew that we would be safe there. When that swirling wedge dropped out of the sky, I thought that we were goners. We huddled in the woods by the base of that tree. Debree was flying all around us. But we were left untouched. Somehow, you knew that."

Jordy remembered being drawn into the woods instead of making a run for it. Somehow, he knew to take cover by that tree. It was not even a thought in his head, it was like he had been operating on pure instinct. He never questioned it but followed where it led. In the end, they walked away with nothing more than a few scratches. "Ok, but I can't control it. I don't see how it will help."

"We will have to wait and see," Cesar said.

Chapter 38

ordy was getting ready to leave for the fields when Petunia came running up to him, looking frantic. "Daddy, daddy, Walter is missing," she said. "His pen door is open, and I can't find him."

"Did you check the garden?" Jordy paused by his truck.

"I did. I called him over and over. Someone stole Walter." Fat tears ran down her cheeks.

"Petunia, I'm sure he is around here. You go inside, and I'll look for him in the field. He's probably rooting around in the field someplace." His tempest coiled, making him frown. Now his gut was alerting over a lost pig, great.

Petunia hesitated before turning. "I just know he is in trouble and needs me."

Jordy ruffled her hair. "We will find him."

Getting into the truck, he decided to get gas before heading to the fields. On his way to town, he scanned the roadside for Walter. Though he never wandered beyond the yard, there was always a first time. Slowing his speed, he looked along the edge of the road and into the yards as he passed by but saw nothing.

Pulling the truck into the service station, Jordy got out and started pumping fifteen dollars of gas into his tank. He stood by the pump, watching people in town as they went about their business. Kids were heading to school, people were walking to work, and some were stopping by Winslow's to get a coffee. The heartbeat of the town beat normally.

His mind drifted back to his Walter problem. Sometime during the night, Walter had escaped out of his pen. So, either Petunia hadn't fixed the latch, or Walter had figured out how to pop it open. It would be another thing to add to the long list of things that he needed to do. Fix Walter's pen. Petunia was beside herself with worry. He would search the fields when he got home, convinced Walter was rooting around somewhere in the cornfield.

Jordy was just finishing up when two of Evander's men, Aiden and Ethan, pulled up to the pumps behind him. Jordy's tempest flared in a warning. He watched them from under the rim of his ball cap. They were smiling but there was nothing welcoming or friendly in it. Their eyes slid over him and again that smile, a smile that was not a smile at all, but a challenging smirk. Something was up.

He kept his eyes glued on the pump, as he silently willed it to stop so that he could hop into his truck and leave. The dial kept spinning. Three more dollars to go, and he could be on his way. He just needed to stay cool, but his tempest had other ideas. It flared in his gut.

"Oink, oink," Aiden said, under his breath.

Jordy froze. They had Walter. They must have come onto his property during the night and taken him. Images of Jed's cows raced through his mind. Did they roast Walter over an open pit and eat him like they did the cows? The pump emitted an audible click as it stopped pumping gas. Jordy secured the nozzle and turned slowly to face them.

He eyed them both, and when they looked at each other and then laughed in his face, a rage lit a fire in his blood, unlike anything that he had ever experienced. It built, as his tempest flared, spreading through his body like an unholy infernal. His whole body vibrated with an unleashed energy. There was no fear as he faced the two-armed men before him, only fury. He struggled to hold onto the rage building, and at that moment, he knew what Jed had felt that day when he found his beloved cows slaughtered in his field. He wanted them dead. Aiden and Ethan stopped laughing and took a step awkwardly backward, looking confused.

"Where's my pig?" Jordy said between gritted teeth.

Ethan was the first to recover, swallowing hard. "Boss has him at the compound."

Jordy stared into their wide, surprised eyes. "Tell him that I'll be around to collect him."

Aiden nodded. "I'll tell him."

Chapter 39

Jordy drove to Evander's, swallowing hard on the rage that he felt. These people were a curse upon Wormwood. Nothing good would come of them being here. Trying to be reasonable was a joke to them. He was making his stand today. Now. They crossed a line, taking his daughter's pet. Actually, they had crossed many lines, he corrected.

When Jordy reached the gate, the men opened it to let him through without saying a word. The first stirrings of apprehension stirred in his gut. This was not one of his best ideas, he reasoned. He had not thought this out, letting his emotions take control. It was a trap, he knew. But he was invested now all in, as Laz would say.

Jordy pulled into the driveway and parked by the house, looking around for Walter. There was no sign of him in the yard. His eyes rested on the barn, in there. They had him in there if he was not already slaughtered. When he got out of the truck, Evander came outside on the porch. Jordy ignored him and instead walked towards the barn.

"You can't get in there," Evander called.

Jordy stopped, turning to face him. "I'm not in the mood for games. Give me my pig, and I'll be on my way."

"Not until, we talk." Evander walked down the steps, facing Jordy in the driveway.

It reminded Jordy of two gunslingers, facing off to see who was the fastest to draw. Jordy was out of his league, he knew. But his tempest was still running the show. He would not, could not, back down.

"Then talk," Jordy spat.

Evander was watching him. "I need you to calm down, first."

Was that weariness that he detected in Evander's eyes? "I'm not in the mood for talking. Give me what is mine, and I will be on my way."

Evander put up his hands in surrender. "All right, but you must promise to talk when you are calmer."

"Why?" Jordy ground out. God, how he wanted to slap that look off his stupid face. "Why should I promise you anything? You came onto my property and took my daughter's pet. Walter is family. But you don't get that, do you?"

Evander took a step backward. "Yes, that was a mistake. I see that now."

"Then do something about it," Jordy bit out. The tempest swirled in agitation.

Evander walked past him to the barn and went inside. Jordy could feel unseen eyes watching him, though he saw no one in the yard. Whoever they were, they were hiding—watchful, and undoubtedly armed. When Evander came outside, one of his men was pulling Walter behind him. There was a rope tied around the little pig's neck, and he squealed and huffed when he saw Jordy.

"Bastards," Jordy said under his breath.

The two men stopped before reaching Jordy. "Now, I have admitted this was a mistake," Evander said. "I would like us to sit down and talk about this."

"I'll think about it," Jordy said, just wanting to collect Walter and be on his way.

Evander smiled. "Yes, you are calmer. That is good." He took the rope from the man at his side and walked Walter the rest of the way to Jordy.

Jordy refused to take the rope from Evander. Instead, he yanked the rope off Walter's neck and pointed to the truck. The little pig didn't hesitate, he trotted to the truck. Jordy turned his back on Evander and walked back to his truck, opening the passenger door to put Walter inside. He felt their eyes drilling into his back but ignored it. If they were going to make a move on him, there was not much he could do about it. For whatever reason, they seemed to hesitate. Jordy didn't take any time to think about it. Whatever the reason, it was fine with him. He just wanted to get out of here.

He climbed into the cab behind the wheel and drove. In the rearview mirror, he saw Henry stepping out from behind one of the parked cars to stand beside Evander. They watched as Jordy pulled away, out of the driveway. He drove up the incline, passing through the armed gate, with the men standing there watching him. When he came to the road, he took a long, shaky breath as he headed for home.

Walter was stretched out on the passenger seat, napping beside him. From the telltale scratches and scrapes on Walter's skin, Jordy guessed that the little pig had put up a fight when he was taken. Poor thing had to be terrified. "Bastards," he whispered.

He drove down the driveway, parking in front of his house before getting out of the truck with Walter. Amelia came running out of the house, a grin splitting her face, when she saw him with Walter. She skidded to a stop, looking at him with concern. "What happened to you?"

"I found Walter," Jordy said, confused by the concerned look on her face.

"Yeah, but what happened to you? Your face."

Jordy frowned, backing up to look at his reflection in the truck's mirrors. His face was vivid red, like he had been out in the sun all day. Amelia walked up beside him, touching his cheek with the cool palm of her hand.

"Hmm. I have no idea what that is. It's like a sunburn, but it doesn't hurt." Jordy probed the scarlet skin with his fingertip.

"Your skin is hot," she said. "Let's get Walter settled back in his pen and then come in for a cold drink. Where did you find him? Petunia is going to be so happy."

Jordy was still frowning at his reflection wondering how the hell he got a sunburn. "Walter must have wandered off," he said absently. "I think that I'm going to move him into the barn. It's safer."

Amelia frowned at him. "Is everything ok?"

"Yeah, everything is fine." He hated lying to his wife but why worry her over this, he reasoned.

"Ok, let's take care of Walter and then I want a better look at that burn."

"Deal," he forced a smile.

Chapter 40

Jordy sat on the porch with Cesar, staring out into the darkness. "Go over it again," Cesar said.

"I told you; it was weird. I met up with Evander's men at the gas pump in town after looking for Walter. They pulled in after I did. One of them said oink, oink. I knew they had Walter." Jordy was frowning. Even now, his tempest coiled in his gut.

"So, they were rubbing it in that they had taken the pig." Cesar was looking at Jordy much in the same way that a doctor looks at his patient.

"Yeah, they were trying to get a rise out of me. But instead, they woke my tempest." Jordy turned to look at Cesar, being careful to keep his voice low so Amelia would not hear from inside the house. "I have never been so angry, Cesar. I wanted to kill them where they stood."

"From there, you went to Evander's place. Why did you go there alone, Jordy? They could have beaten you up or done something even worse."

"I did think that it was not my brightest plan on the trip over there. But I had no fear. Uneasy, sure. But I was never afraid. I was too angry." He had thought about it a lot since it happened. Adrenalin, he thought. Whatever it was, he was not going to back down even though reason told him he was being foolish facing all those men on his own.

"What was their reaction?"

"That's the weirdest part, they seemed uneasy, too." He remembered the uncertain look in their eyes and was puzzled by it.

Cesar scoffed. "Of what…a pissed-off farmer?"

Jordy shrugged, shaking his head. "I have no idea, but I sensed that they did not want to mess with me. When I got home, my face was scarlet red, and hot like I had a sunburn. It disappeared in an hour. I can't explain that either."

"It's got to be connected to your gift, right?"

Jordy snorted. Was it a gift or a curse? He was undecided. "Some gift. It's going to get me killed."

Cesar chuckled. "Whatever it is, it made them back off, right? The way things are going in town, we are going to need that secret weapon of yours."

Jordy looked over at him. "Are things worse?"

Cesar nodded. "Esmae was in the store this morning picking up supplies. People are scared. Evander's men are becoming bolder. They are threatening people. Much in the same way that they did with you at the gas pump. They are looking for a fight."

"But to what end?" Jordy sighed. It was senseless to him. Wormwood was a peaceful place with good people.

"That is the million-dollar question. They cornered Phil at Hadley's, too. Just blocked him down one of the aisles. The way Phil tells it, they were just waiting for him to make a move. They kept talking about his wife and how she was a pretty piece of ass. Jack Hadley came down the aisle with a cart full of grain sacks and pushed it between them so Phil could make for an escape."

"Jesus," Jordy whispered, running his fingers through his hair. He worried now about Amelia going into town.

"Yeah, it's heating up. Just a matter of time before the tension overflows and someone gets hurt."

"Laz brought up a point about destroying our faith and community. Maybe he has a point. If they want the town and the people to be too terrified to move against them, then they win. Laz thought it was infrastructure that they were after."

Cesar tipped his head at Jordy. "Yes, I remember. What are you thinking?"

"I think Laz has it partially right. I think that whatever they are doing on that compound requires them to wipe out any threat. Once they control the town, the threat is eliminated.

"I've wondered about that. Do you think it is drugs?"

Jordy shrugged. "It could be any number of things. None of them good."

Chapter 41

Jordy was working in the cornfield the next afternoon. The warm nights, along with the rain, had been good for the crops. Where every place around them was experiencing near drought conditions, Wormwood was blessed with enough rain so that he only had to irrigate sparingly. No one understood it, but Jordy was glad for it.

His father always told him to never question good fortune, because asking why could somehow end it. Instead, he said a silent thank you each morning. Sometimes, you get lucky, he thought. After last year's crop, he could use a good one coming for Fall. He knew Cesar was in the same position. The money from last year's crop barely pulled them through. Like all farmers, there were good years followed by the inevitable bad year. As long as the good ones outnumbered the bad, he could stay ahead.

Walking through the cornrows, he ran his hand gently up the cornstalks. There were hardly any stalks that did not come up. All of them are strong and healthy. The same was true of the wheat field. This could be his best year since he started. If it were not for the trouble brewing in town, he would be a happy man.

He was halfway down the path when a voice called his name from behind. With a sigh, he looked up at the clear blue sky. Evander. Slowly, he turned, spotting Evander standing about ten feet away, right in the middle of the cornrow.

"Why are you here?" Jordy asked. His tempest was coiling in his gut.

Evander smiled at him like a friend. But Jordy knew better. "I told you that we needed to talk. I thought that I would stop down here and save you the trip delivering the food."

Jordy wanted to tell him what he could do with his food and the talk but kept that to himself. "If this is about your job offer, I'm afraid you came here for nothing. I'm going to have to pass on it. I'm a farmer and will remain a farmer."

Evander smiled. "Yes, I'm not surprised. You are at home here in this field." He looked around. "I can see why. It must give you pleasure looking around, knowing that all of this is because of you."

"Something like that," Jordy said, wondering where he was going with this. Was he threatening his crop or was he reading too much into it? His tempest quivered in his gut.

"I brought us food and drink. Let's sit and finish our talk." Evander turned, expecting Jordy to follow him.

Jordy hesitated. "I have a lot to do."

Evander looked at him from over his shoulder. "Give me fifteen minutes. Think of it as a work break."

Jordy wanted to argue. He didn't have anything to say to Evander after what he did by taking Walter. But drawing a line in the sand with someone like Evander was not wise. That whole thing about keeping your enemy close was ringing true. "All right," he said, walking behind him.

There was a picnic blanket spread out beneath the oak tree at the edge of the cornfield. A basket and cooler were in the center. Cesar and Laz were sitting at the side of the blanket, eating sandwiches, and drinking pop. Jordy frowned. So, this was going to be a conversation that included all of them. When Jordy walked to the edge of the blanket, he spotted two of Evander's men, standing on the hill a short distance away., watching them.

Evander sat on the blanket, looking up at Jordy. "Here," he said, opening the basket and cooler. "Help yourself. I'm afraid the sandwiches are not the best. They came from Finn's. But they will do."

Jordy reached in, took a sandwich and a pop and sat down on the ground beside the blanket. He did not miss Evander's smile. Evander helped himself to a sandwich, and they ate without speaking. Jordy thought it was better that way. He was hungry after working in the fields since dawn.

Evander put down his half-eaten sandwich on the corner of the blanket. "Henry has a friend from his village back home, though a friend isn't exactly the right term for it. He is a very old man."

Jordy glanced over at him but kept eating. He sensed Evander was going to tell them a story. So, he stayed quiet, listening. Cesar and Laz glanced at Jordy but said nothing.

"The man is very wise," Evander continued. "He is gifted."

If Evander was expecting a reaction, he didn't get one. Jordy was aware that Cesar and Laz were listening to every word just as he was. He wondered where Evander was going with his tale.

"The man is what we would call a fortune teller. He is remarkably accurate with his predictions. He told us when we came here that we would meet a man with a powerful gift. A man who can turn even the most fearsome warriors into frightened children. He said that this man was blessed by the gods and that his powers came from them. What do you think of that story?"

"I think it is fanciful thinking," Cesar said, keeping a blank expression.

"It is just a story told by an old man," Jordy said, finishing his sandwich.

Evander nodded. "He said that the man does not know the true strength of these powers. The man is humble yet brave."

Jordy shrugged. "So, what is the moral of this tale?"

"I would say that one must use great care around such a man," Evander said, staring at Jordy.

"Live and let live. That sounds like the right move. If such a man existed." Jordy didn't like where this was going.

Evander laughed, rising to his feet. "Yes, live and let live. Well, I must be going. I have taken up enough of your time."

Jordy rose to his feet. "Thanks for lunch."

"It was my pleasure." Evander stood still, staring at Jordy. "I hope that we can be friends, Jordy. Someday, I hope that you will tell me a story about a man with gifts."

Jordy gave him a lopsided grin. "I'm not much for telling stories."

"But I'm sure that you have a good one to tell." Evander looked at his men and nodded. His men walked down the hill and packed up what was left of the picnic. Evander was turning to leave but turned back to Jordy. "Henry can help you explore your gift if you are curious."

That was never going to happen. "Nope, I'm good." Jordy waved it away, not needing any time to think about it.

Evander shook his head and chuckled. "If it were me, I would want to know."

See, Jordy thought, Evander was nothing like him. That is what separated them. For Jordy, he was content with not knowing. Evander would sharpen his skills like a weapon to use against people. Pastor Ezra said that some people would covet such a power given by God. Jordy would never do that. To him, the gift was a burden that he wished was not his.

Once Evander was out of earshot, Laz turned to Jordy. "What do you make of that?"

Cesar snorted. "It was a warning."

Jordy nodded. "Yeah, I think so too."

Chapter 42

Dominos at Finn's was a tradition that they had shared for over five years. But to be honest, Jordy would have rather skipped it altogether and gone fishing. Jordy sat with his back to the wall, watching the door. The plan was that they would play until Evander's people showed up. Once they did, they would call it a night and go home. At twenty past nine, Jordy's tempest curled in his gut.

"I think we should make this our last game," Jordy said, his eyes glancing from the game to the door.

Cesar looked over his shoulder at the door. "We got company coming?"

Jordy nodded. "Yeah, I think so."

Ten minutes later, five of Evander's men walked through the door. The men looked around the bar, their eyes coming to rest on Jordy for just a second as they strolled inside. Some people were dancing to music that was playing on the stereo, while others were seated at the bar and tables, laughing, and talking. But the moment the men entered, a hush fell over the bar, the lively atmosphere suddenly growing tense.

One of the men walked over to where people were dancing. Jordy recognized him as one of the guards who watched the fence on the road into Evander's place. His name was Cole. He walked straight up to Molly Harold, who was dancing with her husband, Andy. "Dance," he said, grabbing Molly by the arm.

Andy confronted him. "Please release my wife's arm."

"Or what?" Cole said, glaring at him.

Jordy's tempest twisted into a knot as the growing current passed through his body. "We should go," he whispered.

"Yeah." Laz nodded, starting to gather the dominos from the table.

Andy stared up at Cole, who was at least four inches taller than he was. "I'm not asking you to let her go. I'm telling you to let go of my wife's arm."

Molly stood between them, looking like a frightened doe, glancing from Andy to Cole. "Please, let me go," she begged, withering. "You are hurting me."

Finn's grew deathly quiet with everyone holding their breath as the tension ratcheted up. It was like lightning had struck, and they were all waiting breathlessly for the crash of thunder that was sure to follow. For Jordy, the storm was building from within him. He was in the vortex of a building rage, waiting to be set free.

Andy lunged, swiping at Cole, but Cole deftly sidestepped him. "Big mistake," Cole said, laughing at the much smaller man.

Cole took a swing at Andy. It connected, breaking his nose with an audible, wet snap, as Molly screamed. The other four men were watching, circling around like hungry sharks looking for prey, waiting for anyone stupid enough to step into it. No one did. Andy was on his knees, cupping both hands over his damaged nose as blood gushed out between his fingers. Molly was on her knees beside him, crying. Cole shoved Molly out of the way and kicked Andy in the ribs, sending him face-first onto the floor.

Jordy rose to his feet and slowly walked onto the dance floor facing Cole. "Enough," he snarled. His tempest was raging through his body, pumping his blood hot with fury.

Cole raised his fist for the knockout blow, but his arm hovered there in midair. His eyes fluttered, as the expression on his face went slack, void of emotion. Then he collapsed like a broken doll onto the floor. Jordy looked around, stopping when his eyes rested on the other four men. They backed away, looking terrified, before heading for the door. Seconds later, they heard the roar of motorcycles racing out of town.

Danny, the bartender, was the first to spring into action. "Let's get these guys to Doc's for medical attention."

Jordy returned to his chair and sat down heavily. He was out of breath and his face felt hot and flushed as he glanced at Laz and Cesar in confusion. "I'm not sure what just happened."

Laz smiled, setting the dominos back up on the table. "You just kicked their ass," he whispered with a sly smile curling his lips.

Cesar flagged the server. "Another round," he said, smiling.

Chapter 43

"It felt like when you stand beneath high tension lines. There was an electrical vibration in the air." Laz said from the backseat of the truck on their way home.

"Yeah, the hairs on my arms were standing up," Cesar agreed.

"Then you got up and walked to the dance floor. Your eyes were narrowed but alert as you homed in on target. Your face was red like a sunburn." Laz laughed. "It was awesome, dude."

"Did anyone else notice in the bar?" Jordy was nervous. "Did they know it was because of me?"

Cesar shook his head. "Most people there were too busy shitting themselves. No, they didn't know it came from you. But they saw you were the only one willing to stand up to them."

At least that was good, Jordy thought. "Evander's men knew."

"Yes, I'm sure they did," Laz agreed. "It was focused on them. They looked terrified. Like they were going to be evaporated or something."

Jordy groaned. "I don't know what happened. I was struggling to hold onto it. I don't even remember getting up or walking to the dance floor. The next thing that I knew, I was standing there, and Andy and Cole were on the floor."

"What does it feel like?" Laz asked.

"Not good, I can tell you that much." Jordy ran his hand through his hair in frustration. "I can feel this pressure growing inside of me. It's like it is building, and I try to control it, but it takes on a life of its own. There is this rage building, and it feels like I am going to explode. But then there is this clarity that comes with it and a need to do something to stop whatever sets it off. There is no fear. Only a complete focus on what is causing harm."

"When you let it go? How does that feel?" Cesar was looking at him strangely.

Jordy considered the question. "There is a sense of relief. It's like the air being let out of a balloon."

"Once, I told you that you have never tested it to see what it can do. I guess we have an answer."

Jordy was not so sure. "Yes and no. I have the sense that there is more."

"More?" Laz said, sitting up straighter.

"Yes, I feel it. It's a little like standing at the precipice of a great divide. The power that I feel is immense, but I think I'm only experiencing a tiny piece of it. And it scares the shit out of me."

Cesar sobered. "I never considered that."

"Personally, I hope it scorches all those assholes," Laz said. "It was pretty satisfying seeing that big piece of crap crumble to the floor on his face. Poor Andy. I hate to think what would have happened if you didn't stop it. They remind me of wild dogs by the way they circle their prey. They deserved a good ass kicking."

Jordy chuckled. "That was pretty satisfying to see him out cold on the floor."

"Hold on to that thought. I'm sure Evander isn't going to share your joy." Cesar sighed.

"Yeah, there is that. I'm sure there will be another conversation." Jordy was not looking forward to it.

Laz snorted. "Oh, the hell with him. If he does not like it, let him keep his tin soldiers on the compound."

If only it was that easy. Jordy wondered. He knew Evander would escalate things soon enough. What would his next move be? He was sure that he wouldn't have to wait long to find out.

Chapter 44

Jordy sat out on the porch sipping an iced tea. It had been two days since that night at Finn's playing dominos. He had learned that the man, Cole, had a cerebral hemorrhage and was sent away to a hospital. Doc said it could have happened anytime. But Jordy wondered. Had he caused it? He felt a measure of guilt until he saw Andy with a broken nose and busted ribs. The town was helping the young couple while Andy was laid up, unable to work. Doc said Andy was lucky that his broken ribs did not puncture his lung. One more kick could have ended Andy's life.

It's a funny thing, Jordy thought, as he listened to crickets and the breeze whispering through the grass, how things seemed to work out. Andy will recover, but Cole's recovery is uncertain. Sometimes, it does not matter how strong you are, life has its own plan for everyone. For Cole, there was a ticking timebomb in his brain, waiting for the right moment to explode.

Jordy was not at all surprised when he saw the black Mercedes rolling up the driveway. Evander. Jordy sighed. He was not looking forward to this conversation. He watched as Evander got out of his car and slowly walked to the porch. The moths that were dancing in the light paused their aerial dance as he climbed the stairs. Almost like they sensed the undercurrent of conflicting emotions. Jordy's tempest pulsed in his gut.

"You have changed, Jordy, since we first met," Evander said, taking a seat beside him.

"How so?" Jordy asked, still looking out into the darkness.

"I can feel a vibration coming from you. I had hoped that we could be friends."

Jordy was aware that his tempest was brewing. It warned of danger, and Jordy had no doubt it was right on the money when it came to Evander. "I don't know what you are talking about. I'm just a simple farmer."

Evander snorted, stretching his long legs. "You are far more than just a simple farmer. Cole would agree with me on that. Well, if Cole had a thought left in his head, that is."

Jordy turned to look at him. "Cole was out of line."

"Cole was following orders."

"Yes, I guessed as much."

"I don't get you, Jordy. You are wasting your talent. You could be rich and yet you are content to break your back day after day toiling in those fields. Think of how your family could benefit."

What about my self-respect, he thought? What is the price for that? "Leave my family out of it."

Evander sighed heavily. "I've come to tell you that things are going to get more difficult for the town. You need to stay out of it. Stay on your farm, and don't get in the way."

"What have you done?"

"What is necessary. If you interfere, there will be pushback. I have tried to run interference for you. I have tried to bring you into the fold. Now you are on your own."

"You come here and threaten me?" Jordy's tempest grew in intensity.

Evander rose to his feet. "Not a threat, Jordy, a warning."

Evander walked unsteadily to his car. The headlights dimmed when he started the Mercedes, its engine was running rough. As he pulled out of the driveway, the headlights became brighter. Jordy watched it roll down the road. Trouble was coming.

Chapter 45

Jordy went into town to pick up supplies at Hadley's store. On his drive through town, he noticed that the streets were nearly deserted. What people he saw scurried across the streets, seeming not to linger. The usual coffee crowd outside Winslow's was nonexistent and the vegetable stand set up by some of the farmers to sell in town was all but abandoned. So, whatever Evander meant by things getting tougher in town was at play. He wondered what was happening.

Jed and Phil were inside Hadley's when Jordy opened the door. They were standing near the window when Jordy walked inside. From the look on their faces, he knew that something bad had happened. "Good morning," Jordy said, tipping his head at them.

"It's anything but a good morning," Jed mumbled.

"Evander's guys are now patrolling the town, some with long guns. There is a curfew, now. No one can be out on the streets after midnight. The Sheriff is behind them. There was a meeting of the town council, and we were told to comply or face the consequences." Phil's hand shook as he drank his coffee.

Jordy rocked back on his heels. "Did they say why they need to patrol the town?"

"They said it is for our own safety." Phil snorted.

Jordy knew it was bullshit. It was the first step to take over. "Now, why would they want to do that? For what purpose?"

Phil grunted. "They are running their trucks through town after it gets dark. Lenny Dawson told us that they stop and gas up their trucks at night. Whatever they are up to, they don't want us seeing it."

"I wonder what is in those trucks?" Jed asked.

"Nothing good," Phil grumbled.

This is what Evander had meant when he warned things would get tougher. So, now they were being policed in their own town. People were scared. "Did they say for how long they were going to do this?"

Phil shrugged. "They said until further notice."

Phil and Jed ducked away from the window. "A patrol is going by."

Jordy took their place in the window, looking outside, ignoring Phil tugging on his sleeve. He stood watching as Ethan and Aiden walked by. They stopped and stared back at Jordy through the window. Draped over their shoulders were automatic weapons. Aiden reached up and patted the rifle, his eyes staring at Jordy. Jordy smiled back at him as his tempest flared. Ethan must have sensed something because he elbowed Aiden, and the two men walked away.

"Are you crazy, Jordy?" Phil hissed. "You're going to get yourself killed. Evander has a small army."

"I'm not afraid of them," Jordy said. He wasn't, even though good sense told him differently.

"Jordy, it makes sense to use caution," Jed reasoned.

"Someone has to stand up to them," Jordy said, not backing down.

Jack Hadley walked over. "What can I help you with, Jordy?"

Jordy was relieved to talk to Jack. The truth was that he was not going to allow Evander or his toy soldiers to interfere with his life. Maybe it was the tempest fueling his rebellion, but he didn't think so. The fiber of a man is engrained in his soul. Jordy had learned from an early age that there is right and then there is wrong. He would stand by what is right. "I need some nails and some wood. I need to finish the pen for the pig."

"Right back here," Jack said, walking down an aisle.

Jordy followed. "I need some fence rail."

"Yeah, I know what you need," Jack muttered.

Jordy smiled. "I expect you do."

Jack opened the back door, and they stepped out into the lumber yard behind the building. "Your daddy was one brave son of a bitch. I guess you get that from him."

Jordy nodded. "I expect so."

Jack turned to him. "These dudes are not playing games, Jordy."

"I'm aware."

"You got a nice little farm and a family. Just remember that if you take on this fight all by yourself."

Jordy started picking out the wood that he needed. "I think of nothing else but my family. But what kind of man would I be if I turned my back on what I believe in?"

Jack chuckled. "You're one stubborn son of a bitch, too."

"Yeah, I get that from my mother."

Chapter 46

Pastor Ezra gave a thought-provoking sermon on facing evil together as one people. It was like a cool balm to shredded nerves. People sang as one, filling the old church with hope. As always, Pastor Ezra took Jordy's hands in his on the steps when it was over. "I would like to have a word with you, Jordy. Can we meet?"

"Come for dinner," Jordy said, smiling at him.

"I would enjoy that, my boy. I'll stop by after this evening's sermon."

Amelia was frowning as they headed for the truck. "Why does that man always stare at the pastor like that?"

Jordy looked over his shoulder and spotted Henry sitting in his car. He was staring at the pastor with that same grimace etched on his face. "Henry is complicated. I would suspect he does not favor religion."

"I don't like it. I'll be glad to go home. Being in town is scary now." Her eyes rested on three of Evander's men standing near Winslow's.

"Yeah, they want you to feel like that. Pay them no mind."

Amelia sighed when she got into the truck. "I just want things to go back the way it was."

"Me, too."

Jordy drove back to the farm, feeling relieved when he pulled into the driveway. Life was normal here. Eggs to gather in the hen house, animals to feed, and the fields needed to be worked. But the growing tension in town loomed in the shadows. There was now an uneasy undercurrent pressing against his little slice of heaven. Jordy sensed it was going to get worse.

Amelia was starting to bake bread for dinner. The smell of it reminded him of his mother. He remembered when he was a kid, how his mother would bake bread. His father would wait around to snag a piece when it came hot out of the oven, just like he was doing now. He glanced over and spotted his son sitting on the stool.

"What are you waiting for?" Jordy asked with a knowing smile.

"Ahh, nothing," Brian said, smiling.

"You both are full of it," Amelia said, laughing. "I need to save some of it for when the pastor comes tonight."

"I saw you put in two loaves," Jordy pointed out.

"One was for Evander."

"Not today," Jordy said,

Amelia nodded in agreement. "Not today."

Chapter 47

Jordy was playing catch with Brian when a car pulled into the driveway. "Who's that?" Brian asked, frowning.

Jordy tipped his head as he watched the car roll to a stop in front of the house. It was Henry driving, and sitting in the passenger seat was Pastor Ezra. Henry gave Jordy a curt nod from inside the car.

"That is Henry Lee. He works with Evander," Jordy mumbled, wondering what this was about.

Pastor Ezra stepped out of the car, looking strained; his expression tense despite the outwardly calm demeanor that others might have mistaken for ease. But Jordy knew him too well. He could see the way his mouth was turned down, that the good pastor was not happy. He tipped his head to the side and thanked Henry for the ride before closing the car door. Henry didn't hesitate, backing out of the driveway.

Jordy tossed the ball to Brian. "Henry gave you a ride from town? I thought that I was picking you up."

The pastor shuffled over to where Jordy was playing ball with his son. He stood, leaning heavily on his cane. "Something like that. Henry didn't give me much of a choice in the matter. It's part of what I wanted to talk to you about."

"Let's go up and sit on the porch until dinner," Jordy said, gesturing to the porch.

"Yes, I'd like that." Pastor Ezra turned and slowly walked, leaning heavily on his cane, to the steps.

Jordy watched as he held tightly to the railing with his gnarled hand, taking one stair at a time. The pastor had aged since Evander's people came to town. He looked gaunt and thinner. The tension in town was weighing heavily upon him. Pastor Ezra was a man of peace who truly loved his congregation. Like Jordy, he hated to see what was becoming of their town and community.

The pastor sat heavily in his chair. Amelia brought out a tray of iced tea and set it down on the small table that was between the chairs. "Dinner will be ready shortly," she said, smiling.

"Thank you, my dear," Pastor Ezra said, reaching for one of the glasses.

Neither Jordy nor Amelia missed the tremor in his hand as he picked up his glass. They exchanged knowing glances. "Just relax, Pastor Ezra, I'm cooking up something that I think you will love."

"If my nose is telling me the truth, it smells like roast chicken." Pastor Ezra grinned at her.

"Well, your nose is telling you true," Amelia said, laughing before she went inside.

"You have a nice family," Pastor Ezra said, his eyes softening.

Jordy nodded, sitting down with a glass of iced tea. "That I do."

"Where is Petunia?"

"In the kitchen helping her mother."

"I look forward to hearing more tales about her super pig." Pastor Ezra chuckled.

Jordy saw the sadness enter back into his eyes. "What's on your mind?"

"Mostly the town, I suppose. Henry is pushing me to leave. My wife is buried here, and I plan to rest beside her once it is my time. I told Henry as much."

"I'm guessing that he had an answer for that."

Pastor Ezra nodded. "You guessed right. He said that they would dig her up and move her." He flinched.

Jordy was not surprised. "It sounds like them."

"How did such men come to be? There is no compassion in them. When I was a younger man, I used to hold a service once a month at the prison. There were some hardcore men there, but they were nothing compared to these men. I don't mind telling you, Jordy, I worry over the town."

Jordy understood and shared his concerns. Mostly, he worried for the pastor's safety. "I'm worried, too."

"Yes, I can sense that. I'm at a loss as to what to do. People ask me, and I have no other words but to tell them it is in God's hands. I just wish I had an earthly answer."

"Your words carry weight with people, Pastor Ezra. You are the calm amongst the chaos. You just keep doing what you do best."

"What is that?"

"You give people hope and a sense of belonging." That is why Henry and Evander want the pastor gone. Jordy knew it and felt helpless. "If ever people needed guidance, it is now."

"Now we are to the place where I must ask something of you."

"What is it? Anything."

"Jordy, if something should happen to me, I want you to step forward and assume my place."

Jordy flinched. "I'm no preacher, Pastor Ezra. I'm a farmer."

"You are a farmer of men, Jordy. People respond to you. God gave you many gifts, my boy."

He was wrong. Leading people was not his strength. "Pick someone else. I'm not the one."

"I didn't pick you. God did. Jordy, do you think Moses chose his path? Or was it chosen for him?"

Jordy scoffed. "I'm no Moses, Pastor Ezra. I'm not a hero or a leader. I'm a simple man who only wants to support my family doing what I know best. No, you must choose another. Besides, why are you asking this?"

"I have a feeling that I'm…not long for this place."

It was an honest answer that reverberated through Jordy's mind. Jordy knew that the pastor was right. How many times had he witnessed with his own eyes how Henry watched the pastor? "Henry would not dare."

The pastor smiled at him. "There are many roads leading the way out of town. Some are more direct than others."

Jordy understood where the pastor was going with it. The pastor could suffer any number of accidents along the way that would not directly point to Henry. Jordy's tempest flared. "They are not that foolish."

"On the contrary, my friend. They are focused on winning. To do that, they will remove all obstacles in their path. It's the smart thing to do."

Chapter 48

Jordy woke from a deep sleep, wide awake. The fields. Fire. He leapt from bed, pulling on his clothes. Oh, God. Fire! It screamed through his head, pushing away the sleepy haze, and leaving complete clarity.

"What is it?" Amelia asked, rising onto her elbow. Her beautiful face scrunching into a frown. "What's happened?"

"The field is on fire. Call Cesar and let him know."

"Oh, my God." Amelia threw off her blankets and got out of bed.

Jordy shoved his feet into his boots and ran out the door. It was still dark outside, as he ran across the yard. From the hill near the oak tree, he saw the fire's glow at the end of the lower field. It had already devoured half an acre, and it was growing fast. He raced to turn on the irrigation system, but when he turned the handle, nothing happened. God. They had disabled the pumps. It screamed through his mind, instilling even more panic.

"What the hell happened?" Cesar said, coming to a stop next to Jordy. Cesar was half-dressed, and his hair was in disarray, signaling he had leapt out of bed the same as Jordy.

"Pumps are not working." Jordy grabbed a shovel and started down the cornrow.

"Jordy, where are you going?" Cesar yelled.

"Work on the pump, I'm going to try and dig a berm and save what I can."

"Jordy, that won't work. Stop."

Jordy paused knowing every second that went by meant more damage to the crops. "Work on the pump," he yelled, from over his shoulder.

He didn't stop to say anything more, feeling the rising tension as he slipped into the cornrows. His heart was racing as he ran through the dark rows of corn with a shovel in hand. When he got to the edge of the lower field, he was met by a wall of fire. The heat made him stop going any further, as he tried to dig a trench to stop the fire from spreading. It seemed useless, like digging a grave with a soup spoon. The fire was traveling so fast, consuming more and more of his crops. The leading edge on the other side was creeping towards the wheat field. He could lose everything.

The tempest jolted him awake with a searing pain that raced through his body, sending him gasping to his knees. Dropping the shovel, he cradled his pounding head with both hands. Not now, he silently panted. He felt the energy building in intensity like a great snake uncoiling deep inside of him. It was more intense than anything he had ever experienced. Panic crept in as fear gripped him, and the fire crawled closer, scorching the ground just inches away, destroying everything in its lethal path.

The acrid smoke was choking him as he tried to clear his head, fighting against the pain that overwhelmed him. Sweat mixed with soot ran black smeary, rivulets down his face, stinging his eyes. Through parched lips, he wheezed, "Rain."

Above him, the clouds darkened and boiled, sending down a torrent of water from the bruised sky. Jordy was kneeling, and the earth beneath him became soaked, turning into thick mud that soaked his pants. The pain was now a dull ache as the rain washed down his hot body, cool and refreshing. All around him he heard the hiss as the water drenched the fires that were sent to consume him. "Rain," he said with more strength.

Chapter 49

Cesar, Laz, and Jordy walked the burnt section of the field, finding the remains of charred glass jars that still smelled of alcohol. Someone had tossed Molotov cocktails into the field, setting it on fire. This was no act of nature and Jordy wanted payback. It was one thing to deal with all the intimidation, but this threatened his livelihood. He could not let it pass.

"So, what do we do now?" Laz asked, tossing the jars in a pile at the edge of the field.

"First, we prepare the soil for planting. Then we get the irrigation pumps working." Jordy shrugged. He had not told them about what happened in the field with the rain because he was still trying to reconcile it himself. Was it possible that he actually called for the rain?

"What are we going to plant?" Cesar asked, kicking the blackened remains of cornstalks with the toe of his boot. "Vegetables?"

Yeah, cabbage, carrots, or kale, was a possibility, but Jordy was leaning towards planting more corn. "I have some seed for corn that matures early. I bought it by mistake. I want to try it."

"That could work," Cesar agreed. "I've never seen anything like that rain last night. I thought the fields were gone."

Jordy nodded. "Luck was on our side."

Cesar picked up another charred glass jar. "What are we going to do about this?"

"I'm going to talk to Evander after I've finished up here. I'm done with playing this game with him." Jordy was determined to take no more shit.

"How do you think that he will react?" Laz said, leaning on the handle of a shovel.

"I don't know. But it's got to be said. I asked them to stay clear of my property last time when they stole Walter. Now I'm going to issue him a warning."

Cesar and Laz exchanged glances. "What if he just laughs?"

Jordy grinned. "Then I will have to give him a little taste of what happens if they don't listen to reason." His tempest was always close to the surface whenever Evander was nearby. Instead of controlling it, maybe he would let it go.

"I think that we should go with you this time," Cesar said. "A united front and all that."

Laz was nodding his head. "Yeah, they threatened our crops too. We need to make a stand."

"I'm good with that," Jordy agreed.

After clearing the burnt vegetation from the field and turning the soil, they tackled the irrigation pump. They were exhausted but pushed to keep going. After removing the housing, they found that the wires were cut, rendering it useless. Sabotage. Jordy swore under his breath as he and Cesar got to work on repairs.

Bastards meant to destroy him by letting his fields burn. Without the income from the fields, he would be forced to find a job to support his family. He had no doubt that setting the fire was done for that reason. It would force him to go to work for Evander. Not this time, Evander, Jordy thought. These people would need to be taught a lesson, or it would happen again. He wasn't sure how to use his gift, but he would learn. His family's life depended on it.

"Let's fire it up and see if it works," Cesar said, after replacing the housing.

"Here goes nothing," Jordy said. Flipping the switch, a fine spray of water pumped through the jets to rain down on the field. Jordy stood, looking around the lush fields that were untouched by fire. "Could have used that last night."

"It was lucky it rained, or we would be looking at a blackened mess. I'm not even sure how we would get through this winter if it all burned." Cesar stood next to him, hands on his hips.

"I don't even want to think about that." Jordy groaned.

"It would be tight, but we would get through it," Laz said, coming up beside his father. "We always find a way. That is what separates us from Evander's people. They just take to survive, where we use our wits and experience to scratch a living out of the dirt the honest way."

Cesar glanced at his son. "When did you become so wise?"

Laz chuckled. "It's inherited from my mother."

Jordy laughed at Cesar's look of surprise. "Esmae is a very smart woman."

Cesar smiled. "I agree, she married me."

They all laughed good-naturedly.

Chapter 50

Jordy, Cesar, and Laz were in the truck, heading to see Evander. The question was if the guards at the gate would let them pass through the checkpoint. As Jordy turned onto the long gravel road leading to Evander's place, he said, "I think we have a fifty percent chance of gaining access."

Cesar huffed. "You're an optimist. I give it only a twenty percent chance at best."

"They will let us in," Laz said, confidently. "After trying to burn us out, they will wonder if we are here to make a deal with them. Given their numbers, they are not going to expect a fight. They will think that we are here to strike a bargain with them or capitulate. This is going to go one of two ways; they will meet us with force to reinforce our surrender, or they will try to strike a bargain."

Cesar was watching Laz while he spoke. "What makes you say that?"

Laz sighed. "It's what I would do if I were them. We are the problem children for them. They must eliminate the threat."

Jordy shook his head in dismay. "Why can't they just leave us alone? Live and let live."

Laz snorted. "Because eventually, we would not be willing to stand by and watch them destroy the town. It's already hard to watch what they are doing. People are frightened, and rightly so. There is only so much that we would stand for before making a move to stop them. The guards harass women just for walking down the street. Even Mom and Amelia are not immune to it. They intimidate the men in town, emasculating them in front of their families. They made Dan Howard beg like one of his dogs outside of Hadley's the other day."

"Sweet Jesus," Jordy whispered as his tempest twisted to life in his gut. "I only go into town for gas or to pick stuff up at Hadley's. Amelia never told me anything. I see the way people act in town but had no idea it was that bad. Pastor Ezra is worried."

Cesar nodded. "I worry for the pastor. He looks so gaunt and thin. This has aged him, I think."

Jordy turned into the driveway. "Well, let's see what the guards do."

Jordy eased the truck to a crawl as they approached the gate, rolling down his window, he made eye contact with the guards. The men eyed them warily, their hands resting on the guns at their hips. Jordy brought the truck to a stop in front of the gate and waited, tension thick in the air.

"What's your business?" A guard that Jordy did not recognize asked tersely.

"I'm here to talk to Evander." Jordy watched the guards as he spoke. One of them looked uncertain. The new one was just all business.

"Is he expecting you?"

"Most likely. Tell him Jordy, Cesar, and Laz are here."

Jordy felt the energy pass through his body and swallowed hard as the pain increased when the tempest stretched out and spread. The guards frowned at him as they spoke into the military-style radio that crackled and hissed.

"He will see you," the guard said, opening the gate.

Once it swung open, they drove through and started down the hill, heading to the house. "I wonder what it feels like for them?" Laz asked absently.

"What it feels like?" Jordy asked.

"We can feel the vibration of electrical pulses," Cesar answered. "It feels like standing under high-tension lines just before it rains. A tingle that passes through your body."

"Does it hurt?" Jordy asked, concerned.

Laz frowned. "It does not hurt. I sat in a vibration chair once at the mall in Colten. It's kind of feels like that."

Jordy chuckled nervously as he came to a stop in front of Eveander's house. "Well, let's hope that is all you feel."

Evander walked out onto the porch with several armed men with their guns drawn. Jordy sensed that there were more men hidden around the vast property. He opened the door of the truck and got out. Cesar and Laz did the same. "We got that thing happening again," Laz whispered. "Like that time with the drink at the Morrison's tribute. I can hear you inside my head."

"Interesting. I wish I had a manual for this thing." Jordy exchanged nervous glances with them before facing Evander and his men.

"So, what do I owe this visit to, Jordy?" Evander said, not moving from the porch.

"Seems that you did not get the message from the last time your people found their way onto my farm," Jordy said, facing him.

Evander frowned. "Could you be more specific? I don't know what you are talking about." He walked to the steps and paused there, not wanting to come any closer.

Jordy walked to the back of the truck and picked up a box filled with the charred, glass jars used to burn his field. He emptied it out onto the ground, scattering blackened jars by his feet. With the toe of his boot, he kicked one, rolling it across the gravel. "It seems like your boys like to play with fire."

The men on the porch became alert, pointing their weapons at him. He could feel their intentions. They were waiting for the signal to shoot them. In Jordy's head, he heard the word hot. He felt a pulse of energy run through his body.

Evander's men winced and dropped their weapons, shaking their hands like they had been burned. Jordy frowned. What was happening? He glanced at Laz and Ceasar. "Hot," Laz whispered, having heard the word, too.

"Enough!" Evander yelled. His men were writhing in pain, some dropping to their knees.

"Try thinking cold," Cesar suggested.

"Cold," Jordy whispered.

The chilly wind came from out of the north, leaving Evander's men shivering on the porch. To Jordy, Laz, and Cesar, it was just cool, but for Evander and his men, it was like being submerged in ice water. Jordy felt lightheaded as the power surged through his blood. *Control*, he heard in his head. "Stop," he whispered.

The wind stopped, leaving a pleasant breeze in its wake. Jordy leaned against his truck, tired after the energy ebbed from his body. "Do we understand each other?" he asked in a strong, steady voice.

Evander straightened up, leaning against the porch rail for support. "Yeah, you have made your point."

"Stay off our land. Leave the town's people and the pastor alone." Jordy knew that he was declaring war but left open an option for them. "Live and let live."

Evander straightened up and walked down the stairs, stopping a scant two feet away from Jordy. "I know about the fire. I found out about it too late to stop it. But I'm going to give you a warning of my own. There are things at play here that you don't understand. People that will do what they may that I have no control over. Things could get out of control fast. I will pass along your message and see how it is received. You know what this means?"

Jordy straightened up, stepping away from his truck as the energy once again uncoiled inside of him. "Do you know what it means?" he repeated the question, turning it back on Evander. "I will be pushed no further. I gave you a chance, and you tried to burn me out. And if your man in the barn wants to live, he will put down his freaking rifle, or I will pop his head like a zit."

Evander raised his hand, signaling to the man hiding in the barn to put down the gun. "So, you have figured out how to use it," Evander said more as an acknowledgement to himself than a question to Jordy.

"It's a work in progress. I have said all that I've come here to say." Jordy turned to leave.

"Jordy, I'll do what I can," Evander said, not taking a step.

Jordy opened the door of the truck to leave. "I'd appreciate it."

"I'll be seeing you, Jordy." Evander walked back to the porch.

Jordy sagged against the seat as he guided the truck up the incline. "I'm beat," he said.

"That was amazing," Laz said.

"How did you know about the guy in the barn with the gun?" Cesar said. "I nearly shit myself."

"I can sense them. He was the only one that was serious. The others were too afraid to make a move or were still recovering. I think that I draw their energy from them when I am dishing out shit."

"What makes you think that?" Laz leaned between the front seats from the back.

"I can sense them growing weaker." Jordy shrugged.

"So, they are like an added power source for you?" Cesar looked thoughtful.

"Maybe. Your guess is as good as mine."

"Well, now it is their move. Laz, you got an opinion?" Jordy glanced at him.

"They will pull something. Right now, they are thinking about it. It's not over. We need to be careful. Jordy, you are a major target. They will be coming for you."

Jordy knew it was true. But standing on the sideline proved to be as dangerous as dipping his toe into the shark-infested waters. Hell, they were going to burn him out. If they want a war, then he would give them a war.

Chapter 51

Jordy sat on the porch after dinner, listening to the night. Far off in the distance, he could hear the lonely call of a barn owl. The sound of the train passing by on the tracks outside of town blew its warning horn at Brown's Junction as it did every night at about this time. It all seemed so normal, he thought. It relaxed him as he relished the cool breeze dispelling the heat of the day.

His mind was still troubled by what had happened at Evander's place this afternoon. For someone who made a point of keeping his nose out of trouble, he sure found it today, making up for a lifetime of staying on the fringe. This gift had only brought him problems, and he knew there was more to come.

Amelia came out onto the porch, handing him a glass of iced tea. "You look tired," she said, sitting down beside him.

He glanced at her, the soft glow of moonlight making her look even more beautiful. Once again, he found himself wondering how he got so lucky to have her as his wife. "I am. It was a long day."

"Do you want to talk about it?"

"Not really." It was the truth.

"I saw Jed in town today. He said that you went over to Evander's place with Laz and Cesar. Jed thought that there was trouble."

Jordy frowned. "Jed is still spying on Evander?" This was not a conversation that he wanted to have. All his life, he wanted only to protect his family from harm.

"Apparently. So, tell me what happened. Was this about the fire?"

Jordy took a long, slow breath. "Partially, yes. I went there to tell them to stay off our land. I told them to leave the town and the pastor alone, too."

Amelia nodded slowly. "I'm going to guess that they didn't take that well."

"I didn't give them a choice." He remembered Evander's face when he unleashed on his men, burning their hands to disarm them. Evander was stunned, yes, but also impressed. It was curious, and it made Jordy uneasy.

"What did you do?"

He may have been keeping a secret from Amelia, but he had never lied to her. But how can he tell her about it without sounding crazy? In the end, he decided to tell her the simple truth. "I used my gift."

Amelia said nothing for a moment and then nodded. "The tempest."

"Yes. I can do things with it. Make things happen."

Her face scrunched up into a frown. "Like what? Show me."

He had never tried to awaken his tempest on his own and wasn't sure if it would work. "I can try."

The night was clear as he gazed up into the sky at the full moon. "Rain," he whispered. He felt a stirring in his gut that spread like warm marmalade through his body. It was not painful or unpleasant. That surprised him.

Wispy clouds appeared and grew thicker. Amelia sat next to him, watching as the clouds darkened and boiled. The shy moon hid behind the clouds, extinguishing its golden light, and plunging the night into total darkness. The raindrops fell from the sky, making a light pitter-patter sound on the roof before becoming stronger and increasing into a downpour. "Stop," he whispered, feeling the energy, leave his body. The clouds dissipated and dissolved in the night sky, revealing the moon and the stars once more.

"Wow," Amelia whispered. Her eyes were like bright jewels in her beautiful face. "Did you really just do that?"

Jordy nodded. "I think so."

"It's a little scary," she whispered.

"Agreed."

"I think that you have always had it, but it was dormant or something until Evander's people arrived, causing all of this chaos. I remember once when we were in the field, and it was so hot and then how this breeze came out of nowhere and cooled it down. Then, there was another time when Petunia cut her hand. Do you remember that? You held a cloth over the wound, and when you lifted it to look, the wound was nearly healed. I think now that you did that."

He remembered. "Maybe? I don't know. Sometimes, I feel like I have a hook in me and that I'm attached to something that I don't understand. It's like this whole other side of me, and I don't know how to control it."

"That must be scary. I've known you for most of my life, Jordy. You are a good man. You will figure it out. I think the reason you were given this gift is that you will only use it for good. It is safe in your hands."

Jordy nodded. "That is true. I would never abuse it." He would be afraid of the consequences if he ever tried. Deep down, he felt there was a punishment that came with using it for bad.

"So, did Evander's men agree to leave the town alone?"

"I'm not sure. I made a convincing argument for change. Why didn't you tell me about how bad it was in town?"

"Probably for the same reason you hid your gift from me. I didn't want you to worry. You have the farm to worry about. I was handling it ok on my own. But it is getting worse."

Jordy nodded. "Did they ever touch you?" He held his breath as his tempest coiled.

"No. Nothing like that. I think Esmae and I are off-limits because we cook for Evander. But it is the way they treat everyone else that is upsetting to see."

Jordy was relieved that so far Evander's men did not hassle his wife, but it ate at him that they were nasty to the town's people. "Well, hopefully, it will change."

Amelia sighed, taking his hand. "That would be nice."

Chapter 52

The Fourth of July dawned, spilling sunshine across the land. It was warm but not hot, with a cooling breeze making it very pleasant. Jordy loaded the last of the food into the truck, taking a minute to lean against the driver's door to look up at the clear blue sky above. It would be the perfect day for the barbeque, he thought. The town would all be there. The kids would play games and have a massive water balloon fight. There would be pie-eating contests, the chili contest that Bree would undoubtedly win as she did every year, dunking for apples, a game of horseshoe toss, softball, and then there was the food. It was fun for the whole family. At night, Phil and Lenny Dawson would light off fireworks over the pond. Families would gather together by the water's edge on their blankets to watch as the sky was lit up in a myriad of colors, ending a perfect day.

Jordy just hoped that Evander and his crew would not show up and ruin it. He had been torn between going through with the celebration or canceling it altogether. The townspeople wanted—no, needed—the event to bring a sense of normalcy back to their lives. Things in town had quieted down after his showdown at Evander's place. But in Jordy's heart, he knew it was only a temporary ceasefire. People like Evander would not go away quietly. They lived to spread chaos and fear.

"Daddy, can I bring Walter?" Petunia begged, walking Walter on a leash with red, white, and blue ribbons tied around the little pig's neck. "He'll be good, I promise."

Jordy rolled his eyes. "Petunia, you know once you get there you are going to want to go play with all the other kids. Leave him here in his pen. Besides, there are going to be fireworks tonight. He'll be afraid."

Petunia pouted, puffing out her lower lip. "I'll protect him. Please, please, Daddy."

Jordy looked away, knowing that he would regret this. "Ok, but he is your responsibility."

Petunia brightened, her face splitting into a smile that could light up the world. "I will take care of him."

But Jordy already knew that he would be dragging around Walter for most of the day. "I'm going to hold you to that, young lady."

Brian came out of the house carrying his guitar. "We almost ready?"

"Are you going to be supplying today's music?" Jordy smiled down at his son.

Brian nodded as he stored his prized guitar in the truck. "There are a few of us that have been practicing for today. It should be fun."

Amelia came out of the house with another basket of food. "I think this is the last of it," she said, handing the basket to Jordy to put in the back of the truck with the others.

"I hope so, unless you are planning to singlehandedly feed the whole town," Jordy joked.

Amelia huffed. "Not likely with Dan Howard's appetite."

Jordy chuckled. "You got a point. You know that he will win the pie-eating contest, hands down."

Amelia laughed. "Only man I know that asks for seconds after devouring a whole pie in less than a minute." She frowned when she looked into the truck and spotted Walter sitting beside Petunia. "Why is that pig in the truck?"

"Oh, Mom, he has a name," Petunia said, grimacing.

"That does not answer my question."

"Daddy said that I can take him."

Amelia turned to Jordy. "Remember, you agreed to it."

"Yes, and I already regret it."

Amelia smiled. "Good, because you are going to be stuck with him."

Jordy knew only too well that it was true, flashing a glance at the little pig, nestled up close to his daughter. Some things are worth the pain, he thought, seeing how happy it made his little girl. "Let's get going. I want to try and get a seat under the trees in the shade."

As they drove into town, there were cars lining the street all the way up to the park. Jordy pulled over to unload before finding a parking place. The park was already crowded with people. He spotted Cesar and Laz under the tree, carrying baskets of food with Esmae leading the way. Phil and Bree were standing by the picnic tables, arranging the food. It looked like everyone was showing up to celebrate.

After unloading the food and picnic blanket, Jordy wove his way back through town to find a parking place. As he got out of the truck, he spotted Evander and some of his men, parking close by. His tempest coiled in his gut in warning. Evander waved, smiling at him. Jordy would have liked to just walk away, but he knew that they would only follow him. He waited by his truck, wondering what this was about.

"What a great day for a party," Evander said, leaning on Jordy's truck.

Jordy got to the point. "So, you and your men are going to the barbeque?"

Evander smiled good naturedly, like they were friends. "Sure, the whole town is welcome, right?"

Jordy nodded. "Yes, that is right."

"I brought drinks and toys for the kids. This should be fun."

Jordy wished that they would turn around and go back the way they came, back to their compound where they belonged. "Very generous," he muttered, turning to go to the park.

Evander matched Jordy step for step. "Maybe we can talk today at some point. I've missed you."

Not likely, Jordy thought. "It's a party, Evander. A family day to enjoy with the kids."

"Yes, but while we are eating and enjoying the festivities, surely, there is time to chat."

Surely, Jordy thought wryly. "Let's see how it goes." He was unwilling to agree to anything. His tempest coiled foretelling of the looming trouble that was sure to follow.

Chapter 53

Jordy set up a spot for his family beneath a large oak tree near Cesar's family. As he set up his lawn chairs, he watched as Evander's men hauled in the many coolers of drinks. The red coolers were filled with beer, while the blue ones were filled with pop and bottled water. Like anything that had to do with Evander, it was over the top.

"Looks like our friend is back," Cesar said dryly.

Jordy nodded. "Yeah, I met up with him while parking my truck."

"I was kind of hoping that they would stay on their compound and leave us alone," Laz said, leaning forward in his chair. "This was supposed to be a good time."

Evander and his men were like a dark cloud blotting out the sun. The town's people were leery and standoffish. Many of them just stopped to stare at the newcomers with open skepticism as their children hung by close. But who could blame them after what they had experienced? Evander set up his campsite close to Jordy's, bringing in chairs and a table. He even set up a portable fire pit.

When his men brought in boxes filled with gift-wrapped packages, Jordy wondered what this was about. Then he remembered, Evander had mentioned toys for the kids. Jordy had assumed that he meant squirt guns and balls to play with at the picnic, but this looked like more. Evander sat in his chair surrounded by the colorful gift-wrapped packages like a rock and roll Santa. Though his merry elves still looked like trained killers.

Evander picked up a package and held it in his hand. "This one is for Petunia," he said in a loud, clear voice.

Petunia looked at her mother and father, uncertainly. "Go ahead," Jordy whispered reluctantly.

Petunia walked to Evander, with Walter trailing behind until she got nearer. The little pig stopped, locking up his back legs, pulling away hard against his leash, refusing to get any closer to him. Jordy went and retrieved the leash and brought Walter back to his chair. Pigs were incredibly intelligent. Walter remembered what they did to him and wanted no part of Evander. Like Jordy thought, pigs are smart creatures.

After hesitating, Petunia walked up to Evander and stopped just before him. Everyone from town was watching. Evander leaned down closer to Petunia, holding out the gift-wrapped box. "I have a gift for you, Petunia," he said with a smile.

Petunia looked back over her shoulder at Jordy and Amelia. When Amelia nodded, Petunia took the package. "Thank you," she said in a tiny voice.

Evander ruffled her hair affectionately. "You are welcome, sweetheart."

Petunia scampered her way back to her parents and sat down on the ground beside Walter.

Next, it was Brian's turn. When his name was called, Brian walked up, stopping in front of Evander. He handed Brian a large, gift-wrapped box. "This is for you," Evander said, flashing another smile.

"Thanks," Brian said, accepting the package.

Evander played Santa, calling out each child by name, and handing out toys to all. The kids were shy at first but when they saw the toys that he was handing out, they warmed to him. Jordy bit his bottom lip when Petunia and Brian unwrapped their gifts. Evander gave Petunia a stuffed pig that looked remarkably like Walter. It oinked and walked, making Petunia giggle with pure joy. For Brian, he bought him a new guitar and strings. Brian was on cloud nine as he strummed it, tuning it with loving fingers. All the kids got something that they wanted. It was personal and very unsettling.

"How do you suppose he knew what to get them?" Amelia whispered.

Jordy frowned, not liking it at all. "I don't know, but it was not by accident, I can tell you that much. Nothing Evander does is put to chance."

With the kids preoccupied with their loot, the town's people relaxed and went back to their celebration. Phil announced the pie-eating competition. Everyone started gathering around the long table. Five pies lined the tabletop, along with the contestants readying for competition. Jordy stayed behind to watch Walter as his family went to play in some of the games.

"So, who do you think will win the pie-eating contest?" Evander asked, opening a beer, and handing it to Jordy.

Jordy accepted the beer, reluctantly. "Dan Howard. The man is a human vacuum cleaner."

Jordy noticed that some of Evander's men were mingling with the town's people. Some were eating food while two others were playing horseshoes. But there were always two standing close by. "Dan Howard? The guy with the dogs?"

"Yes, he has search and rescue dogs. He has won the competition three years straight." Jordy was watching Petunia dodging away from water balloons.

Evander gestured to Walter. "Did you get stuck watching the pig?"

Jordy turned to look at Evander. It was like having an annoying bug buzzing around your head, waiting for the right opportunity to sting. "Not stuck. I offered. Why are you here?"

Evander smiled. "You are never one to play with small talk, are you?"

"And you are never one to indulge in small talk unless you want something." Jordy tossed it back.

Evander chuckled. "Touche. I was hoping we could talk. Bury the hatchet, as they say."

Yes, except he had the creeping suspicion that Evander wanted to bury it in his head. "What do we have to talk about?"

Evander leaned back in his chair, stretching out his long legs. "Many things. I want us to go back to being friends. I don't have very many here. I miss our conversations."

Bullshit, Jordy thought. Besides, the only conversations that they had always came back to his gift. Jordy had no interest in talking about that. "Your track record on being my friend is pretty poor. I like it the way that it is now. You do whatever it is you do on your compound and leave me out of it."

"Now, is that any way to treat a friend, Jordy? I will admit that I fucked up. I pushed too hard and made mistakes. I'm trying to make amends."

Why did this feel like he was talking to an old girlfriend after a breakup? "Look, you are a dangerous man, Evander. I think for the safety of my family, we should remain as we are."

"A man with your powers has nothing to fear from me. I'm the one taking all the risks here. I would imagine that you could stop my heart just by thinking about it."

Jordy narrowed his eyes as he stared at Evander. Here, they were going into a subject that he didn't want to talk about. "First, I'm not that kind of man. You know that, or you would not be here. I think you are very good at figuring out people. What I will tell you is that you are not in my circle of friends and never will be. The trust factor between us is nonexistent. I'm not willing to talk about my gift, do you understand?"

Evander grinned at him. "But here we are, talking about it. Do you not realize how special it is? With the right inspiration, you could do anything. Be anything. Have anything. Do you not see that?"

Jordy glanced at Cesar, aware that he was listening to every word. He glanced back at Evander. "The true test of a man is in the decisions he makes. My decision is to work with my two hands to care for my family and my farm. I don't need magic to know who I am and where I belong."

Evander picked another beer out of the cooler left by his chair and popped the top. "With the right motivation, I think I could change your mind."

What the hell did that mean? Jordy sighed. "Evander, I understand your curiosity and fascination. Whatever this is and wherever it comes from, it is not a toy. I think there are dire consequences for misusing it. I don't know how I know that. It's more something I feel. So, if it is all the same to you, I don't want to talk about it."

Jordy rose from his chair along with Cesar and Laz. "Where are you going?" Evander asked.

Jordy looked back at him from over his shoulder. "I'm going to get something to eat with Walter. Then I'm going to join my family, maybe toss a few water balloons at my daughter and wife."

"I'll be waiting," Evander said, raising his chin.

Jordy shrugged. "Suit yourself."

Chapter 54

At dusk, Jordy rolled out the picnic blanket closer to the pond. Petunia was playing with her friends at the water's edge. Brian sat close by, playing his guitar, serenading the townspeople before the fireworks. Amelia and Esme were helping with the cleanup and putting out still more food. The pastor was sitting close by, sampling the sweets that they piled onto the table. As for Jordy, he was still stuck watching the pig.

"You and that pig make quite a team," Cesar said, chuckling, sitting on his blanket next to Jordy's.

Jordy glanced at the little pig, sound asleep, curled up on the corner of the blanket. "Petunia has me wrapped right around her little finger. She just has to make a pout, and I turn to Jello."

"Daughters will do that." Ceasar agreed, patting Jordy's shoulder in mock sympathy.

"I see your fan club is still in place," Laz said, glancing over his shoulder at Evander.

Evander was still sitting in the same spot from the afternoon, his gaze fixed on Jordy like a predator watching its prey. "Stubborn son of a bitch," Jordy muttered under his breath.

"He has to know by now that you will not work for him. Besides, you have to wonder what he wants from you." Cesar took another beer out of the cooler and handed one to Laz and Jordy.

Jordy popped the top of his beer. "Whatever it is, I'm not interested. The one thing that I'm sure of is that it would be nothing good."

Laz nodded in agreement. "I can't help it, I'm curious. Aren't you? What does he have in mind?"

"I'm a little curious," Jordy admitted. "But peeking into Pandora's Box can only mean trouble. If it were something simple and harmless, Evander wouldn't bother. He would have moved on after our visit the other day. He is even more determined now after witnessing what I'm capable of. So, whatever he has in mind, can't be good."

Cesar was looking at him with a serious expression, etching deep lines into his sun-tanned face. "Hmmm, I think you are right. Do you really believe that if you use it for bad, it will have consequences?"

Jordy nodded. "I do. I feel it. Don't ask me to explain it further because I can't."

The first rocket streaked golden through the air over the pond before exploding into a dazzling burst of red, white, and blue shimmering lights in the sky. The loud pops awakened the pig, startling him. Without hesitation, Jordy scooped him up onto his lap. Cesar chuckled, and Jordy rolled his eyes with a sigh. The things a man does for this child…and his pig.

Amelia and Esme joined them on the picnic blankets, each with a plate of treats. This is the way it should be, Jordy thought. Simple, country folk, enjoying a night as a family with the rest of the town. The pure joy of watching your friends and family together. Memory building for the little ones. This is what Wormwood was supposed to be. What it had always been, and if Jordy had any say about it, Wormwood would be this way always.

After the fireworks, Petunia crashed on the blanket, having a hard time keeping her eyes open after a full day of playing. Walter curled up by her side, giving Jordy his first taste of freedom for the day. He helped Amelia pack up to go home with Cesar and Esme. They walked out to their trucks, stopping to talk after everything was packed. Petunia and her pig were fast asleep in the back of the truck within seconds. It had been a great day for everyone, Jordy thought. People were smiling and laughing as they packed their vehicles to head home.

There was a commotion across the street in front of the church that drew Jordy's attention. One of Evander's demons, Jordy thought he remembered him being called Marty, was hassling Brooke Porter and her grandmother. Brooke was a sixteen-year-old girl from town just trying to get to her car. Her grandmother stood looking on helplessly as Evander's goon was standing in their way.

Marty had Brooke by the elbow, and Brooke was trying desperately to pull free. When did being young and pretty become a curse here? Jordy's tempest coiled.

"Man, why can't Evander keep his people on a shorter leash?" Cesar grumbled.

"I saw that man at the festival," Amelia said. "He was drinking heavily all day."

"No excuse," Jordy said, watching as the scene was escalating. Brooke was getting more animated, trying to get away from the persistent Marty.

"I'm going to go over there and put a stop to it," Laz said, starting to walk across the street.

Pastor Ezra beat him to it, stepping onto the sidewalk. "Stop that. Let her alone."

It all happened like it was in slow motion. Pastor Ezra put his hand on Marty's arm. Marty growled, "Get off me, old man."

Marty turned, slamming Pastor Ezra in the face with his beefy fist, knocking him down, hard onto the sidewalk. Laz was on him instantly.

Chapter 55

It was an emotionally charged, chaotic scene with people gathering around. Some were crying, and others were venting their anger. The outpouring of raw emotions from friends and family for the love of the pastor solidified the town in grief and concern more than anything Jordy had ever witnessed. Attentions were divided between the man who hit the pastor and Pastor Ezra's prostate body stretched out on the sidewalk. Cesar and Laz had Marty sitting on the curb at the edge of the sidewalk while Phil and Jed ran to get the sheriff and Doc Willows. Jordy knelt beside the pastor. He was unconscious, and there was blood seeping from the back of his head.

When people tried to instinctively move him, Jordy held tight, saying, "No, we can't move him. Wait for Doc Willows."

"Look, I didn't mean any harm to come to the old man," Marty growled. He was rubbing his swollen eye where Laz had hit him.

"Just shut up," Laz growled back at him. "You knew exactly what you were doing."

"How is he?" Amelia asked softly as she knelt by Jordy's side.

"I don't know." He looked at her and saw how pale she was. Concern etching her beautiful face. "You and Esme should take the truck and get the kids home. Emotions are high, and this is going to take a while to straighten out."

Amelia nodded, getting to her feet, and glancing at the gathering crowd. "Yeah, I don't want the kids seeing this. I'll see you when you get home." Bending, she lovingly stroked the pastor's face. "Be ok for us," she whispered.

Doc Willows ran up the road with his medical bag in hand, followed by Phil, Jed, and the sheriff. Jordy stepped away from the pastor's side letting Doc Willows do the needful. Cesar and Laz stood next to him, looking on as Sheriff Clancy led Marty away. The townspeople were all watching Marty and did not hide their fear and loathing, showing it clearly in their thin-lipped expressions. It was raw and real. The pastor was a beloved man of peace who touched the hearts of everyone in Wormwood.

"Jordy, go get the gurney in my office. Bring it here." Doc Willows gave nothing away with his expression as he worked on Pastor Ezra.

Without hesitation, Jordy, Laz, and Cesar followed Doc's request, making their way through the solemn crowd of onlookers to retrieve the gurney. As they walked to the office, Jordy spotted Henry Lee sitting in his car across the street. It reminded him of a vulture circling his dying prey.

Was this planned? Jordy considered it. Yes, it was likely. Marty stopping Brooke right outside the parsonage now seemed planned. Anyone who knew the pastor would know that he would not sit idly by and watch one of his lambs being attacked. It was a setup. But there would be time to speculate more about it later, he thought. Inside the office, they found the gurney and wheeled it outside.

"I see Henry has left," Laz said.

"You caught that?" Jordy asked, not surprised.

"He was returning to the scene of the crime to admire his handy work," Cesar agreed.

On their return, if anything, the crowd of people had increased as more people heard about the pastor. As they wheeled the gurney through, Jordy heard grumbling about how someone had to pay for this. Karma is coming. Time to take a stand. True, some of it could be alcohol-fueled rage from the festival, but they were not saying anything that he himself wasn't feeling.

When they got to the pastor, Doc was still knelt beside him. "Good, help me lift him onto the gurney," Doc said, rising to his feet.

"How is he?" Jordy asked. The pastor looked deathly pale. His lips had a bluish tint to them that set off alarm bells ringing in Jordy's head.

Doc looked at them, and for the first time, Jordy saw the shadow of concern cross his features. "I'll know more when I get him back to my office, where I can run some tests. I'm going to transfer him to the hospital in Dalton once I'm sure that he is stable."

"He's got to be ok," Phil said, not hiding the panicked concerns.

Doc nodded in understanding. "Let's get him to my office. Ok, I want you to support his neck; he has a gash on the back of his head. So, lift him carefully."

Jordy, Laz, Cesar, and Phil gently lifted the pastor onto the gurney. Jordy was surprised at how light the pastor was when they lifted him. He was all bones. Over the last few months, he had noticed that he looked frail, but this just drove it home. Marty had to outweigh the pastor by at least sixty pounds. What kind of man strikes an old man like that? A hot rage grew in him, awakening his tempest to stir in his gut. The pastor stirred on the gurney, opening his eyes to look up at Jordy.

"Pastor," Jordy breathed.

Everyone around him stopped what they were doing and looked. The pastor had his eyes locked on Jordy. He tried to raise a shaky hand to touch Jordy, but he didn't have the strength. Instead, Jordy took his hand.

"Come closer," Pastor Ezra whispered in a raspy, paper-thin voice. Jordy leaned closer, and the pastor whispered, "Yes, I feel your power. So strong… You must take care of the town, my boy. It is your destiny."

With that said, Pastor Ezra fell unconscious once more.

Chapter 56

Cesar dropped Jordy off at home after things settled down in town. The pastor was resting easy with doc taking care of him. The townspeople had calmed down, but tensions were still running high. He was tired and only wanted to crawl into bed beside his beautiful wife and sleep. It was dark as he climbed the stairs. It wasn't until he crossed the porch to the door, did he noticed Evander sitting in one of the Adirondack chairs, drinking a beer.

He sighed, dropping his head. The last thing he felt like doing was having another word game with Evander, especially after what had happened to the pastor tonight. "Why are you here?" he asked grimly.

Evander chuckled. "It's nice to see you, too, Jordy. I'm here to talk. I had nothing to do with what happened to Pastor Ezra. I like the old man. How is he?"

Reluctantly, Jordy sat in the chair next to Evander. "The pastor is holding his own; no thanks to you. I was there. I saw your guy hit the pastor."

"My guy? Are you sure about that?"

Jordy looked at him, trying to read his expression in the gloomy darkness. "Where are you going with all of this?"

"Sometimes what we assume is not always true."

"Look, I'm tired and not in the mood for games. If you have something to say, then say it. I want to go to bed."

"Always right to the point." Evander sighed. "I'm sure you have some idea who might want the good pastor out of the way."

"Henry Lee. Yes, I saw him sitting in his car tonight."

"Well then, you think on that. I'll let you go inside and get some sleep." Evander rose to his feet and stretched. "One more thing before I go for you to think about. Things are going to get worse, not better."

What the hell did that mean? "Is that a threat?"

"Some people do not know where to draw the line, Jordy. There are people in this world that are void of right and wrong or good and evil."

Henry was such a man. Jordy had sensed it from the first time they met. There was a darkness about him that emanated from his being like a dark cloud shrouding his soul. "If you know that, then why is he your partner?"

Evander laughed without humor. "Is that what I am to him? Sleep well, Jordy." Evander walked down the stairs and down the driveway, disappearing into the darkness.

"Sure," Jordy mumbled. Sleep would be a long way off, with his mind churning over everything Evander had told him, yet it was what Evander left unsaid that gnawed at him. Evander had said that Jordy was jumping to conclusions. There was something not right with this, like a puzzle with missing pieces. He could make out the big picture, but the fine details were missing. He had a feeling that he was going to find out, and he was not going to like it.

Chapter 57

Jordy was working in his lower field. Most of the corn that he reseeded after the fire was growing back well. The accelerated seeds had worked their magic, growing better than he had hoped, though the stalks were smaller. He had written off this end of the field as a loss. Any farmer will tell you that harvesting anything is better than nothing. He was pleased.

At lunch, he was sitting under the big oak with Cesar and Laz. It was hot today, and the shade felt good. "Any news on the pastor?" Laz asked, holding his water bottle.

Jordy shook his head. "Last I heard, he is still in the hospital. Amelia bumped into Doc Willow's wife at the store. She said that he is improving but that he has a long way to go before they release him."

Cesar sighed. "I sure hope he gets better soon. I don't know how much longer I can take Phil replacing the pastor on the pulpit. His sermons are long and out there."

Jordy laughed. "Last Sunday's was the best, though. The whole comparison of God to superheroes was great."

"Yeah, if you are twelve," Laz said, laughing.

"Well, having a service, any service, seems to bring the town together," Jordy said, taking a bite from his sandwich.

Cesar was frowning. "Jed is coming up the backfield road in his truck."

Jordy looked over his shoulder with a frown of his own. He never remembered Jed ever visiting him in the field. He watched as Jed parked his truck next to his and got out. The look on Jed's face was telling. Something was wrong.

Jordy glanced at Cesar and Laz. "Something is up."

"Yup," Cesar agreed.

Jed sat beside Jordy and sighed. "I need a favor."

"What do you need?" Cesar asked.

"You guys have the largest farms. I need to ask you if I can bring my cows here for a while."

Cesar and Jordy exchanged glances. "Why?"

"Man, I fucked up. I was still spying on Evander's place, and they caught me. They made threats. I need to move my cows because I'm afraid they might retaliate against them. You won't have to feed them or anything. I'll take care of everything. Jordy, you already have that gated area near your barn that would work for most of them."

Cesar nodded. "Yeah, we have a spot to take a few near my barn. Fence might need some work if you are willing."

Jordy tipped his head. "Yeah, it could work. But what about you and your family?"

Jed sighed. "We will be fine. It's the cows that I'm most worried about. They were already helping themselves to one here and there before this. This morning, I noticed that I'm missing another calf. Now I worry about the whole herd."

"Ok, bring them over," Jordy said. He didn't doubt that Jed stepped in it with Evander's people or that the cows would be a major target.

"Thanks, I'm going home and start getting them loaded. I really appreciate this. Hopefully, this cools off in a month or so, and I can bring them back home."

"What are neighbors for?" Cesar said, shrugging.

They watched Jed leave a lot happier than when he came. "I told him to stop snooping on those folks," Cesar said. "Never wise to poke a snake."

"I think everyone told him that. So, cows."

"Yup, cows."

Chapter 58

Jordy sat on the porch after a long, hot day in the fields. He could hear Jed's cows near the barn. Jed was calling his girls for supper. Jordy smiled. There hadn't been cows on his land since he was a kid. He remembered the sounds and smell. For him, it was oddly nostalgic and pleasant.

It reminded him of his grandfather. Gramps was a true farmer down to the bone. Back then, it was a real farm with cows, chickens, goats, and pigs. They grew crops, but the cows were the main source of income. It was also working sunup to sundown, twenty-four seven. He decided a long time ago that he would concentrate on growing crops.

Jed came up the steps and slumped into the chair beside him. Jordy passed him a glass of iced tea that he had waiting for him. Jed happily accepted it, draining half of it. "I didn't anticipate how hard it was going to be with the cows here," he said.

Jordy nodded in understanding. "Yeah, hauling grain and hay for them and then all the rest of it that goes into it must be tough."

"Yeah, my wife is pissed at me. Hell, I'm pissed at me, too. It was stupid spying on those assholes."

"Yup, not your best move. Anything coming from them?"

Jed shook his head. "Not so far. I hope it stays that way."

Jordy hoped so, too, but his tempest told him it wasn't over. It was a sense he had that warned of more to come. "Just keep your eyes open."

"Yeah, I don't trust them. I put up some cameras at the house. I'll keep watch." Jed leaned back in his chair and closed his eyes. "I wish things were back the way it was before they came to Wormwood."

"You and me both, brother."

"Bree and Linda Dawson went to see the pastor in Dalton at the hospital. They said he is getting better. He might be released from the hospital next week. So, there is some good news. No one in town has seen Marty since the night that he hit the pastor."

"I heard the sheriff released him."

"Yeah, he said it was an accident. Can you believe that shit? An accident?"

Jordy scoffed. He never believed for one minute that the sheriff would charge Marty. "I'd believe almost anything these days. But that is good news about the pastor."

"Well, I'm going to get home before it gets any later. Thanks for the iced tea." Jed rose to his feet.

"Be careful, Jed."

"Always. See you tomorrow."

Jordy watched as Jed walked over to his truck and hopped inside. He felt uneasy. Should he warn Jed? And say what? It was only a…feeling he was getting. A vague awareness that something was brewing. He wasn't even sure what it meant or what the danger was. When Jed backed out of the driveway, Jordy rose to his feet and stretched. He was tired. It was a deep, bone-weary tiredness not born from a hard day's work. It was deeper and more profound. He felt dread seep into his pours. It grew stronger. He walked inside and took his truck keys off the hook by the door.

Amelia looked up from the book that she was reading at the kitchen table, frowning at him. "Where are you going?"

"Jed forgot something; I'm going to go catch up to him. I'll be back in a few minutes."

Jordy walked to his truck; a storm brewing in his gut, poised to erupt. He could feel something dark looming, something inevitable and wrong. There was an acrid taste coating his mouth as he drove through town, heading to Jed's house. The car in front of him was doing no more than twenty. Old lady Harris plugging along at a snail's pace. His fingers curled around the steering wheel like he was trying to hold on to the fury that coursed through this bloodstream. Finally, she turned off into her driveway, giving Jordy the space that he needed to get by on the narrow road. He felt his time was short. Something was wrong.

As he pulled into Jed's driveway, he slowed his speed, rolling up the driveway with his headlights off. When he pulled up to Jed's truck, the driver's door was open, but the truck was empty. Jordy got out and looked around. The hairs on the back of his neck were standing up on end as the cold chill of fear went down his back. *In the field,* he heard a voice say in his head.

He turned away from the trucks and walked into the field. I should call the sheriff, he thought. Going into the field alone like this was foolish. His tempest led the way, and he followed. It was calling the shots, pulling him in the direction without any help from him. It was like he had no control. It was unsettling.

When he crested the hill, he heard the voices, harsh and guttural. It reminded him of when coyotes were hunting their prey. In the dim light, he could make out Jed and his wife, Diane, on their knees, both wearing blindfolds over their eyes. They were surrounded by three men wearing black hoods covering their heads. The men circled them, snarling at them about how they knew how to take care of snitches. One of them kicked Jed in the face. Jordy stopped, trying to think of what to do. He knew these men were going to kill them. The torture would be long and painful. He could almost hear the men's thoughts, all of them vile. One of the men raised a bat to hit Diane in the head. *Stop,* slammed through his head.

The man holding the bat stood frozen, the bat raised like he was waiting for a pitcher to throw the ideal ball so he could bat it out of the park for a home run. He stood perfectly still, not a single muscle twitching, only the slight breeze, fluttering his shirt. The other men were confused when the batter just stood there. "Hit her," one of the men yelled. "Smash her face in, stupid."

Blind, he heard the voice again. The power cursed through him before he let it go, focusing on the men at the bottom of the hill. It felt like a warm breeze filtering through his body in the direction of the men.

"What the fuck," one of the men shouted, tugging to get off his hood. "I can't see. I can't see."

The men had their hands on their faces, rubbing their eyes. The man with the bat, dropped it onto the ground, pulling at the hood to get it off. They were all stumbling over the uneven ground, falling, and panicked, their hands stretched out, pawing the air. "I can't see," they repeated.

Jordy walked around their outstretched hands to where Diane and Jed were kneeling. He knelt beside them. When he touched Jed's shoulder, he winced. "It's Jordy," he whispered. "Just be still. I'm going to untie you both, and then we are going to get out of here."

Jed and Diane nodded. Jordy pulled out his knife from his pocket and cut through the ropes that bound them. Quietly, they rose to their feet and followed Jordy around the men, wandering around with their outstretched hands. "Is someone there?" one of the men asked. "Please. Is someone there?"

Jordy, Diane, and Jed said nothing as they climbed the hill. Diane let out a single sob but then straightened her spine and walked on. When they got to the driveway, Jordy asked, "Where are the kids?"

"Spending the night at a friend's house," she said, leaning heavily against the truck. "What just happened?"

"Yeah, I thought we were goners," Jed said, fishing around inside his truck, and finding his cigarettes.

Diane grabbed them out of his hand before he could light one, crushing the pack in her fist. "I thought that you quit these."

"I did…sort of," he said, turning to Jordy. "We can't stay here tonight."

"I think it best if you stay at the parsonage tonight. Do you need a doctor?" Jordy gestured to the gash on Jed's forehead.

"I'll be fine." Jed waved it away.

"But those guys roaming around in the field probably need one," Jordy pointed out. He didn't know if the blindness was permanent or temporary.

"The hell with those guys," Diane said. "I'll call the sheriff when we get to town. They can be his problem."

"Why are you here?" Jed asked in confusion.

"I had a bad feeling." Jordy shrugged.

"What do you think happened?" Diane asked, keeping a wary eye on the field for the men.

"No idea," Jed said. "There must have been something in those hoods that blinded them."

Sure, that was as good an answer as any, Jordy thought. "We should get going."

"Yeah, agree. Thanks, Jordy. I can take it from here. You are a good friend." He slapped Jordy on the back.

Jordy looked around. "If it's all the same to you, I'll follow you into town."

"Good," Diane said. "I'm going to run into the house and grab a few things."

"We will come with you. But let's hurry up. We don't know if it was only the three of them." Jed looked around uncertainly.

The house was trashed. The men had gone through it looking for anything of value. Jed knelt and picked up a broken picture frame with a picture of his children. "It looks like a bull went through here. Why just break shit?"

"My guess is that they wanted this to look like a robbery," Jordy said, looking around in disgust.

"It's replaceable," Diane said, coming out of the bedroom with a bag. "Let's get out of here before they come back and finish what they started."

Jordy's instincts were heightened. There were only three men that came here. No one else was coming, at least for right now. He knew the road to town was clear, that no one was waiting to jump them. Just like he knew the blind men were still falling all over themselves in the field. Now that the energy was spent, he was tired. Once he got Jed and Diane settled in town, he looked forward to his bed. For now, they were safe.

Chapter 59

Cesar and Laz sat on the porch beside Jordy, having a beer. "That was something about what happened to Jed," Cesar said, popping the top on the can.

"Yup, it was something," Jordy agreed, not wanting to talk about it. He knew Laz and Cesar wouldn't have it. They would want all the details even if Jordy was unsure of what happened there himself.

"Doc says those guys are blind. It was like their retinas were fried." Laz looked at Jordy.

"That's too bad." Jordy took a drink of his beer, saying little.

Cesar nodded. "I wonder how something like that could happen. Doc is at a loss on how to explain it."

Jordy rolled his eyes. "Ok, ok, I can see that you're not going to let it go until I tell you about it."

"Hold on. I love a good story. I've heard Jed's, but I'm betting yours is better." Laz took another beer and popped the top.

"What did Jed say happened?"

Laz shrugged. "Three guys had him and Diane in the field and were getting ready to beat them to death when they suddenly went blind. Then you showed up and cut them free. But I know there is more."

Jordy nodded. "I knew something was wrong when Jed left my house after feeding the cows."

"How did you know?" Cesar asked, turning to look at Jordy.

"I sensed it. There was trouble. So, I went after him. When I got there, Jed's truck was parked in the driveway with the door open, but no Jed. I heard a voice in my head, telling me he was in the field."

"Like before when we heard the voice that day at Evander's?" Laz asked.

"Yes, but the voice is stronger now than before. It was directing me where to go like I was on autopilot. It, whatever it is, took over. I was just along for the ride. When one of the guys was going to hit Diane with his bat, I heard it say... *stop*. The guy was standing there frozen with the bat in the air. He just stood there unmoving. The other men were getting pissed at him. They wanted him to smash Diane in the head. To kill her. Then I heard it say,... *blind,* and you can guess the rest."

Cesar sat back in his chair. "So, you had nothing to do with it. Now, this thing is running the show. It's a little scary."

"Tell me about it." Jordy ran his hands through his hair in frustration.

"I think it's cool," Laz said.

Jordy snorted. "If I could, I'd give it to you."

Laz raised his hands in surrender. "I didn't say that I wanted that. I just think of it like a guardian angel. If it was not for you, Diane and Jed would be dead."

Cesar glanced at Jordy. "He does have a point. It seems to only do good."

Jordy was not so sure. "You're assuming that it will only do good things. What happens if it wants to do something bad? I'm not sure that I could stop it."

"I guess, we will just have to see," Cesar said. "Whatever it is, we are here to witness. We are in a bad place with these people, Jordy. All we have between us and them is your gift. The sheriff sure isn't going to help us. Whatever it is, I feel better with it here."

Well, that made one of them. Jordy felt trapped by it. The immensity of the power that he felt was inhuman. It was all-consuming, and that terrified him. But Cesar was right about them being defenseless against the small army of Evander's men. Farmers with shotguns were no match for trained assassins. They were outnumbered and outgunned. "I guess you are right," he agreed reluctantly.

"I think it picked you for a reason," Laz said reflectively. "Some men would try to misuse the power. The temptation of wielding that kind of power would be too much for them. See, you're not that kind of man. You would only use it for good."

Jordy looked at him. "That is true. I would never do that. Besides, I feel there are consequences in misusing it."

"You have said that in the past," Cesar pointed out. "Like what?"

Jordy shook his head. "I don't know, it's just a feeling."

"Nothing good, I'd wager," Laz said.

"Agreed," Cesar said.

Chapter 60

Jordy was going to the parsonage to visit the pastor. He was home from the hospital but in rough shape. Amelia told him that he was so weak that he now used a wheelchair. She had warned him how weak and frail he looked. They were all taking turns watching over him while he got his strength back. Amelia had sent him to deliver some food that she had cooked for him. It was nice having him back home, where he belonged with people who cared for him.

As Jordy made his way up the walk, he spotted Elma Watkins sitting outside. Amelia had told him that Elma had taken it upon herself to be the pastor's main caretaker. It was odd because Elma was not much of a churchgoer. She often said she doesn't need a church to find God. God is everywhere and in all things. She was dressed in her usual jean bib overalls, her long, white hair twisted into a bun at the base of her neck, smoking a pipe and no doubt there was whiskey in that glass she was drinking.

"Hey, Elma, is he awake?" he asked, smiling at the way that she looked him up and down, her eyes landing on the basket in his hand.

She scoffed. "Tell me you are not bringing more food. Just how much food do you people think that old man is going to eat?"

"Amelia loves to cook." Jordy shrugged.

"Suit yourself. My pigs got to eat, too."

Nice, Jordy thought sarcastically but only smiled. "Can I see him?"

"Sure, once he is done talking to him."

Himself?"

"Yeah, Evander is here talking to him."

Alarm bells rang in Jordy's head. Why was he here, he wondered? "Is he alone with him?"

"Yup, they are sitting in the back. Evander helped the pastor outside to get some air."

"If it's all the same to you, I'm going to go check on them."

"Figured you would. Leave the basket. I'll take it inside with the rest."

Jordy followed the walkway around to the back. Evander and the pastor were sitting under the oak tree in the shade. Evander was the first to spot Jordy. He waved, flashing a smile at him. The pastor turned and looked at Jordy. Amelia was right, the pastor looked like he had aged ten years.

"Jordy, my boy. I was hoping that you would come to see me." The pastor reached out, taking Jordy's hands in his.

"How are you? You are looking better."

"I look terrible. I know. But I'm feeling better. Sit and join us." The pastor gestured to the chair beside Evander.

"He can take mine," Evander said, rising to his feet. "I need to be going."

Jordy was glad to see him go. "Fine, thanks."

"Jordy, I'll see you later. We need to talk." Evander turned to the pastor. "I'll see you later, Pastor Ezra. Try and get some rest."

Jordy watched Evander as he walked away. "What did he want?"

The pastor was watching Jordy. "Evander stops by to see me now and again. He visited me in the hospital. He would read to me."

"Evander? Really?"

"That surprises you?"

"It does."

"You don't like him?"

"I don't trust him."

"He's a complicated man. There are many sides to some men, Jordy."

"Enough about him. How are you really?"

"I'm weak as a kitten. I'm just glad to be home where I belong."

"People will love that you are back. We have missed your sermons."

Pastor Ezra chuckled. "Phil tries."

"Yes, he did," Jordy agreed.

"I thought comparing God to superheroes was very creative."

Jordy laughed. "It was totally Phil."

"I heard about what happened to Jed. He is lucky that you were there."

"Yes, it could have turned out badly."

"The night Marty hit me, I was unconscious. Do you remember?"

Jordy nodded. "I do."

"I heard you calling me back. When I opened my eyes, you were there. You took my hand, and I felt this power flowing from you to me. It was so strong and healing. There was a profound pureness about it. I think you saved my life, Jordy."

Jordy looked away from the pastor's searching eyes. "I did nothing but hold your hand."

Pastor Ezra slowly shook his head. "No. It came from you. Perhaps you are not even aware of it."

"To be honest, I hate it. I wish it would go away. It haunts me. I feel like some kind of freak. It's too much responsibility."

Pastor Ezra laughed. "God does not give us what we cannot handle. You were chosen for a reason."

Jordy was tired of hearing that. Chosen? Cursed was more like it. "I know you believe that. I would just like to go back to what I was."

"Don't you see, Jordy? You have always had it. Born with it, more than likely."

"If it were up to me, I would give it away to someone else. Let them deal with it. I'm tired."

"Something has happened. What is it?"

The pastor was always a wise man who could read people well. The tempest now had a mind of its own; that's what happened. Jordy didn't want to talk about it anymore. "Not today, pastor. Let me help you inside. I need to go work my fields."

Pastor Ezra looked like he wanted to argue but only nodded. "Ok, Jordy. But we will talk about this. You can't keep it locked up inside of you."

Yeah, that pretty much sums up the problem, Jordy thought.

Chapter 61

Jordy grimaced when he saw Evander pull into the driveway. He knew it was coming, but that didn't make it any easier. This was all he needed after working in the fields all day. Sitting out on the porch at night was his time to relax. This was when he decompressed from the work and worry that went with farming. Though the crop yield looked better than he had seen in years, it was his job to keep it that way. Last year had been tough. He needed a good harvest to pull him out of the red and back into the black. So, the stress was never far behind him. Evander waved to him when he got out of the car. Jordy just nodded to him.

"Nice night," Evander said as he walked up the stairs and sat beside him on the porch.

"It will do," Jordy said, sipping his iced tea.

"Do you think that I could get one of those? I don't know what Amelia does to it, but that iced tea is the best."

"Peach juice." Jordy groaned, getting up from his chair from stiff muscles.

Evander frowned. "Are you injured?"

"No, just stiff. Hard day." He walked to the door intending to refill his and bring Evander a glass.

When he opened the door, he was not expecting Evander to follow him inside, but there he was, right behind him. Amelia looked up, startled by the table loaded with canning jars. "Hello," she said, shyly.

"What is all of this?" Evander said, picking up one of the jars to look at it.

Jordy ignored him and concentrated on filling glasses. Amelia glanced at him and shrugged. "Corn relish," she said.

"Corn relish?" Evander said, turning the jar in his hand. "I don't think that I have ever had it."

"Take one. I hope you enjoy it." Amelia went back to labeling the jars.

Jordy turned, handing Evander a glass of iced tea.

"Thank you. So, you are canning for winter." He gestured to all the jars lined up on the table.

Jordy walked to the door with Evander following him. "Some of it is for winter. Others are for bartering."

Evander sat down, still clutching the glass and the jar. "Bartering?"

"All the townspeople do it. Bree for her pies, Amelia for canning or vegetables, Esme bakes bread, some do eggs or apples, and Diane barters milk from the cows. Whatever you have that others will want to trade for. People have been doing it for years."

"Fascinating," Evander said, deep in thought. "Your home is very homey inside. You are a lucky man, Jordy."

"Luck is only part of it, and the other part is hard work."

"You could make it easier on yourself by using your gift." Evander pointed it out to him.

"So, you keep telling me. People here work hard for what they have. It's a lesson your people should learn. Nothing worth spit comes by having it handed to you or taking it from people."

"I had nothing to do with what happened to Jed. And while we are on that subject, let me point out that you don't have a problem using your gift in helping others, so why not use it to help yourself?"

Jordy sighed. "It does not work like that. I told you before, to use it for the wrong reasons comes with consequences."

"You can't be sure of that. Unless you have tried it? Have you?"

"Look, I don't need to try jumping off a cliff to know what will happen, just like I know using the gift for selfish reasons comes with consequences."

"But have you tried it?"

"I have not, and I don't plan on testing it."

Evander sipped his tea. "What if I had something that I wanted you to do? Something that would bring good to Wormwood? Would you consider it?"

Jordy glanced at Evander, measuring his response. "It would depend on what it is and how it would help the people here."

"I want you to think about something, Jordy. Things are only going to get worse. Yes, what happened at Jed's has people thinking twice, but that will change in time. I see you are protecting Jed's cows here, but how are you going to protect everyone in town? Because there are things at play that you don't know or understand. I could be wrong, and this will blow over in time. Either way, it will all be over by the time October rolls around."

"What are you talking about?"

"I've already said too much. I should be going." Evander drained his glass and put it down with a thump on the tiny table near his chair before rising to his feet. "Thank you for the tea, and please thank Amelia for the corn relish."

Jordy tipped his head at him, narrowing his eyes. "I wish you would just say whatever it is for once without playing these word games."

"Some things are not mine to tell. Just think about what I said about using your gift."

Jordy watched as Evander walked to his car, a nagging sense that this wasn't over. Evander wanted something from him—something he knew was no good. By October, it would all be over, Evander had said. What did that mean? Were they planning to leave town? If so, why was it so important to Evander? One thing was for certain, whatever Evander wanted would mean crossing a line that he was not willing to cross. But what was it, and what did it have to do with the safety of the town?

Chapter 62

"Brooke Porter is missing," Cesar said. "So is her car. Her grandmother said she left for work but never showed up. Everyone in town is looking for her. Tomorrow, after church services, there is a search party."

"Are you planning on going?" Jordy asked.

Cesar nodded. "Yeah, it's the right thing to do. Brooke is a good kid. Her gran is worried sick."

Jordy grimaced. "God, I hope this doesn't end the same way as Kelly Morrison. You don't think that Marty has anything to do with it?"

Laz groaned. "Lord, I hope not. One is enough. The sheriff seems to think that she ran away."

"What makes him think that?" Jordy asked, stretched out under the shade of the oak tree.

"Some of her friends said that she always wanted to be an actress. She dreamed of going to New York or Hollywood." Laz shrugged.

"So, she leaves without telling anyone?" Cesar was shaking his head.

"What does your famous gut tell you?" Laz asked, looking at Jordy.

"Nothing," Jordy said, frowning. "It doesn't always tell me when something is wrong."

Laz shrugged. "Maybe she did run off."

"Would not be the first one. Remember Debbie Watkins? She just got up and left. I thought Elma was going to toss a fit." Cesar chuckled.

Jordy nodded. "I saw Elma the other day at the pastor's. It surprised me."

"Yeah," Cesar said. "She has been caring for him."

"I saw Evander there," Jordy said. "Pastor Ezra told me that he visits quite often. He even reads to him."

Laz scoffed. "It's some kind of trick."

Jordy shook his head. "I can't figure him out. Pastor Ezra told me that men can have many sides."

Cesar huffed. "The only side I want to see is his backside heading out of town."

"Funny you should say that. Evander told me something about it all being over by October. I was not sure what he meant by it."

Cesar and Laz both sat up straighter. "Do you think that means that they are leaving?" Cesar asked.

"Maybe," Jordy said, leaving out the rest of what Evander had said.

Cesar wistfully looked out at the fields as the wheat swayed in the breeze. "That would be great. We are looking at what might be the best harvest yet. We could finally move ahead and buy that land from Ralph White. I can toss Laz's ass out of the house into his own place."

"Thanks, pop." Laz rolled his eyes.

Cesar reached over and playfully tapped the visor of Laz's hat down over his eyes. "But just think of it. It would be great. With no more bastards running around messing with the town, things can get back to normal."

"Yeah, that would be nice," Jordy agreed, but he felt they would need to run a lot of miles before October came. He sensed that Evander was not wrong about more to come before it was over.

Chapter 63

The church was packed to capacity to hear Pastor Ezra's first sermon since getting released from the hospital. The pastor sat in his wheelchair at the front of the church, looking pale and gaunt. Jordy frowned at the sight of him. The incident with Marty had taken a lot out of the man. He worried about if he was rushing things and not waiting until he was stronger. But Pastor Ezra had a will forged in steel even if his body was not.

People were pressed together on the wooden benches inside the stuffy church. It had to be already eighty degrees outside with high humidity, making it feel like a sauna inside. Jordy's shirt was already plastered against his body like a damp second skin. Petunia sat beside him, playing air drums, her bony elbows bumping rhythmically into his rib cage.

He reached over, covering her hands with his to make her stop. "Petunia, settle down," he whispered.

She looked up at him. "I want a set of drums," she whispered.

Jordy smiled down at her. "Flip over a couple of buckets when you get home and have at it. But right now, you need to sit and be still."

She pouted at him, her bottom lip trembling. "It's hot."

"I know, but you need to show respect for Pastor Ezra." Jordy gestured to the front of the church.

Petunia was still pouting as she crossed her arms over her chest and sat back. "I will."

"My children," Pastor Ezra began. His voice was soft and raspy. "Today, I want to talk about Wormwood. We have gone through many trials and tribulations these past few months. I fear the bitter waters are still to come. Currently, we all have Brooke Porter on our minds. Let us pray for her quick return." The pastor bent his head in silent prayer, and the congregation followed his lead.

After a moment of silence, the pastor looked up. "Wormwood is more than a town; it is a community of people that are more family than neighbors. As a family, we care for each other in the way God has willed it. We are facing challenges together. We are overcoming obstacles. We are solid in our faith."

Pastor Ezra's voice grew weaker and thinner as he spoke. Jordy wondered how long they would have him. His stay in the hospital did not heal the pastor as he had hoped. He thought about what Evander had said about ridding the town of evil with his gift. He glanced around at all the people sitting beside him. The pastor was right. They were more like family than neighbors.

The pastor's voice grew louder and more forceful as he talked about the bitter waters of Wormwood. "The star will come from the heavens and with it will follow the bitter waters. But we are warned not to drink from those waters. God has warned us, and we will survive while the evil is vanquished. That is God's will."

Pastor Ezra looked over the people sitting before him. "Go now, my children, before you all melt." He smiled.

Everyone stood and clapped. Their faces showed the naked emotions that they felt. The love for the pastor shone brightly in their eyes. Elma pushed his wheelchair to the doorway so the pastor could greet his congregation as they left.

Jordy waited in line for his turn. Petunia, however, was pushing her way through the crowd to get outside. With a sigh, he glanced at Amelia, rolling his eyes. "She is your daughter," Amelia whispered.

It was not lost on Jordy that Amelia always pointed that out whenever Petunia acted up. "I recall that you were there when she was born."

Amelia pursed her lips. "Don't blame the gift giver."

Jordy laughed. Petunia made it to the pastor vigorously, shaking his hand before running outside. "Do you have a return policy?" Jordy muttered.

Amelia chuckled. "Sorry, no refunds."

When Jordy's turn came, Pastor Ezra took both of his hands, as he always did, and pulled him close. He leaned in and whispered, "I feel the power. The strength."

"I have no control over it," Jordy whispered.

The pastor continued to hold on to him. "It's amazing. It flows through me like a river of healing strength. I'm feeling much better now." He released Jordy's hands reluctantly.

"Rest, old friend," Jordy said and moved on to let others behind him have a turn.

Cesar was waiting outside. "I figured we could take my truck to search for Brooke. I already have our search grid in the truck."

Amelia held out her hand for the truck keys. "I'll take the kids and Esme home."

Jordy fished the keys out of his pocket and kissed his wife on the cheek. "I'll be home after we get done."

Amelia nodded. "Good luck."

Jordy watched as his family got into the truck, wishing he was going with them. He glanced at Cesar from over his shoulder. Still, his tempest was dormant. He hoped the girl really did run off to follow her dreams. Finding her dead in a field would be soul-crushing for not only him but the entire town.

Laz had brought cold drinks for the search. Jordy rode shotgun beside Cesar, with Laz taking the backseat. Their search grid would take them out near Evander's place. He opened his water bottle and took a long drink from it. "So, what's the plan?" he asked Cesar as he pulled onto the road.

"I figure, we cruise the streets looking for the car. They are forming a group of volunteers to do a ground search on foot. We save Evander's place for last."

Jordy nodded. "Sounds good."

"Do you suppose that they gave us this area to search because they knew it would pass by Evander's?" Laz asked, studying the grid.

"Yup, that was not lost on me, either." Cesar glanced into the rearview at Laz.

"Hopefully, she is not there." Jordy looked out the window, feeling the gloom settle over him.

"Anything buzzing from your early warning system?" Cesar asked, glancing at Jordy.

"Nothing." Jordy glanced back out the window.

It bothered him that he felt nothing. If the girl was really in trouble, surely, he would sense it. The fact that he didn't, made him wonder if she really did run away. As they traveled down the streets of Wormwood, seeing no sign of her or her car, it seemed to confirm that she had left the area either on her own or by force. He focused on the miles of roadsides, searching for anything unusual. The tall, tangled scrub grass on the side of the roads made it hard to see if there was anything hidden. The car would be visible, but if there was a body, the scrub grass held that secret. Later, when they did a ground search, the volunteers would find it if it was there. But Jordy didn't sense there was anything here. Right now, Brooke Porter might be having a latte in New York City for all they knew. Living the dream.

"Ok, we are just about done here. What do you say we stop at Evander's place and get this over with before heading back?" Cesar had pulled over, his arms resting on the steering wheel.

Jordy nodded. "Let's do it and get it over with."

As they drove up the winding, dirt road, the familiar tightening in his gut signaled the awakening of his tempest. His senses sharpened. He knew there were two men guarding the gate up ahead. Just like he knew, there were at least twenty men at the compound standing alert and ready for their arrival. They knew they were here, judging by the fluttering in his gut.

When they turned the corner and the gate came into view, the two guards were standing at the ready. One of the men was on his com while the other held up a hand, signaling them to stop. Cesar glanced at Jordy. Jordy only nodded. "It's fine. Don't worry. I'll be back after I chat with our friends behind the gate."

Cesar sighed heavily. "I hate coming here. It's like walking into a rattlesnake's pit."

Laz was leaning in between the front seats. "Good description. Very true."

Jordy got out when the truck stopped. As he walked up to the guards, the guards stepped back hesitantly. He felt their fear as he faced them. The tempest was tapping into their strength, uncoiling, and reaching out with invisible tentacles. Jordy had never felt that before. It was like a parasite, identifying its host, looking for a weakness.

By the time he got to the gate, the tempest's lock on all the targets was complete. It had identified all threats and was ready to strike. Jordy was aware of it but not in control. It was like that day at Jed's. The tempest was running the show.

"What do you want?" the guard asked.

The fear coming from the guard was tangible. "I'm here to see if you have seen a missing girl. Her name is Brooke Porter."

The guard shook his head. "I ain't seen nothing."

He was lying about the girl. "I think you have seen her. Where is she?"

The guard backed up a step. "I don't know anything about where she is. I had nothing to do with that shit."

"Do you want to try again?" Jordy stared at the man, watching the sweat bead up on his forehead as the tempest probed deeper. He wondered if the guards could feel it. Was there some feeling like a vibration running through their bodies, or was it a primitive instinctual warning of danger? Jordy wondered.

The car coming from the compound interrupted them. Evander was sitting in the front passenger seat of the jeep. When it came up to the fence, Evander hopped out with a smile. "Jordy, what brings you here?"

"We are looking for a missing girl." Jordy's eyes slid over the four men, noting their hands were hovering inches away from the guns holstered at their hips.

Evander flashed an easy smile. "Oh, yes, I heard about that. Brooke Porter. Pastor Ezra told me about her. We have not seen her. Maybe she ran away like the sheriff thinks."

He could not tell if Evander was lying, but he didn't think so. "Ok, let us know if you stumble across her. Her grandmother is very worried."

"Of course. Why don't you come down to the house and have a cold drink? It's hot today." Evander casually leaned against the fence.

"No, we are still searching. Thanks for your time." As Jordy turned away, he felt the relief filter through Evander's men and smiled.

"Well, what did they say?" Cesar asked when Jordy climbed back into the truck.

"They say that they have not seen her."

"Do you believe them?" Laz asked skeptically.

"No." Jordy stretched out his legs, reclining in his seat. "Some of what was said rang true, but something is off."

"If they have her, you know she is dead," Cesar said, as he turned the truck around.

"I don't think so," Jordy said.

"Because you would sense it," Laz finished for him.

"Yes, I think so." Jordy nodded.

Cesar glanced at Jordy as he navigated the truck down the dirt road. "When you were at the gate, we felt something. It was like a tingling that ran through our bodies. It was not unpleasant, but we felt it."

"The tempest was working its magic. I'm not entirely sure what it was searching for."

"So, the gift is now more of an it?" Laz asked, frowning.

"Yeah, like it has a life of its own." Jordy looked out the window, feeling more like an unwilling host to whatever was inside of him.

"Awesome and yet terrifying," Laz whispered.

Chapter 64

Jordy sat out on the porch after a tiring day in the fields. The crops were looking the best that he had ever seen them. Harvest time was approaching, and the yield was going to be better than he ever could have predicted. He would be a happy man if it wasn't for the feelings of uncertainty that plagued him.

The ongoing problems in town were overwhelming. Brooke Porter was still missing, having disappeared into thin air. There was no trace of her. It weighed on Jordy that someone from town could just vanish like that. It could happen to anyone. Maybe even someone that he loved. There was also the failing health of the pastor that was troubling. Then, he still had the cows roaming his property and the added worry about the safety of Jed and his family. All these things weighed heavily on Jordy's mind.

The cool breeze was a welcome balm to his tired body, as he tried to relax. He stretched his legs, listening to the night's chorus of crickets and the soft melody of the chimes swaying on the porch. Two white moths were doing an aerial ballet around the porch lights. All of this should be calming. Then why was his tempest coiling in his gut? The car rolling up the driveway soon gave an answer to that.

Henry Lee parked in front of the porch and got out of his car. He stood staring at Jordy for a moment before climbing the stairs. "Nice night," he said.

Jordy felt his tempest searching, as it reached Henry. "Yup," Jordy said. "What brings you here, Henry?"

Henry leaned lazily against the porch railing. "You can relax, Jordy. I'm only here to talk."

That was not quite true. He was here to test him. Jordy sensed that he, like his tempest, was probing for weaknesses. "I am relaxed," Jordy said.

"Hardly. I can feel it, you know."

Jordy decided to play dumb. "Feel what?"

Henry stared at him, measuring his response. Jordy could sense conflict and uncertainty inside Henry. He had never dealt with anything like Jordy before, and it perplexed him. "You have grown much more powerful. I'm here to tell you to back off, Jordy. I have business here, and nothing is going to stand in my way. Do you understand?"

"Stand in your way…" Jordy repeated slowly, as his anger stirred the tempest into full alert. "You come to my house and make veiled threats?" His tempest coiled tighter. "I think you should leave."

Henry straightened and stood facing Jordy, all traces of this being a relaxed little chat evaporated. "This town is still vulnerable even with you in it. Do you want to be the cause of more trouble? More missing girls? More random beatings? You can't always be everywhere. My suggestion to you is to stay on your farm and leave the town to survive on its own."

"So, basically, let you torture people in town." Jordy rose to his feet, intending to ram his fist down the pompous, little bastard's throat.

He felt the energy push away from him, and with it, Henry was tossed from the porch, landing ten feet away by the front of his car. As Henry scrambled to get up, he was held there firmly in place. Jordy stomped down the stairs and walked over to him. "Now you will listen. I don't know how powerful this thing is or all that it can do. But what I do know is that if anything more happens in town, I will hold you responsible. And here is something else for you to think about, I don't have to come and find you in order to dish out a little kickass. You can't hide anywhere that I can't find you. So, if you want to be a hard ass, so be it. You call down the thunder, Henry, and you will find lightning will follow."

Henry looked up at him, his eyes glinting with open malice. "I could end you for this," he hissed.

"Not if I end you first." Jordy stared down at him. "The decision is yours."

"Fine, you win this round," Henry conceded.

Jordy felt the pressure ease, and Henry got to his feet. There was an internal struggle going on inside Henry, Jordy sensed. He wanted to lash out and challenge Jordy, but reason won out, and he went to his car, and opened the door.

"This is far from over," Henry said, looking at him, trembling in anger and fear. He had wet himself while he was pinned to the ground.

"I know," Jordy said, standing his ground.

He watched Henry back out of the driveway. It was Henry who brought all the evil into town. Evander was just a frontman. They came here because it was a manageable little town that they could control and run their criminal empire. To anyone passing through, it was a cute, small town used as camouflage. He had read many things inside Henry's mind while he was held on the ground. His business at the compound was locked there until whatever they were doing was completed. Weapons, drugs…a whole buffet of illegal activities with a complex hierarchy of dangerous hidden investors. It was like fighting a monster with many heads. By eliminating Henry, he would do nothing because another monster would step up to take his place. So, now, what does he do with that?

Chapter 65

Jordy was just finishing the next day in the field, when he saw Evander driving up in his jeep. He had not mentioned anything to Cesar or Laz about his visit with Henry. What was the point in worrying them? Seeing Evander was not a surprise. No doubt Henry vented to him about being tossed off Jordy's porch last night. The memory of Henry slinking away to his car with urine-soaked pants, made him smile.

"What do you think he wants?" Cesar asked, leaning up against Jordy's truck.

Jordy shrugged. "Nothing good."

Evander stopped the jeep when he reached Jordy's truck. "Hop in, let's take a ride and talk," Evander said, lacking the usual charming smile.

"I'm tired. Come by later. You know where I'll be." Jordy continued to stow gear in the back of his truck.

"Jordy, it's important and won't take long." Evander refused to go.

Jordy sighed, turning to Cesar and Laz. "I'll see you guys tomorrow."

"Jordy, are you sure you want to go with him alone?" Laz asked, concerned.

Jordy glanced at Evander from over his shoulder. "I'll be fine. I'll see you tomorrow."

He walked over to Evander's jeep and got into the passenger side. "Ok, let's go."

Evander turned the jeep around and drove back the way he came, driving along the edge of the field back to the road. "You met with Henry last night?"

"Is that a question?" Jordy asked sarcastically, tired of playing games.

"No, I know you met with him, I want to hear your side. He's pretty pissed off."

"Good, that makes two of us then."

"What happened?"

"He came issuing threats, and I tossed him around like a ragdoll and sent him home."

"Henry is a dangerous man, Jordy."

"So am I." He was tired of playing nice with them, too. It was time to show them that he was serious.

"I suppose that you are. He's not done, you know."

"Yeah, I know."

"What will you do?"

Jordy looked at him. "Why would I confide in you, Evander?"

"Ok, then. That's fair. Let me confide in you. I want you to kill Henry and all his men. Focus your powers and take them all out. I will handle the fallout from it. I will convince them that we need to move our operations out of Wormwood."

"Now, why would you do that?" Kill Henry? Was he for real?

"Because I've grown attached to the place and the people. Kill him, Jordy. It is the only way. Better yet, wait until next month. On September twentieth there is a meeting at the compound. All the decision-makers will be there. Kill them all."

Only a part of what Evander said was true. The part about being attached to Wormwood was a lie. He wanted out of this deal. It had turned into more than he had bargained for, and he was trapped.

"I told you that I can't do that."

"Damn the consequences. People are going to suffer. You know that I am right."

It was not just the consequences any longer that worried him. The storm within had a will of its own, a dark agenda he doubted he could control. Further, he didn't want to murder anyone. What would separate him from them if he did that?

"There has to be another way."

"Well, I'm all ears if you have a better solution."

"I'm tired. I want to go home, take a shower, and get something to eat."

"At least think about what I said." Evander turned the Jeep around to take him back to his truck.

"I'll think about it, but my decision will be the same. I could never do that."

"Never say never. You have no idea what these people are capable of doing. They are monsters. There may come a time that you will change your mind, Jordy."

He did not take that as a threat. Evander was being truthful with his warning. "When and if those times come, then we will see what happens."

Chapter 66

Pastor Ezra sat across from Jordy at the dinner table, looking deep in thought. Amelia had made the pastor's favorite dinner, but he hardly touched it. There was a visible tremor in his hand, making it challenging for him to eat. He spilled more than made it to his mouth. He was painfully thin and ashen. Over the meal, Pastor Ezra kept looking thoughtfully up at Jordy but said little. Something was troubling him, and Jordy knew he wanted to talk.

"Daddy, I'm trying to teach Walter to speak," Petunia said. "I thought I heard him say apple."

"Well, Walter is one smart pig," Jordy said, laughing.

Petunia turned to the pastor. "What do you think?"

"I think if any pig can learn to talk, my bet would be on Walter," he said, smiling.

"Mine, too," Petunia said, eyeing the pastor's untouched peach cobbler.

The pastor pushed it over to her. "I'm going to let you have this. My appetite is not that good these days."

Petunia's eyes grew large. "Really, are you sure? It's really good."

The pastor chuckled. "I'm sure."

Petunia didn't hesitate to pull over the plate and dig into it. Amelia rolled her eyes. "She's a bottomless pit these days."

"She's growing," the pastor said, looking at Petunia affectionately.

"I'll send some of this home with you, Pastor Ezra," Amelia said, smiling.

"Would you like to go out and sit on the porch for a while?" Jordy asked the pastor, rising from the table.

"Yes, I would love that." He backed the wheelchair away from the table.

Jordy pushed the wheelchair out onto the porch and sat down beside him. "It's nice out here today."

"It is." The pastor agreed, looking out over the yard.

Jordy waited patiently for the pastor to begin to speak about whatever was troubling him. The lines on his face deepened into a frown as he turned and looked at Jordy. "I'm dying, Jordy," he said.

Jordy was at a loss for a second as he absorbed it. "You're just healing, Pastor Ezra. It might feel like you are at your end, but give it time."

He slowly shook his head. "I had a dream. In it, I was being called home."

Jordy reached over and took his hand. "You can't think this way. People need you."

"That is the hardest part about leaving. I feel that my work here is not complete."

"Then you need to fight to stay."

Pastor Ezra chuckled. "Sometimes there is a time to fight, and then there is a time that we must accept what is to be. Jordy, I feel something is coming. Something big. I feel it even stronger now with your hand on mine. You are in for a great battle, my boy. I want to be here when it comes so that I can help you."

Jordy frowned. He felt an energy coming from the pastor. A spark of something undefined. "I can tell you that you will be here." How he knew this, he could not say.

The pastor was looking at him earnestly. "I believe you. Can you see what is coming, Jordy?"

He could not see it, but he felt it. It was a feeling of dread so deep that it had no ending. "I can't see it. I can only feel it coming."

Chapter 67

Jordy was standing overlooking the fields, waiting for the combines to show up. It was his favorite day of the year. Harvesting day! He looked over at Cesar and Laz doing the same. His chest puffed with pride at what he had grown with his own two hands. All his hard work came down to today.

Amelia was home planning a celebration dinner for tonight. They would celebrate tonight as a family, as they always did on harvesting day. But this year will be special. It was his greatest harvest ever. Winter would be gentle with all the extra money.

In the field, he spotted a boy, no more than nine or ten. "What is he doing there?"

"Who?" Cesar said, frowning.

"That boy. In the field standing in the cornrows." Jordy squinted to see him better. He was dancing in the cornrows.

Laz and Cesar were craning their necks to see what Jordy was looking at. "I don't see anything."

Jordy started walking down the slope to get the boy out of the field. "I'll be right back."

When he got to the cornfield, he lost sight of the boy. He was a pretty boy with a head of golden curls. Jordy peered in through the burgeoning cornstalks, trying to spot him. "Hey, boy, you need to get out of there. The combines are due here any minute."

He spotted him twenty feet away, walking barefoot down the row. Jordy followed him. "Boy, did you hear me?"

"I heard what you said," he said in a sing-song voice followed by a musical giggle.

Jordy sighed. Just what he needed, a kid playing in the corn with combines ready to harvest. He walked more determined. When he caught up to him, he reached down and grabbed the boy's arm just above his elbow. The second his fingers encircled the boy's arm, he felt an electrical jolt pulse through his body, making him gasp. The current was so powerful, it brought him to his knees.

"You are Jordy Hart," the barefoot boy said, not pulling out of his grasp. "You have great power. I can feel it as you can feel mine. Pastor Ezra has taken a bad turn. You must go to him. He needs you."

Jordy looked into the bluest eyes that he had ever seen. In them, there was a pureness that was not of this earth. He could not speak so he nodded that he understood. When the boy pulled free, Jordy collapsed to the ground, smelling the damp earth and sweet corn. His equilibrium returned, and he looked up; the boy had disappeared. Vanished into thin air. "Pastor Ezra," he whispered, getting shakily to his feet.

He walked out of the cornfield, uncertain if any of it had even happened. His mind struggled to focus, to make sense of it all. As he climbed up the bank, he noticed Cesar and Laz watching him with strange expressions, "What happened?" Cesar asked, confused.

"How did you get that sunburn?" Laz asked, backing up a step.

"Pastor Ezra. I need to go to him." Jordy mumbled.

"Pastor Ezra?" Cesar asked, confused.

"Can you guide the combines into my fields?" Jordy asked, leaning heavily against the giant oak.

"Where are you going?" Cesar asked, perplexed.

"I need to see Pastor Ezra."

Cesar stood with his hands on his hips, looking at Jordy with deep concern. "Yes, of course, I can handle the combines. What is wrong with the pastor?"

"I'll be back as soon as I can."

Jordy walked to his truck, feeling better. The weakness from his encounter with the boy was ebbing. On his way to the parsonage, he passed the combines rumbling their way down the narrow street. He drove past with only the pastor on his mind. The boy had said that Pastor Ezra needed him. What had happened?

He parked on the street outside the parsonage and ran inside the building. Elma Watkins and Doc Willows were standing near the pastor's bed. "What's happened?" Jordy asked, coming into the room.

"He's had a setback but refuses to go to the hospital," Doc said, turning to Jordy.

"Jordy?" the pastor wheezed. "Is that Jordy, my boy?"

Jordy rushed to his bedside. The pastor was lying on his back on top of the bed. He was deathly white with lips that were nearly blue. "Pastor, you must go to the hospital," Jordy whispered.

The pastor tried to raise his hand to Jordy but only made it halfway before his arm dropped back to the bed. Jordy took his hand in his and held it. "Jordy. I knew that you would come."

"Rest, pastor. You need to go to the hospital."

"No. I want to stay here. The hospital is for the sick. I'm not sick, just old and tired. If I die, I want to be here and not in some hospital." He closed his eyes. "I'm feeling better. Just stay with me for a short while."

Doc Willows shook his head. "You are stubborn."

Pastor Ezra chuckled and winked at Jordy. "The hospital cannot heal me. It can't give me better care than I'm getting right here."

Doc shook his head. "If your blood pressure drops any lower, I'm not going to give you a choice."

Doc listened to Pastor Ezra's heart through the stethoscope. "Hmm," he said. Pulling out the blood pressure cuff, he attached it to Pastor Ezra's arm and pumped it up, watching the needle. His bushy eyebrows drew together. "Well, call me dipped," he muttered. "That is a nice improvement."

Pastor Ezra, glanced at Jordy. "Yes, I'm feeling better."

"You are not out of the woods, Pastor Ezra. This is temporary at best." Doc took off his glasses and cleaned them with the hanky he snaked out of his pocket. "I think you should go to the hospital to be evaluated."

"I'm staying here. Elma is here to help me. And I have a town full of friends for support. There is nothing for me at the hospital." Pastor Ezra struggled to sit up, looking to Jordy for assistance.

"Are you sure?" Jordy asked, helping him up.

"I am sure. I think that I would like some tea and toast."

Doc rolled his eyes. "I'm not sure what just happened here. But ok."

Elma nodded, smiling at Pastor Ezra. "I'll go get you something to eat. See, I told you it would pass."

"Well, I'm going to go," Doc Willows said, picking up his medical bag. "I'll be back to check on you later."

"Thanks, Doc," Jordy said, turning to the pastor.

"I'm so glad that you came," Pastor Ezra said, squeezing his hand. "Why did you come?"

Jordy didn't know how to explain it himself. "A little voice told me that you needed me."

"Must be heaven sent." The pastor sighed.

"Could be," Jordy said, thinking about the beautiful boy in the corn.

Chapter 68

Jordy returned to the field after settling down with Pastor Ezra. When he left, the good pastor was sleeping peacefully. He stood on the bank under the big oak tree in the shade, watching the combines. By the time he got there, the combine harvesting the corn was halfway through his field. It was something to see. They had already finished harvesting the corn in Cesar's field and they were doing the first pass through his wheat field.

"How do the numbers look?" Jordy asked watching as the corn shot out the grain outlet into the harvesting truck's trailer.

"They look better than I have ever seen them," Cesar said proudly.

Jordy smiled. "Let's call Ralph White and see if he is still interested in selling."

Cesar chuckled. He was like a kid at Christmas. "I talked to him last week at Winslow's. He is extremely interested. I told him that we would be in contact after the harvest, and we see the numbers."

"Great, this time next year, we will be harvesting that acreage, too." Jordy could not hide his excitement.

"We'll have to hire some people to help," Cesar said.

"Yup, but it will be worth it."

"And I get a house out of the deal," Laz piped in, grinning.

"So, what happened?" Cesar asked. "How is the pastor?"

Jordy sobered. "He had a setback but for right now, he is holding his own."

Cesar pushed back his cap and wiped the sweat from his brow. "That's good. What about this morning in the cornfield? What was that?"

Good question, Jordy thought. "I don't think you would believe me if I told you. Hell, I don't even know what to think, and I was there."

"After everything that I have witnessed over the last few months. Give it a shot."

"I saw a boy in the cornfield, remember?" Jordy said, uneasily. It was like repeating what he saw as some kind of secret that he was revealing.

"Yeah, but we didn't see him," Laz added.

Here goes nothing, Jordy thought. "Yes, well, I don't think it was a normal boy playing in my cornfield. I…I think it might have been an angel or something."

Cesar looked at Laz, and they both started laughing. "That's a good one."

Jordy cleared his throat. "I'm serious."

Cesar sobered. "What makes you say that?"

"When I caught up to the boy, I grabbed him by the arm and a current shot through me like a lightning bolt. It was so powerful that it sent me to my knees. That's when the boy told me about the pastor. He told me that he needed me."

Cesar made a low whistle. "But an angel? Why did you settle on that?"

Jordy stared off into space as he recalled it. "There was something about his eyes. There was a pureness there that was not of this earth. I could not read anything from him. He was a blank slate. But it was a being with immense power. God-given."

Cesar made the sign of the cross. "This is really getting scary."

"Not as long as they are on our side," Laz drawled. "This angel sent you to help the pastor?"

"Yes, and the pastor was in a bad way." Jordy nodded.

"Do you think the pastor could have died if you hadn't gotten there?" Cesar asked.

Jordy frowned. "I don't know. Doc was determined to send the pastor back to the hospital. Maybe I was not sent there to save his life, as much as to keep him from being sent there. Maybe the powers that be, want the pastor to remain here in town."

"Why?" Cesar asked.

"I don't know. I'm not sure of anything. But the pastor told me that he has been getting a feeling that something bad is coming.

When I touched his hand, I felt something." Jordy frowned, remembering it. "There was an undercurrent of power, and with it came this intense foreboding feeling of dread. I could sense something coming. Something bad."

Cesar shivered in the heat. "That's terrifying."

"I think it is amazing," Laz said.

"I'm with Cesar on this. This whole heaven and hell thing has me a little freaked out." Jordy ran his fingers through his hair in frustration.

Laz slapped him on the back. "At least the kid that you saw didn't have horns and a pitchfork."

Jordy flinched, looking at Laz, but laughed beside himself. "True."

Cesar chuckled. "Hey, they are done with the corn. Let's go talk to them and get the rough numbers before they take it to the grain elevator."

"Let's do it," Jordy agreed. Such a weird day filled with so many ups and downs. What will tomorrow bring?

Chapter 69

The land that they bought from Ralph White was better than Jordy remembered. The acreage doubled what Jordy and Cesar had, making theirs the two biggest farms in the area. Laz and Cesar took the southern field and the farmhouse. Jordy took the rest, including the stream and water rights. Ralph had not done much with the property in the last few years. It was left unfarmed and wild.

Walking through the field overgrown with tall grass, he stopped by the stream. The water ran clear and soothing over the rocks. He crouched down, dipped his hand into the cold water, and watched as it trickled through his fingers. In his head, he heard a voice say, *the bitter waters will never touch this stream.* He stood up, looking around to see if he was alone. All he saw was the long grasses bending in the breeze.

"The bitter waters," he whispered, feeling a chill of apprehension. Now, why would he hear that in his head? What did it mean? Nothing good, he thought, turning away from the tranquil water.

He walked back the way he came, done with the enchantment of his new property for now. Cesar and Laz were working on the tiny farmhouse where Laz would soon live. Like the property, Ralph had done little upkeep on the house. He found Cesar on the roof making repairs, and Laz was busy fixing dry rot on the sills.

Jordy shielded his eyes from the bright sunlight, as he looked up at Cesar on the roof. "Where do you want me?"

Cesar looked down at him, pulling the nails out of his mouth. "Come on up."

Jordy climbed the ladder and hunkered down next to Cesar. "Roof needs work."

"Yup, everything does. I don't think Ralph touched the place in years. We got to rip it apart. We will do a patch job for now to keep out the water."

"I'll start over here and work it down from the peak." Jordy grabbed a bundle of shingles and a hammer.

"Sounds like a plan. Next summer, I'll get a new roof for the place. But this will get Laz through winter."

Jordy was busy and didn't notice the car pulling up the long, gravel driveway. He heard his name being called and looked down to see Evander standing by his Jeep. He seriously was not in the mood to talk to him. Reluctantly, he put down the hammer and climbed down the ladder.

Evander was leaning against his Jeep with his arms crossed over his chest. To anyone else watching, he looked relaxed. But Jordy knew him well. Something was up. "What brings you here, Evander?"

"I heard that you bought this place. So, I decided to come and take a look." Evander straightened to stand away from his Jeep, looking at the house. "Looks like you got your hands full fixing up this place."

"You didn't come here to talk about house repairs," Jordy pointed out.

Evander chuckled. "True to form. You never like small talk."

Evander had something on his mind. Jordy sensed that he was troubled. "So, what is it?"

"They are planning something. It seems Phil and some men from town are looking to stage a rebellion of sorts. Word has leaked down to Henry. They will squash it, and people could get hurt."

Now, why would someone say that to Henry, knowing that all hell would break loose? Jordy had not heard anything about it. "You said Phil was involved?"

"That is what I hear. I'm telling you so that you can head it off."

Evander was telling the truth. If this was true, it was foolish. October was the next month. This could be over by then. "I'll look into it."

"You didn't know."

"This is the first that I'm hearing of it."

"You should work quickly. Henry is planning something. It won't be good."

"It never is."

"Have you thought about what we talked about?"

"I'm not going to kill Henry for you."

"We will see." Evander turned back to his Jeep. "Good luck," he said, before he got in behind the wheel.

Jordy climbed back up the ladder and squatted down beside Cesar. "Do you know anything about some of the guys around town looking to make a stand against Henry and his men?"

Cesar looked up at him in surprise. "Is that what Evander wanted?"

"Yeah, he said that Phil is involved."

Cesar snorted. "It's probably all talk if Phil is involved."

"Well, someone brought it to Henry's attention, and he is taking it seriously."

"It's foolish. Who do you think the rat is?"

"No idea. But this could make trouble for everyone."

"And if you are right about October and them leaving, it is really stupid. We are so close to seeing our way out of this mess."

"I agree. We need to talk to Phil."

"Agreed." Cesar was swinging the hammer down with more force.

Chapter 70

Jordy, Laz, and Cesar drove out to Phil's place. "What if he won't listen to reason?" Cesar asked.

"Let's find out if it is true, first," Jordy said, driving down the street where Phil lived.

Laz snorted. "It's true. At the fourth of July festival, I heard a couple of guys saying that they should all get together and kick their ass out of town."

"But it's suicide," Cesar said.

When they pulled in, Phil's car was parked by the side of the little farmhouse. Jordy parked his truck next to Phil's, got out and walked up the flowered walkway. There were kid's toys scattered all over the porch. Phil answered the door on the second knock.

"Hey, guys, what's up?" Phil said, smiling.

"Hey, Phil, we wanted to talk to you about something we heard," Jordy said, getting to the point.

"Come in; I'll put on some coffee." He turned to go to the kitchen, leaving the door open for them to come inside. "Bree is at the school with the kids. I was just about to go out, but I still have a little time before I need to leave. Besides, there is something that I want to run by you."

Cesar glanced at Jordy. They could guess what he wanted to talk to them about. "I'm good on the coffee. We won't stay long."

Phil stopped and turned to face them. "Oh, ok, good. What's the problem?"

Cesar cleared his throat. "We heard that you and some of the guys are looking to make a stand against Evander and his men. Is that true?"

Phil tipped his head at them. "Where did you hear that?"

"It does not matter who told us," Jordy interjected. "Is it true?"

Phil eyed them suspiciously. "I'm not sure that I like this line of questioning. What if it was? What would be wrong with us standing up for our rights in this town?"

Laz sighed. "There is nothing wrong with it except that you are seriously outgunned. Going up against these men is going to get you killed, and who knows how many innocent people hurt."

"If you are scared, stay out of it then," Phil shot back. "Let the men in town oversee it. Besides, we have the element of surprise on our side. They will never know what hit them."

Jordy read him clearly. Phil was determined to raise a battle that they could not win. "Henry knows about it."

"How the hell do you know that?" Phil snapped. Some of the bravado went out of him.

Jordy met Phil's anger with patience. "I was questioned about it. Someone tipped off Henry."

"Who would do that? I don't believe you."

"Then how would I know about it?" Jordy returned.

"Get out. Stay out of it. You are no longer friends of mine. Your problem is that you are all chicken."

Chicken, Jordy thought. Is that really what he thought? "Phil, stop this. For the sake of your family, don't do this. Think about it."

"Leave and don't come back." Phil stood, pointing to the door.

This was useless. They were not going to get anywhere with him. Jordy turned to leave, followed by Cesar and Laz. "Good luck."

They walked down the stairs and got into the truck. "He's determined to do this thing," Cesar said angrily.

"I know who the other guys are," Jordy said, getting behind the wheel. "One of them is Brooke Porter's older brother, Danny Porter. Phil thinks Danny is the one who ratted them out. Big Mike Wilson, Jack Milton, Sam Comings, Will Benton, and a few others are part of this group. They call themselves the Wormwood Warriors."

"This is not a high school football game," Laz said. "Most of those guys played football in high school. This is war with real guns and bullets."

"What can we do?" Cesar asked.

"Nothing," Jordy said. "Stay out of town."

Cesar glanced at Jordy. "Maybe we could try and talk to the other guys."

"From what I read from Phil, this is a determined crew. Phil is not a leader, we know that. Maybe Jed could try talking some sense to him. They are pretty tight."

"It's worth a try," Cesar agreed. "He should be at my place feeding his cows. Let's see what he says."

Chapter 71

They drove back to Cesar's house. Jed's truck was parked in the yard by the barn. "He's here," Cesar said, the muscle pulsing along his jaw, showing his irritation. "Hopefully, he can get through Phil's thick skull."

"He'd be the first," Laz said under his breath.

Jordy only smiled. Phil had a well-earned reputation for being stubborn. "Let's be vague about it and see what Jed knows first. The fewer people that know about this the better. We don't want to start a panic."

"True." Cesar got out of the truck.

"Here we go," Jordy said. He knew his friend, but going gently was not his way.

"Pop is ready to rip someone a new asshole."

"Yup," Jordy got out of the truck and caught up to Cesar.

Jed was shoveling feed into large bins for his girls. He looked up as they approached and put down the scoop. "Hey guys, what is going on?"

Cesar looked at Jordy and nodded for him to begin. "Jed, do you know if anything is going on in town involving Phil?"

"No." Jed looked away at his cows.

He knew. Jordy glanced at Cesar and nodded. "Jed, you are Phil's friend, right?" Jordy asked.

Jed looked down at his shoes. "I'm guessing that you know what those idiots are looking to do."

"It's foolish and irresponsible," Cesar spat.

Jed held up both hands in surrender. "I'm not disagreeing with you. I learned my lesson the hard way from playing with those guys. They play for keeps and show no mercy. I've tried to talk to Phil, but he is riding this ego trip. I told him that the only trip he was going on was to the cemetery. He thinks that he will be the town hero if he defeats them. I'm not mentioning any names, but the guys he is hanging around with are high on macho power."

It was all true. Jordy was disappointed. He knew Henry better than most, and the hell he would unleash without mercy. "People will die."

"That's what I told Phil," Jed said.

"All right. I guess we see what happens." Jordy could almost see it and pushed it from his mind.

"It's pure stupidity," Cesar grumbled, walking away back to his house with Laz following behind.

"I was planning to get the cows back home next week. Now, with this, I'm skeptical."

"You know that we bought Ralph White's property."

"I heard that. Congratulations." He held out his hand.

"Thanks," Jordy said, shaking hands. "What I wanted to run by you is that I own the field back there near the stream. It's fenced pastureland with enough room for all your cows. I'm not using it until Spring. What do you think?"

"I know that property. I'd love that. It's closer to my place, too. If you are offering, I'm accepting."

Jordy was looking forward to getting the cows away from his house and out of his barn. "Great."

"I'll start moving them today." Jed stepped closer, and patted Jordy's shoulder. "I can't thank you enough for helping me. You are a loyal friend. Tell your wife that I said hello. When this all settles down, we would love to have you over for dinner."

"Thanks, Jed. Be careful."

Jed put up his hand. "Don't worry. I've learned my lesson."

Jordy watched him return to his cows, hoping Phil might learn the same lesson. But trouble was brewing in Wormwood.

Chapter 72

"Let's get this done. I've got squash to pick." Jordy said, as Amelia hopped into the passenger seat.

Amelia frowned at him. "Do you really think it will come down to Phil and the others fighting with Henry?"

Jordy nodded. "I do. That's why we need to stalk up on food and then stay out of town for a while."

"I guess we keep the kids home from school and hunker down, but for how long?"

"As long as it takes." Jordy shrugged.

He pulled into Cesar's driveway. Cesar and Esme were waiting for them outside. Cesar waved and came over to talk to Jordy. "I guess I'll follow you into town," Cesar said. "I could wring Phil's neck for this."

"I don't really blame them for being fed up. The town has been a powder keg for months. Something was going to give."

"Yeah, but we are so close to seeing a peaceful ending,"

"They don't know that, and there is no way to convince them."

"Yeah," Cesar stepped back from the truck. "You lead, I'll follow."

"What did Cesar mean by we are close to an end?" Amelia asked.

Jordy watched Cesar and Esme get into their truck. "It's something Evander said to me. He said this was going to be over in October."

"Curious. Do you think that means that they are leaving town?"

"I hope that's what it means."

"Me too."

Jordy pulled out of the driveway and drove into town, with Cesar following behind. When they got to town, he pulled over in front of Dawson's store to let Amelia and Esme get out. The store was packed with people for a Tuesday. It was like a storm was coming, and people were stalking up on supplies.

"I shouldn't be too long," Amelia said, leaning over to kiss Jordy on the cheek.

"I'm getting gas. I'll be waiting to load the groceries when you come out."

He waited until Amelia walked into the store before pulling into the gas station to top off the tank on the truck and fill gas cans. Cesar followed behind. The town seemed busier than usual, with not just the market but all the shops bustling with activity. Jordy thought it felt like how it was before a storm. People were preparing to hunker down. Jordy could feel the anticipation of something bad pressing all around him. People knew something was coming.

Cesar was looking around apprehensively as he filled his gas cans. "So, is this the bad thing that you felt was coming?"

"I don't think so." What he had felt was more…darker than this.

"What could be worse than war?"

"I don't know. I just feel something…" Jordy finished filling the last tank.

"Let's get a coffee at Winslow's and wait for the ladies to finish."

Jordy nodded. "Lead the way."

They sat on the bench across from the store, sipping coffee. "People are tense. I don't need your superpowers to feel it."

"Yeah, they know something is coming."

Henry Lee and some men drove into town, stopping in front of Finn's. When Henry spotted Jordy, he crossed the street, walking towards them. "Here comes trouble," Cesar whispered.

Henry waved and stopped right before them, leaning lazily against the porch railing in front of Winslow's. "Jordy, why don't you come for lunch? I was out of line that night at your house. Let me apologize by buying you something to eat." Henry made his best attempt at smiling, but it never reached his eyes. Lunch was a subterfuge to sit and talk. He wants something…

Jordy felt the undercurrent of resentment wafting from him. "Not today, Henry. We are waiting for our wives to complete their shopping."

Henry nodded in understanding, glancing over his shoulder at the entrance to the market. "Perhaps another time."

Jordy watched Henry walk back across the street to Finn's. "He wants to talk."

"What do you think he wants?"

"Maybe to find out what I know about the guys here in town. Or to smooth things over."

Cesar gestured to Dawson's. "Check out across the street. Big Mike Wilson is standing across the street by the market. If looks could kill, Henry would be dead."

"It's a losing battle. I feel it. The losses will be heavy."

Cesar shivered in dread. "I wish we could warn them somehow."

"We tried. Phil won't listen. I have a theory about Phil. When he took over as the pastor, he had the respect of the town. People were coming to him with questions, involving him as they do the pastor. My take on this is that Phil liked the attention and respect. If he does this thing and succeeds to rid the town of these guys, he is back to being a hero."

"Makes a lot of sense. None of that will matter, though, if he gets killed in the process."

"Let's cross the street, I want to see what I sense about Big Mike." Jordy rose to his feet.

"I hope it is a change of heart," Cesar said hopefully.

Jordy glanced at Cesar as they got closer to Big Mike. He and Cesar leaned against a light pole not far from Mike. Jordy was watching him standing by the far wall by the door of Dawson's with clenched fists as he stared at Finn in stone, cold silence. "No change of heart there, Cesar. Right now, he is contemplating whether to go inside Finn's for a confrontation."

"Can you stop it?" Cesar asked, glancing at Jordy.

Jordy slowly shook his head. "I told you the tempest runs its own agenda. I'm not feeling anything from it for this. Without it, we are defenseless. Our families will be left defenseless. Men make their own choices, Cesar. Sometimes, the decisions are poor with consequences. My guess is the tempest is not going to interfere with the will of men. If they choose to fight each other, they will do so and pay with their lives. All we can do is try and pick up the pieces later."

"See, that is what I don't understand about Phil. He has kids and a wife. Pushing this thing to violence of this magnitude is foolish. What happens to his family after?"

"Well, Phil might feel this is the right choice. I don't know what they are planning. But given what we know about the enemy, they are outgunned and undertrained. I might be a simple farmer, but I know it's going to end in defeat."

"When do you think this will happen?"

"Soon, very soon."

Chapter 73

Jordy was sitting on the porch sipping his iced tea with Cesar when he heard the first gunshots ring out from the far end of town. "Shit, are those gunshots?" Cesar said, rising to his feet.

It had begun. Oddly, his tempest was quiet. It was not going to throw in on this fight. "Yeah, I think so, unless someone is lighting off fireworks."

There were more. This time, sounding like different calibers.

"I got to go," Cesar said as Amelia came out the door.

"Is that what I think it is?" she said, coming to sit down next to Jordy.

"Very likely."

"You are not going," she said, cuddling closer to Jordy.

"I'm not leaving my family," he said firmly, wrapping a protective arm around her. The sounds of chaos echoed from the town, like a distant battle raging on.

Cesar descended the stairs, his voice steady. "I'm going home through the field. Laz is with Esme and the kids at the house. Do you think Henry will come here?"

Jordy shook his head. "I don't think so. Their fight is in town."

"I guess we just wait and see what happens, then." Cesar winced when he heard the explosion go off somewhere in town. It echoed all around them.

"You are welcome to come here and stay with us," Amelia offered.

"No, I think we will ride this out at home on the farm," Cesar said, before turning to head home through the field.

"I'll call you if I hear anything," Jordy said.

"Same here. Use the house phone."

"Be careful," Amelia said.

"It will be ok," Jordy said, kissing Amelia on the top of her head.

"I hope so. I just can't help wondering what Bree is going through."

"What makes you think that she even knows?"

Amelia looked up at him. "Surely, he would have told her."

"Maybe." Jordy doubted it.

Amelia pushed away from him to look up at his face. "They have been married as long as we have. This is a decision that she should have some say in."

"I agree."

"I honestly don't know Phil right now. I think for them to decide to do this; the town should have some say. It affects us all."

"Yes, it does."

"What do you think will happen?"

Jordy sighed; he had done nothing but think about it. "I think that our guys will lose. I think that things in town are going to get bad. Henry will retaliate on us all."

Amelia nodded. "Yes, I can see that. What can we do?"

"We will do as always. Survive."

The house phone rang, and Amelia went inside to answer it. "Jordy, it's for you; it's Cesar," she said, leaning out of the door.

Jordy went inside reluctantly to answer it. "Jordy, there is a fire in town. I can see it from here."

Jordy took the headset and stretched the cord to see out of the back window. On the horizon, he saw the glow of the fire in the night sky. "The shooting has stopped."

"What can we do about the fire? I wonder if the fire volunteers will put it out?"

"It's going to rain, Cesar," Jordy said, feeling his tempest awaken in his gut.

"Ok, at least we will have something left to go back to."

"Sit tight, we will head into town tomorrow and see what has happened."

"Ok, I'll pick you up early."

"I'll be waiting." Jordy hung up.

Amelia was watching the fire light up the night as the rain started to fall. "I wonder what is burning. It looks like several buildings."

"I'll find out tomorrow." Jordy stood beside her, stroking her hair.

"Be careful, Jordy."

"I will. We have to know what is happening?" His tempest coiled.

Chapter 74

Jordy finished his morning coffee, skipping breakfast. Amelia said little to him at the table, keeping her eyes cast down at her plate as she pushed food around, eating little. He knew she was upset at him for leaving, but he had to know. Last night, he had dreamed about Wormwood. He saw the battle as it unfolded. It was a horror scene, as all wars are. But this was his town and his people. He had to know what was left.

He rose from the table to get ready to go. "I'll be back soon."

Petunia was already outside playing with Walter. Brian went to his bedroom to listen to music. Jordy walked out onto the porch. The sun was glowing in the sky, the birds were singing, and the breeze smelled of sweet honeysuckle. It was like any other morning, but everything had changed.

Amelia came running after him as he walked to his truck. When she reached his side, she threw her arms around his neck and hugged him close. "Be careful," she whispered into his neck.

"I will," he said, kissing the top of her head. "I won't be long."

He got in behind the wheel and drove to Cesar's house. Cesar walked out onto the porch, carrying a shotgun. "Just in case," he said, tossing it on the backseat of the truck before getting in on the passenger side.

Jordy nodded. "Laz staying with Esme and the kids?"

"Yeah, they were not thrilled about this idea about going to town."

"I can go by myself, if you want," Jordy offered.

Cesar looked at him. "Where you go, I go."

Jordy chuckled. "Following me straight to hell."

"Something like that."

They drove in silence. Everything seemed normal on the drive, except there was no traffic. "Stop at Phill's house," Cesar said. "Let's see if he is at home."

Jordy nodded, turning down the road to Phil's. That was where everything changed. All that was left to Phil's house was a burned-out shell. Jordy parked, and they walked up to what was left. There was a gaping burned-out hole in the roof, but some of the walls of the structure were still standing. Jordy peered inside but saw nothing but the charred remains of what was once a happy home.

"No signs of Bree or the kids," Cesar said, pushing a discarded toy with the toe of his boot. "So, what do you think happened?"

"I think that Henry had the house torched to send a message." Jordy turned and walked back to the truck with Cesar following.

"If you are right, we now know what was on fire last night."

Jordy nodded, getting behind the wheel. "Yeah, if I'm right, we will see more burned-out structures."

They passed two more torched houses on their way into town. "That's Big Mike's house, or what's left of it."

"I think we park here, and walk into town," Jordy pulled over and backed into a dirt road.

Cesar nodded, hopping out of the truck. "Should I take the shotgun?"

"Leave it." Jordy patted his gut.

"Hope we don't have to use it."

"Me, too."

They walked into the deserted town, the streets eerily empty. Slipping behind Winslow's, they peeked cautiously around the corner of the building. Across the street, in front of the sheriff's office, five bodies lay on the sidewalk, draped in bloodstained sheets. Jordy quickly pulled back behind the building, his face pale.

"God, they have bodies lined up on the sidewalk," Cesar whispered, shaking his head in disgust.

"It sends a strong message."

Jordy peeked out again. There were people sitting on the sidewalk not far from the bodies. He recognized Big Mike Wilson's father and sister. The Milton's and the Benton's. All families of the men that decided to take their stand against Henry. Then he spotted

Bree, and her children covered in soot, sitting huddled together. Close to them was an armed guard.

"They got Bree and the kids," Cesar whispered.

Jordy leaned his back against Winslow's out of sight. "I'm going after them."

"They are going to take you prisoner if you try it." Cesar was shaking his head.

"I have to try. Stay here. If things go wrong, take the truck, and get out of here."

Before Jordy walked out, Cesar grabbed his arm. "Destroy the bastards, Jordy."

"It's not my choice."

Jordy walked around the side of Winslow's, not giving Cesar's location away. He stood across the street, waiting for the guards to notice him. Raising his hands, he stepped off the sidewalk into the street. Bree looked over at him and started to weep openly. Jordy took a step.

"Stop," The guard snapped, pointing his rifle at Jordy. "Stay where you are."

Jordy's tempest flared to life. "I would like to talk to Henry."

The guards were already talking into their coms. One of the guards pointed at him. "You stay put."

Jordy did as he was instructed, but his tempest had other ideas. Frozen, he heard the voice in his head. Jordy watched in wrapped fascination as the guards stood perfectly still. One with his hand still touching the com at the side of his head.

He crossed the street and knelt close to Bree and her children. The people on the sidewalk were looking around in confusion. Ray Wilson was the first to recover. "What is happening?"

Jordy shrugged, "I don't know," he whispered, turning to Bree. "I'm going to try and get you and the kids out of here."

Tears were tracing a path down her soot-covered face. "They are going to kill you."

Jordy winked. "They will try."

Henry drove up in his black SUV and got out, looking at his guards and then at Jordy. He walked over to where Jordy was kneeling beside Bree. "This was justified," he snarled.

Jordy stood up to face him. "You made your point. Now let the families go home and bury their dead."

"You do not order me around," Henry stepped closer to Jordy.

"Close enough," Jordy said, standing his ground.

He saw the hesitation in Henry's eyes. "Take the woman and her brats. Be gone."

"I want all the families released."

Henry glared at him. "One day, you and I are going to come to terms, Jordy."

Jordy nodded. "But not today."

"Fine, let them go home to what is left of their houses." Henry smiled darkly.

"Let's go," Jordy said. The people on the sidewalk rose to their feet, still looking frightened and confused.

"What about my boy?" Ray Wilson asked, pointing to the bodies on the sidewalk.

"They stay until I'm sure this town understands what happens when you cross me," Henry snarled. He threw Jordy a hard glare.

Jordy met him with one of his own. "As I said, you made your point, Henry. Let them bury their dead."

Henry spun around, coming nose to nose with Jordy. Pain, he heard the voice say. Henry recoiled, backing up a step. "Fine, clean the garbage off the sidewalk," he growled, before limping back to his car.

"Come on, Bree. Let's get you out of here."

Bree did not hesitate, she got up and gathered her children to follow Jordy as he walked away. Henry sat in his car, watching them. The soldiers came out of their trances and looked around, eyes blinking in confusion. Jordy glanced back at them from over his shoulder, and when they raised their guns, Henry stepped gingerly out of the car. "Stand down, you idiots," he snarled.

Jordy nodded at him as they crossed the street. It was not over, far from it, he sensed. For now, though, they were calling a ceasefire of sorts.

Chapter 75

Bree sat at the table wrapped in one of Amelia's bathrobes after showering to clean away all the soot. There were bruises all over her arms and face. Amelia had brought in some old clothes from Petunia and Brian for the kids to wear, before helping Bree load the washer to clean the clothes that they had. Jordy could not imagine losing everything.

Amelia brought over some coffee and rolls she had made. The kids were busy playing with Petunia and Walter outside. Kids are special beings. Resilient even under the harshest conditions. Bree sat sipping her coffee, looking exhausted.

"You can stay with us until we figure something out," Jordy said.

She glanced at Jordy. "What you did today in town was amazing. I still don't understand it, but thank you. I don't know how I will ever repay you. Our house is gone. Everything is gone." She stared off straight ahead.

"Do you want to talk about it?" Amelia asked gently.

"There is not much to tell. I had no idea what was happening. I found out after hearing the shooting and explosions in town when all hell broke loose."

"So, Phil never told you what he was planning?" Jordy asked, Amelia exchanged glances with him.

Bree sipped her coffee. "Not a word. I would have tried to stop him."

"Do you know what happened to Phil?" Amelia asked, gently.

"I only know that he was not one of the dead. They are all dead, so there is no way to know. Phil told me he was going to Finn's last night to have a drink with some friends. That was the last thing he said to me before leaving the house."

"What happened at the house?" Jordy asked gently.

"I had just put the kids to bed and was hunkering down inside with the lights off when the trucks pulled up in front of the house. They kicked in the door and started setting the place on fire with us inside. As the smoke filled the rooms, I grabbed the kids, and we bolted out the back door. But they caught us. They threw us in the back of a truck with everyone else. I watched the house as it burned. Then the rain came, and they drove us to the sheriff's office. There were still random gunshots in town. I worried that one of us would get shot. It was clear that we were prisoners. The sheriff questioned us along with the scary guy from this morning."

"Henry questioned you?" Jordy asked.

"Yes. He is a cruel one. When I did not answer his questions fast enough, he slapped me across the face. He didn't believe me when I said that I didn't know anything. Thank God, he didn't hurt the children. He was interested in Phil and whoever else was involved. If they find Phil, they will kill him. I don't understand what he was thinking. They never had a chance against those men. After they questioned us, they made us go outside to identify the bodies." She closed her eyes to try and block out the memory as fresh tears rolled down her cheeks. "I didn't want to look but they forced us. It was vile seeing that. These are people you know. They died horribly." She pushed her cup away.

"Would you like to lie down and rest?" Amelia asked. "I can pull out the couch for you to sleep on."

Bree shook her head. "No, I'm fine. I think that I will leave here tomorrow and go stay with my sister in Georgia."

Jordy didn't tell her that leaving here was not going to happen. Henry would be watching for that. She was stuck here. There were a couple of houses that stood vacant in town. Tomorrow he would find out if they could move into one of those temporarily. He was also going to see if he could find Phil.

Chapter 76

“I’m going to talk to Jack Hadley about one of the vacant houses in town for Bree and her children,” Jordy said at the kitchen table on the third day after the war.

Amelia tipped her head at him. “Which one?”

“It’s the nice, little three-bedroom on Hill Road. I think it’s even furnished. It would do until she finds something better.”

Amelia frowned at him. “You are going to have to talk to Bree about it.”

“I know. I will.” He had a feeling that Bree was not going to like the idea.

Bree came into the kitchen and sat down with her children. “I’ll help make breakfast,” she said to Amelia.

“No, you sit. Jordy has something he wants to pass by you.” Amelia retreated to the coffee pot.

“What is it? Is it Phil?”

Jordy felt bad as the fear flushed her face. “No. Nothing like that. I think that I may have an idea for a place for you to stay until you decide what you want.”

“I told you that I was thinking of going to my sisters.”

"About that, Bree. I don't think Henry is going to let you just leave town. It's safer if you stay." He didn't want to tell her about the Wang brothers and their sudden fatal crash when they attempted to leave.

Bree stared at him before nodding. "I wondered about that. I'd like to stay at least until we know what happened to Phil. I just don't want to be a burden. What do you have in mind?"

"There is a vacant house on Hill Road."

"The Cane's old house. Yes, I know the place. It's nice. Do you think Jack Hadley would let me have it? I can't pay very much."

"Leave that to me. I'll talk to Jack today." Jordy smiled reassuringly at her.

"That would be great. I think that place is even furnished."

"I believe so," Jordy felt better now that Bree was onboard.

"I think that I'm going to make you guys my famous waffles." Bree smiled for the first time.

"That sounds amazing," Amelia said. "Do you want a hand?"

"I'm living in your house, wearing your clothes, and eating your food. No, you sit. I'm making breakfast. Besides, cooking in a kitchen makes me feel normal."

After breakfast, and some of the best waffles that he had ever eaten, a secret from his wife that he would take to his grave, he decided to go talk to Jack. As he rose from the table, Amelia followed him outside to the truck. "I know, you want me to be careful."

Amelia smiled. "Yes." She cupped her hands around the back of his neck and pulled him down. Placing a kiss on his mouth.

"I promise to be careful."

"Ok, be safe. Come home soon."

"As soon as I'm done."

Jordy got behind the wheel. Amelia lingered by the door of the truck. "What is it?"

"Be careful, Jordy."

He brushed a kiss on her cheek before backing out of the yard. He was a lucky man, he thought as he looked back at his beautiful wife, standing in the driveway, waving at him. Phil was also a lucky man. Bree was a good woman. Why he took such a poor chance at risking it all, still bothered him.

The town had a little more traffic on the third day after the war. More cars roamed the street and people were walking the sidewalks. The bodies draped in bloody sheets were gone from outside the sheriff's office, thankfully. He parked in front of Hadley's Feed and Grain. Jed was there talking to Jack when he walked inside.

"What's new?" Jordy said when they both looked up, startled.

"The sheriff is saying the boys were shot and killed for looting," Jed whispered. "Total bullshit as usual."

"Looting? Looting what?" Jordy frowned.

"That's just it, big fat nothing," Jack said.

"Has anyone heard anything about Phil?" Jordy asked, looking at Jack and Jed.

"Nothing other than they are still hunting for him. He's not the only one missing. Brooke's brother, Danny, is missing, too." Jack sighed. "Poor bastards are probably dead someplace. Lord knows even if they were alive, they have nothing to come back to after they burned their houses down and everything."

Jordy nodded. "That's kind of why I stopped by here. I have Bree and the kids living with us. I was wondering about the vacant house on Hill Road. Is it available?"

"Oh, yeah, I still have it vacant," Jack said, reaching down under the counter and pulling out the keys. "Tell Bree it's all hers for as long as she needs it. I'll work something out with her later."

"She lost everything?" Jed said, frowning. "I'm sure we got some clothes for the kids at my house. I grew up on hand-me-downs when I was a kid. I'll have Helen pack them up."

Jordy smiled. It was so Wormwood to pull together to help people in need. "Thanks, she needs everything."

"You know the house is fully furnished, and the cupboards are full of dishes and shit. All she will need is food. I'm sure everyone will contribute. Bree is good people. Though, I'm still not sure what Phil was thinking."

Jordy and Jed nodded in agreement. "You don't fight a bear with a spoon," Jed said.

"You got that right," Jack agreed. "Now Henry and his gang are out for blood."

"Let's hope it blows over," Jordy said, picking up the keys to the house off the counter.

"I don't know, Jordy," Jack said, looking skeptical. "I have been seeing a lot of new faces in town the last couple of days. If anything, Henry has brought in more people. I always blamed Evander, but now I think the real badass is Henry."

"You got that right," Jed agreed. "I try not to come to town much unless I need food, grain, or gas. I noticed that these new guys are scoping out everyone hard. I think they are up to something."

Jordy's tempest coiled. He felt it, too. "Yeah, I feel it. Well, I need to get back to the farm and move Bree and the kids. I appreciate all the help. I'm sure Bree will appreciate it, too."

"I'll get the word out," Jack said, smiling. "One thing about Wormwood, we take care of our own. By tomorrow, Bree is going to have more crap than she will know what to do with."

"Thanks," Jordy said, walking out the door.

He paused by his truck, scanning the area. Jack wasn't exaggerating—there were plenty of unfamiliar faces in town. What was Henry up to? As he got into his truck, he saw Henry cruise through town like a king overseeing his lowly subjects. He slowed his SUV as he passed by Jordy's truck, pointing his finger at him like he was shooting a gun. Jordy stared him down as the tensions increased. He heard the voice in his head say bowel movement. He smiled when Henry accelerated at a high rate of speed, heading out of town. "When you have to go…you have to go," Jordy whispered with a smile.

Chapter 77

Things seemed to calm down in town over the last two weeks. Oh, people were still scared shitless. Jordy was not fooled into thinking that it was over, either. He felt something bad was coming. Pulling in front of the parsonage to drop off food to the pastor, he noticed that there was a roadblock set up at each end of town, blocking the exits onto the main roads. He was sure there was a bullshit story about how Henry and his boys were keeping them safe from harm.

They had not been to church service since before the night of the war. It was a matter of safety. The pastor was sending typed copies of his sermons to each house. Henry had finally gotten what he so longed for in keeping them from the pastor and the good word. The thing that Henry doesn't understand is that faith lives within us. It is not generated by earthbound entities. He was sure there was a special place reserved in hell for people like Henry and his crew.

Elma was picking fresh flowers in the garden when he met her on the walkway. "Is he awake and up for a visit?" Jordy asked, holding up the basket.

She pointed to the ground for him to put down the basket. "He should be. But I'm going to warn you before you go inside, he is not doing well. Stubborn old bugger won't let me call Doc, either. Maybe you can get it through his thick skull that he needs to see the doctor."

"I can try." He picked up the basket to take inside.

"Leave it. I'll get it when I go inside. Sure, hope your missus packed some more of those peach scones. I dream about them at night." She grinned.

He winked. "I think that you are in luck."

Jordy walked through the door and down the hall to the pastor's bedroom. When he entered the dimly lit bedroom, he stopped. Pastor Ezra is going to die, Jordy thought with great sadness as his eyes traveled over him. The pastor was in bed, swaddled in sheets. He was so tiny and thin. His skin was gray, and his eyes and cheeks were sunken into his face, making him look hollow. It looked like a death mask. The only color in Pastor Ezra's face was from his watery blue eyes. A sad knot formed in his throat.

"Jordy, my boy. Come closer." His voice was a paper-thin wheeze.

Jordy knelt beside the bed. "Pastor, let me get the doctor."

The pastor struggled to raise his hand off the bed. "No, just sit with me."

Jordy took his hand. He felt a push of energy travel down his arm to the pastor. "Is that better?"

The pastor closed his eyes in contentment. "Yes, I feel it. It is a healing warmth spreading through my body."

"You are getting worse."

The pastor opened his eyes and gently smiled. "I'm dying, Jordy. But not yet. God has a plan for us, that, I am certain."

"I feel it, too."

Jordy could feel the slight pulse of power coming from the pastor like before. It was weak but still there. He wondered what it was. He sensed that there was real power here. It was like it was sleeping. Or waiting... The dark feeling of dread that something was coming was there, too.

Pastor Ezra sighed. "I feel much better. Can you help me up?"

Jordy pulled the pastor into a sitting position. "Like this?"

"Yes, that is perfect. Any word on Phil or the Porter boy?"

"Nothing. I went looking for Phil. I visited all his spots. No sign of him."

"He will show up."

"You think he is alive?"

"I do."

"Why?"

"I feel it." He pointed across the room. "Go over to my desk. I have written you a letter. I want you to have it."

Jordy went to the desk, his eyes scanning the top of the desk over the books and papers scattered there. "I don't see it."

"In the top drawer, Jordy."

Jordy opened the top desk drawer and spotted the letter, sealed in an envelope. He picked it up and brought it to the bed. "Is this it?"

The pastor glanced up at it. "Yes, that is for you, but you are not to open it until I am dead. Do you understand?"

Jordy nodded. "I understand."

"Can you let Elma know that I would like something to eat? I'm starved."

Jordy nodded. "I will."

"Now, off with you; I'm sure you have better things to do than spend your time with me."

Jordy chuckled. "I'm glad you are feeling better."

"I plan to go outside in the sun and breathe the fresh air." He smiled at Jordy.

Jordy smiled back at him, noting the color returning to his face. "You do that, Pastor."

He found Elma in the kitchen, unpacking the basket. "Elma, the pastor is hungry. He would like to eat."

Elma slowly put down the last dish on the counter from the basket. "Well, you must have some powerful magic, boy. That man looked like death warmed over this morning."

"He caught his second wind, I guess."

Elma tipped her head at him. "He caught something, all right." She pushed the empty basket to him across the counter.

Picking up the basket, he walked to the door. When he got to the truck, he opened the glove compartment and tucked the letter in there for safekeeping. Whatever was written there could wait. Jordy was in no hurry to read it.

Chapter 78

Jordy and Cesar were sitting on the porch drinking a beer. It was a beautiful night with the first nip in the air. "Fall is here," Cesar said, stretching his legs.

"Yup, I'm still pulling winter squash. My barn is nearly full."

"Same with me. Laz loves living on his own. I hardly see him outside of working the farm."

Jordy chuckled. "He's just enjoying the quiet."

Headlights from a car coming up the drive lit a pathway. "Oh crap, what is this?" Cesar grumbled.

Evander parked his Jeep in front of the house. He got out, smiling and holding up a six-pack. "I was hoping to find you out here."

"At least he brought beer," Jordy whispered, earning him a stern look from Cesar.

"I'm leaving."

"I'll see you tomorrow."

Cesar rose from his chair as Evander climbed the stairs. "Leaving so soon?" Evander said, leaning against the railing.

"Yeah, got an early start tomorrow," Cesar replied, giving a quick nod to Jordy before heading down the steps. Without another word, he disappeared around the side of the house.

"I hope he was not leaving because of me," Evander said, taking Cesar's chair next to Jordy.

Jordy arched an eyebrow. "Would you blame him?"

Evander chuckled. "Not really. He probably thinks that I had something to do with what happened in town."

"Did you?"

"Not me." He pulled out a beer and offered one to Jordy.

Jordy took it and popped the cap. "What brings you out here?"

Evander smiled. "Right to the point."

"Always."

"Well, something is up. I came to warn you about it. They are planning something."

"Like what?" Jordy turned to look at him.

"I saw them working on one of the outbuildings the last couple of days. It's a building that we were not using. They have been bringing bedding. Like cots and stuff."

"Is Henry recruiting more people?"

Evander frowned. "Perhaps, but I don't think so. He already has doubled what he had. The men he brought in are real pigs, too. I hate the sight of them. They are vile creatures."

"I hope they stay on your compound."

"Not likely, he brought them in for a reason."

"Henry always has something, doesn't he?"

"Have you given any thought to what we talked about? He's no friend of yours, you know?"

"I'm aware."

"Well, have you thought about it? September twentieth is in two weeks. It's prime time to take them all out."

"No, I told you, I'm no killer."

"It's not like you would have to kill them with your bare hands."

"My gift does not work that way, Evander."

Evander stared down into his beer. "Too bad. Because if you thought that uprising was bad, you ain't seen nothing yet. Henry is lethal and holds a grudge. He's going to come for you, sure as shit."

Jordy nodded. "Of that, I have no doubt."

Chapter 79

Jordy was driving the tractor in the field with another load of squash for the barn. He stopped as a dizzying wave rolled over him. He held on to the steering wheel with both hands to steady himself. Something was wrong. His heart accelerated as he looked around. What was it?

He heard his name and turned in his seat. Cesar and Laz were running through the field, yelling his name. Cesar was waving his cap like a flag. "Jordy," he screamed.

Jordy turned off the tractor and hopped down, running towards him. When they met, Cesar was out of breath, bending down, with his hands on his knees to catch his breath. "They got," he panted.

"They got the kids," Laz finished for him.

"The kids? Who? Where?" Jordy grabbed Cesar by the shoulders, standing him up so he could see his flushed face.

Cesar looked wild. "At the school. We got to go. They took the kids."

"Buses came to the school, and they loaded the kids on them," Laz said. "Henry took the kids."

"Maria came home from school screaming that they took Jose," Cesar said.

Jordy took off his hat and slammed it on the ground, running his fingers through his hair. "Let's go," he growled.

They ran to his house. When they got in the yard, Brian was running down the driveway, his eyes wide with terror. "Dad! Dad!" he screamed.

Jordy met him in the driveway, his heart was pounding. "Where's your sister?"

"They got her." Tears blazed a trail down Brian's sweaty face.

Jordy held him by his shoulders. "Ok, calm down. Tell me what happened."

Brian took a shaky breath. "Busses came to the school. Men got out with guns. They had a list. They took the kids on the list and loaded them on the bus. He said, if we don't do as they say…we will never see them again."

"Maria said the same thing. They have Jose." Cesar took a deep, shuttering breath.

"So why not take them all?" Jordy said, trying to make sense of it.

"Dad, I think they took one kid from each family."

"Why do you say that, Brian?" Jordy turned to look at his son.

"Tommy West was not taken, but his little sister was. Same with Ben Butler, they left him but took his little brother. Dad, they have Petunia."

Damn them to hell. A rage such as he had never felt cursed through his body. "I'm going after them," he said.

"We are coming with you." Cesar stepped forward with Laz.

Jordy turned to Brian. "Go in the house and stay with your mother. I'm going to go get your sister." He turned to Cesar and Laz. "Let's go."

They ran to the truck, and Jordy got behind the wheel. He thought about what Evander had said about killing Henry. Right now, he could kill him. End his miserable existence on this earth. He swung the truck out of the driveway and headed for the compound. God help whatever got in his way.

As he drove, his tempest was quiet. Why? Why, when he needed it most, did it pick now to be silent? He drove into town, passing people on the street. It looked like the whole town was out there. He came to the roadblock and stopped behind a long line of cars waiting to get through. Six armed men were standing there with guns pointed.

"Damn it!" Jordy fumed, pounding the steering wheel.

"Turn around. If you try to break through, I will shoot." A man was saying over a bullhorn.

Henry took the bullhorn. "Your children are all safe as long as you do as I tell you. You will turn around and go home. You will stay in your houses and do what you normally do when coming to town for the rest of the week. You will be the perfect citizens, do you understand? The perfect small town. If you do that, your children will be safe. If not, they die. Do I make myself clear?"

Jordy watched him leave, surprised by the measure of hatred he felt for Henry Lee. Henry's eyes locked on Jordy's as he smiled, lifting his hand to flash him the finger. Jordy clenched his fists, willing himself to stay calm, but the moment left a bitter taste.

"Use some of your superpower shit," Cesar said.

Jordy stared at the armed men. Do something, he thought. Talk to me. He heard only silence. "It's not responding."

Cesar pounded the dashboard in frustration. "Shit! Why now?"

"I don't know." Jordy looked around. "I'm going to turn around and try getting around them. I think we can cut back onto the main road if we drive through the field."

Cesar nodded. "You might be onto something; the property borders the road. Let's do it."

No, he heard in his head. The voice was loud and strong.

Jordy hesitated. Why? Please, I need help, he thought desperately. As he drove to the new farm, the tempest twisted almost painfully in his gut. No, he heard it again. It's not time.

Jordy pulled into the farm and parked in front of Laz's house. "What is today's date?" he asked, frowning.

"September nineteenth. Why?" Cesar was frowning.

"I know why they took the kids." Jordy rested his forehead on the steering wheel.

"Why?" Cesar demanded.

"Henry is having a large meeting at the compound tomorrow. Important investors for whatever shit they are into."

"How do you know that?"

"Evander told me about it. He wanted me to kill them. He wanted me to kill them all."

"That's surprising. Well, are you going to do it?" Laz asked.

Jordy sighed. "It's not up to me."

"Is that what it meant when it said that it wasn't time?" Cesar asked.

"You heard that?" Jordy was surprised.

Laz nodded. "I heard it, too? So, what do we do now?"

Jordy shrugged. "What choice do we have? We wait."

"We wait?" Cesar asked in disbelief.

Jordy nodded. "Something is coming. We have to wait. The pastor knows it, too."

Laz nodded. "I can feel it."

Cesar sighed. "I can, too. But I want my boy home."

"I want my daughter, too. But we have no choice."

Chapter 80

"We have to get her back," Amelia cried. "I can't live with this. Petunia has to be terrified. I hate them for this, Jordy. I know God tells us to forgive. But I can't find it in my heart to do that. God, she is just a baby."

"I know, sweetheart," Jordy whispered, holding her close. "I know. I'll get her back, I promise."

She looked up at him, her eyes glistening with unshed tears. "Use your gift. Make them give me my baby."

Jordy sighed as every sob that she made cut him deeply. "I only wish that I could."

Amelia curled herself into a fetal ball and cried more tears than Jordy thought was humanly possible. Her grief and misery made Jordy feel useless as a man and a father. He held Amelia until she finally fell asleep at three o'clock. He rose from the bed and quietly left the room.

In the kitchen, he made coffee and took it outside on the porch to drink it. It was still dark. There was a cold snap in the breeze that felt good to his tired body and soul. Petunia, his soul cried. "I'll get you back," he whispered. "Daddy is coming soon."

One of the dogs started barking in the barn. Jordy got up, leaving his coffee cup on the table next to the chair. He needed to quiet the dog before it woke Amelia. Stretching when he rose to his feet, he walked to the barn. It was likely just a critter trying to mess with the chickens again. Though he felt a presence. Someone was here.

"Jordy," he heard a voice whispering in the darkness. "Don't turn on the light."

Jordy hesitated, his hand hovering near the switch. "Who is it?"

"It's Evander. Don't turn on the light. I'm not sure if they are watching your place."

"They aren't. I'd know if it was an unfriendly." It was odd, when did Evander stop being the enemy? Even now, with his daughter dragged off to Evander's compound, he did not feel a threat.

"Are you sure?" Evander whispered, stepping out of the shadows.

"I'm positive."

"Good, I have been waiting in this barn for two hours, hoping you would come outside."

"Care for a cup of coffee?" he asked, holding back the one million questions that he had for him.

"I'd love one. Do you know that pig snores?"

Jordy chuckled as they walked in the dark to the porch. "Yeah, I've been told."

"She's ok, you know. Petunia and all the kids." Evander followed Jordy into the kitchen.

"Sit, I'll pour you a cup."

Evander looked around. "I like this house. It feels like a warm hug in here. A real home."

Jordy nodded. "Right now, it's a sad home." He placed the coffee on the table and a plate of scones.

Evander picked up his coffee and took a long swallow. "So good. Why is everything so good that comes from here?"

"It's all made with care. Tell me about my daughter?"

"Henry has them housed in one of the outbuildings. They are well cared for but prisoners all the same."

Jordy nodded. "Any way we can get them out?"

Evander shook his head. "No. Henry has it guarded twenty-four-seven. There are two inside with them. They will kill them if an escape is attempted."

"Damn him," Jordy growled.

"Can you take them out by using your gift?"

"Not yet. There is something coming, but I don't know what it is."

"The pastor told me about that. He said something was coming. Something bigger than all of us, he said. He told me not to drink the water when it does. I'm not sure what he was talking about."

"The bitter waters."

"Yes, he mentioned that. What does it mean?"

"When the third angel blows his horn, a great star will come from the heavens. And with it will come the bitter waters. It is said that anyone that drinks from the bitter waters will die."

"Wow, that's heavy. But that would be like the end of times, right?"

"Yes. So, I don't think that is it. The pastor must have it wrong. Something is coming. I think it is a human-caused catastrophe that we will deal with." Jordy thought of the strange boy in the cornfield and hesitated. "Though, I don't know."

Evander nodded. "When this is over, I am going to change my ways. At first, this was exciting, you know?"

Jordy didn't know. For him, life on the farm held all the excitement that he craved. "What will you do?"

"I'm still deciding. I should get back before they wonder about me. They are already keeping me at arm's length. I just wanted you to know about the kids. For them, it is like being at camp. Henry has brought in games for them to play with to keep them occupied. I'm sure they want to go home, but they are not being abused physically."

Jordy nodded. "That helps to know that. Thank you."

Evander stood from his chair as Amelia stormed into the kitchen, her eyes blazing with fury. She stopped and glared at him.

"Where's my daughter?" she demanded, her voice sharp with anger.

Before Evander could respond, Amelia lunged at him, hands outstretched as if to claw at his face. Jordy quickly stepped in, wrapping his arms around her to hold her back.

"Amelia, no! Stop, baby," Jordy pleaded, his voice firm but gentle. "He's here to help."She went limp in his arms. "Help?" she whispered, looking around in confusion.

Evander's face was awash in a mixture of concern and regret. "Amelia, I had no part in it. I have only come to tell you that Petunia is fine. Henry has the kids. From what I know, they are ok."

Amelia stood, straightening her spine. "Then use your influence and make him let them go home."

Jordy let her go. "He can't, Amelia. This is Henry's show."

"I will watch and let you know if anything changes. I don't have the power to do anything more. I'm sorry."

"You're sorry," she spat.

Evander nodded solemnly. "Yes, I'm sorry. If I had known this was how this would turn out, I would have left long ago. But I'm glad I stayed to at least be here and try to help."

Amelia's shoulders slumped as she sat down on a chair. "So, what can we do?"

Evander exchanged looks with Jordy. "Wait and see what happens. Do as Henry says."

"Have you seen her?" Amelia asked, dissolving into tears.

"I have seen her. Today, I'm planning to go visit them and read a story to them."

Amelia rose from her chair and took a book out of the bookshelf to hand to him. "Read them this one. It's her favorite."

Evander looked at the book and smiled. "It's about a pig."

"Of course," Jordy said, swiping at the tears that glazed his eyes.

Chapter 81

The morning of September 20th dawned with a spectacular sunrise that seemed to mock them with its beauty. Jordy sat on the porch, waiting for any word on the kids. When the car pulled into the driveway, he inwardly prepared himself for the bad news. Jack Hadley got out of his truck and lumbered up the steps. "Good morning, Jordy," he said, frowning. "Though, there really isn't much good about it."

"Take a seat," Jordy said, gesturing to the chair beside him. "What's up?"

Jack shook his head. "I can't stay. I'm only here to deliver a message. Henry wants everyone in town to put on a show. Everyone is to be all smiles. You know, the happy, small town of Wormwood, welcoming his guests as they arrive."

"Such bullshit."

"Yes, it is. But what the master wants, we must give him." Jack turned to leave.

"We will be there." At least he would be there.

"Yeah, I expect so."

Jordy watched him leave. He was operating on four hours of sleep but felt amazingly awake and alert. He got up to get ready to head into town. Walter was sleeping on the porch next to him. "Well, Walter, let's get this dog and pony show on the road."

He smiled when Walter raised his head and grunted. The pig missed Petunia. When Jordy fed him this morning, he didn't touch his breakfast. "I'll have her home soon, I promise."

Jordy went into the house. To his surprise, he found Amelia kneading dough to make bread. "What are you making?"

Amelia turned around and smiled. Jordy felt a quiver pierce his heart when he saw the dark circles under her swollen eyes. "I'm going to make a big dinner with homemade bread and all the fixings. I have a good feeling about today. My baby is coming home."

Jordy nodded, trying to sound positive. "I hope so."

"Where are you going?" she asked, returning to her dough.

It was funny how Amelia always knew when he was leaving. Being married for so long made it so. They were like two halves of a whole. "I'm heading into town to put on a happy show."

She frowned. "Do I need to go?"

"No, I think there will be enough people to satisfy the requirement."

"Good. I don't think that I could stomach seeing Henry Lee without killing him with my bare hands." She punched the dough with extra force.

Jordy chuckled. "It would be an interesting sight to see."

Amelia laughed despite herself. "It would be memorable."

Jordy nodded, grabbing his keys off the hook by the door. "I'll be back when the show is over."

"Be careful," she looked up, and all signs of amusement faded.

"Always," he said, kissing her on the cheek before walking to the door.

As he got into the truck, his tempest coiled into life. "Now you decide to awaken."

Starting the truck, he drove to Cesar's house. When he pulled into the driveway, Cesar and Laz were sitting outside. Jordy parked in front of the house and hopped out of the truck. "I'm heading into town. I thought I'd stop and see how things are going."

"Probably no different than at your house," Cesar said, gesturing over his shoulder to the house. "Esme has been crying since yesterday. Then, about an hour ago, she started cooking. Go figure."

Jordy frowned. "That's strange. Amelia is doing the same. She's planning a huge meal."

"Maybe they know something that we don't."

"I talked to Evander…"

"I would have shot that son of a bitch…" Cesar raged.

Jordy put up his hands to halt him. "He had nothing to do with it. He says the kids are ok."

Laz nodded. "See, I told you that this is all Henry. What else did he say? Can he help us?"

Jordy shook his head. "No, he says that Henry has them guarded and that any escape attempt will be met with force. Evander is going to keep an eye on the situation."

Cesar sighed heavily. "You headed to town? Jack stopped here earlier and said we need to go into town and put on a show for those bastards coming."

"Yeah, I'm going to play my part for Petunia."

Cesar nodded. "Well, I might as well go with you. All one happy family, right."

Jordy got behind the wheel of the truck with Cesar climbing into the passenger side and Laz taking the back seat. "Well, here we go," Jordy said, pulling onto the road.

As they entered town, Jordy slowed the truck, hardly able to believe what he was seeing. The town had been transformed into an almost surreal vision of perfection. Vegetable and flower carts lined the sidewalks, their vibrant colors creating a picturesque scene. People stood at strategic spots along the street, smiling brightly, as if posing for a magazine cover of the ideal small-town life. It was a picture-perfect façade, but something about it felt unnervingly staged.

Jordy parked the truck, and they got out, still blown away by the transformation. Sheriff Clancy approached them. "You three, stand by Winslow's drinking a coffee, looking happy."

"Happy," Jordy said with a false smile.

Sheriff Clancy looked around at his choreographed town. "That's right…happy."

Jordy, Cesar, and Laz bought a coffee and stood on the sidewalk as they were instructed. Elma Watkins stood behind the fruit cart, cackling at them. "Ain't this the shit?" she said.

"Yeah, it is the shit," Cesar with the worst fake smile that Jordy ever saw. It was more of a leer than a smile splitting his face.

People around them stood in their assigned spots, all with frozen smiles plastered on their faces. Even the people walking their dogs up and down the sidewalks, some with borrowed dogs had the same stupid smiles on their faces.

"These people coming through town are either stupid, or they want to believe their lying eyes for the money," Laz said with a big grin.

"My bet is on the latter," Jordy said, sipping his prop water that Winslow's was supplying instead of coffee.

"Whatever Henry has going with these guys, it must be big," Cesar said.

"Cartel people, I bet."

"Possibly."

The first of the cars drove by. Jordy snuck a look at them. It was a trio of black-on-black SUVs with no-neck men and stern expressions. "They look tough."

"I'm telling you that they are cartel dudes," Laz said, still wearing a stupid grin.

"Scum," Cesar whispered.

An hour later, another group drove through. The lead car slowed to a stop in front of Winslow's. "How's the coffee?" a man in the backseat asked with a heavy accent.

Jordy looked down into his empty cup and smiled. "It's fantastic," he said, holding up his cup.

The door opened, and a man wearing a black suit got out with two men who looked like bodyguards. He crossed the street, lingering by Elma's fruit cart. Jordy noticed that Sheriff Clancy had come to attention. The man with the shiny shoes reached over and picked up an apple. "How much?" he asked Elma.

Sheriff Clancy stepped up before she could answer. "Oh, help yourself," he said. "Wormwood welcomes you."

The man nodded. "I thank you. Wormwood…" he said, with a quizzical expression creasing his face. "That is from the bible, yes?"

"I… I think so," Sheriff Clancy said.

He turned to Jordy. "I'm sure that I have heard it before. It is from the Bible?"

"Yes, it is," Jordy said. "It's about the third angel."

The man smiled with gleaming white teeth. "I thought so. It is the benefit of a good education. Me, myself, I am not very religious." He made a point of lifting his cuff to check the time on his diamond, encrusted Rolex. "Well, I must be going. Nice town."

Jordy watched him walk back to his car with his men. "Why does it feel like I just talked to the Devil?" His tempest coiled in his gut.

"Maybe you did," Laz said.

Sheriff Clancy gave them a sour look before walking off to check on the rest of his actors. Elma laughed from behind the cart. "Cheap bastard didn't even tip me."

Jordy, Laz, and Cesar laughed. It was going to be a long afternoon.

Chapter 82

It was after five when the town was told that they were relieved from duty by Sheriff Clancy. He drove through town on his way to a celebration dinner at the compound. Jordy watched him as he drove out of town where the roadblocks once stood blocking their way.

"He's a traitor," Cesar growled.

"Yes, of the worst kind," Jordy agreed. "Betraying your own people for the sake of a few dollars is unforgivable."

"He will pay for that once they leave him behind," Laz said, with narrowed eyes not concealing the depth of his hatred.

"We should go. We get to do this whole act again tomorrow." Jordy started walking to his truck when he stopped, not believing his eyes.

Pastor Ezra was coming down the sidewalk towards him. But there was no limping, old man using a cane, or someone being pushed in a wheelchair. The pastor was walking! He stood tall and lean, walking with sure-footed steps in an easy stride. It was like the hands of time had turned back ten years.

Cesar looked to see what Jordy was looking at and made the sign of the cross when he spotted him. "My God," he whispered.

"Pastor, what has happened?" Jordy asked, when the pastor reached him, putting a hand on Jordy's shoulder.

"Jordy, my boy. The time is close."

People gathered around him, not believing he was real. They reach out with tentative hands to touch him, as if not believing what they saw. The pastor smiled at them. It was a warm, familiar smile that they all knew and loved. Jordy sensed that there was something even more different about him. When the pastor placed his hand on his shoulder, he felt the power that once was only a glimmer, now teaming with strength.

"My children," the pastor's voice rang out. "The time is nearly upon us. You must go home and fill anything you have with water. Tonight, the bitter waters will come to Wormwood, snuffing out all the evil that plagues our town. After you have done this, come back here to witness the miracle for yourself."

"But pastor, what is happening?" Lenny Dawson asked in confusion.

Pastor Ezra turned to him. His eyes were limpid pools filled with a light that could only be described as not of this earth. "Now is the time to trust in your faith, Lenny."

He turned and walked back to the parsonage, leaving a crowd of people standing in stunned silence behind him. Whispers filled the air as they exchanged uncertain glances, unsure of how to make sense of what they had just witnessed.

"I don't know about you, but I'm going home and filling everything I have with water," Elma said. "This morning, that man was on death's doorstep. I was waiting for him to take his last breath. Something is happening here."

"Yes, whatever it is, it has to be some sort of miracle," Jack Hadley said. "If anyone needs buckets, come over to the shop."

People snapped out of the confusion they were wrapped into, and immediately acted. Jordy, Cesar, and Laz turned and ran to the truck. "We have those five-hundred-gallon water wagons we can fill," Cesar suggested when they got into the truck.

"I'll get started with the one at my place," Jordy agreed.

"Yeah, we will do the same," Laz said.

When Jordy got home, he and Amelia were filling anything that would hold water. "Any idea how long the water will be bad?" Amelia asked.

"I'm not sure. I'm not even sure this is real. All I know is there is no earthly reason that the pastor should look the way that he does. Something is coming. And I believe it is something big."

"How do we warn the kids at the compound?"

Jordy stopped what he was doing to turn and face her. "We are going to hope that Evander figures it out. We will get to the kids as soon as we can."

"You're placing a lot of faith in Evander."

"I'm placing a lot of faith in everything."

Chapter 83

"Are you sure you don't want to come?" Jordy asked. "I'm staying here in case they release Petunia," Amelia said. Jordy nodded. "I'll be back after this is over. I'm not even sure what will happen."

"What does your gut tell you?"

"Something is going to happen. I don't know what." He felt as if it was destiny at work here. Like he was always meant for it to happen, and he was here for this purpose.

Amelia stroked his cheek gently. "Just be careful, Jordy."

"Always," he said, snatching her hand to place a gentle kiss in her palm. God, how he loved her.

Jordy got behind the wheel of his truck, taking one last look at his beautiful wife, before backing down the driveway. His tempest was coiling tight in his gut, teaming with power. Whatever this was, he would be a part of it. It both frightened and excited him.

When he got to town, everyone was there. He parked, by driving up on a sidewalk because there was no more room on the street. The pastor was standing on the steps of the parsonage, bible in hand.

Jordy threaded his way through the crowd to stand by the statue of the third angel. Cesar and Laz arrived shortly after he did.

"My children," the pastor said in a loud, steady voice. "Tonight, you are here as a witness to a miracle. It is the righteous taking back from evil."

Jordy looked down and spotted the boy from the cornfield. He was sitting beside him at the base of the statue. His dangling legs were swinging his bare feet back and forth. There was an impish grin curling his full lips like he had a secret. But it was the crystalline, blue eyes staring up at him that held his attention. Jordy looked around to see if anyone noticed him. No one did.

The boy hopped down from his perch on the statue and came over, taking Jordy's hand in his. The power jolt was immediate, matched in tempo with his own tempest. The sheer intensity of it buckled Jordy's knees as the power amped up. He wondered then if he was dying as the immense power surged through his body. Then, the boy lifted a golden trumpet to his lips. The sound was deafening. He realized that the sound was coming from inside of him. It got louder and louder, rising in pitch until he thought his head would explode. A great stream of power whooshed from his body like it was blown by a gale force. It rolled and vibrated up into the heavens, making a crackling sound as it thrust through the air.

There was a flash of light that pierced the darkness. It was brighter than the sun and lightning combined. It grew brighter in intensity, forming a ball that rolled in the sky like a giant top spinning above them. With a crack of thunder, the bright, bluish ball hurtled across the night sky in an arc of pure, brilliant light, leaving everyone spellbound. It was like a comet with a long gleaming tail trailing behind. And then it was gone.

When Cesar lifted Jordy to his feet, the boy was gone. "Are you all right, my friend?" Cesar asked, the concern glowed naked in his eyes.

"Yes, I think so," Jordy said, but still was not sure. His ears were still ringing.

"Did you see it?" Laz asked.

Jordy nodded. "I did."

"It was the greatest experience of my life," Cesar said, humbled.

Everyone was looking at Jordy. In their eyes, he saw amazement. "What's happened?" he whispered to Cesar.

"You were glowing, Jordy," Cesar explained gently. "And then there was a flash of light that came from you that streaked into the sky. Soon after, the great blue ball arced across the sky."

Pastor Ezra came to his side. "You asked for a miracle," he said, placing a firm hand on Jordy's shoulder. "Jordy was the vessel that was chosen for the star."

The people around him came up and either hugged him or patted his shoulder. Jordy had worked hard to keep his secret. Now, everyone in town knew. He was not sure how he felt about it. It was like standing naked with all your secrets exposed to the world.

"Are you ok?" Elma asked with uncharacteristic gentleness.

"I think so." Jordy looked at her uneasily.

"Good, always knew there was something about you," she said, cackling.

"You did, hah?" Jordy said, trying to make it less weird.

"It could have been any one of us," Jack Hadley said, hesitating before patting his shoulder.

"Tomorrow, let's bring our children home," Pastor Ezra said, raising his arms victoriously into the air.

Jordy winked at the pastor, silently grateful for shifting the attention away from him. He joined in the cheering with the rest of the crowd. "Daddy's coming, Petunia," he murmured softly.

Chapter 84

"Did you see the comet?" Amelia said when he got home. "Yes, I saw it." "Is that the star that brings the bitter waters?" Brian asked. "I thought it would be bigger."

Jordy nodded. "That is what the pastor thinks."

"When will we know?" Amelia asked.

Jordy sat down; he was exhausted. "It will be soon. I'm heading out tomorrow morning with Cesar and Laz to check out the compound. We will see what we get for a reception from Henry when we get there."

"What if they fight you? "Amelia said, biting her lower lip.

"They have the kids, and that is all the leverage they need. We can't risk any of them getting hurt. If they are able to still fight, we go home and wait."

Amelia nodded. "I wish the town was not just sending you guys."

"We talked and decided it was best to send a small scouting party out there to check things out." Besides, they think that I'm protected by God," Jordy thought to himself grimly.

"It makes sense," Amelia reluctantly agreed.

"Good night, I'm heading to bed," Brian said, stifling a yawn.

When Brian disappeared into his bedroom, Amelia reached across the table and took his hand. "Are you hungry? I made enough to feed a small army."

"Not really." He threaded his fingers through hers.

"Are you going to tell me what really happened tonight?"

"Maybe tomorrow after I get my daughter back."

Amelia smiled at him. "You think this was all real. A true miracle?"

"I know something happened. I felt it."

"Then tomorrow, there will be a celebration. I'm going to start baking." She rose from her chair and went to the counter.

Jordy rolled his eyes. "It's nearly eleven."

"Yes, I know. This will give me plenty of time, then."

Jordy rubbed his face with both hands. "I'm going to sit out on the porch with Walter."

"Good, he will love the company." She made him a sandwich. "Here, you need to eat to keep up your strength."

He took the plate as Amelia was already pulling out baking dishes from the cupboard. He walked outside on the porch and sat in his chair, placing the plate on the small table. Walter got up from his spot and curled himself around his feet. Jordy reached down and patted him on the head. Tomorrow, he would find his daughter and bring her home to her pig. He smiled and took a bite of his sandwich, feeding half of it to Walter.

Chapter 85

Jordy parked next to Cesar's truck in front of Winslow's early the next morning. "Ready for this?" Jordy asked, as Cesar handed him a cup of coffee.

"I'm ready." He sipped his coffee as the crowd gathered around them.

Doc came up and stood beside him as the townspeople gathered. "Now, I'm preparing for mass casualties; just don't you three be a part of that."

Laz chuckled. "Not planning on it."

Doc took his glasses off and wiped them with his hanky. "Just be careful out there. You don't know what you are driving into. Any signs of them looking to fight, you turn around and get your asses back to town."

"That's the plan," Jordy said.

"Sheriff Clancy never returned last night," Jack Hadley said. "I'm not sure what that means, but I hope that bastard took a nice, long gulp of water."

Laz smiled. "Me, too."

"Well, we should get going?" Jordy asked Cesar and Laz.

"Ok, we will follow your lead."

Jordy nodded, getting behind the wheel, and waving to the crowd that had gathered. The people were yelling good luck, as Jordy pulled out, heading down the road to the compound. He had butterflies in his stomach as the nervous anticipation grew inside him. What would they find? He silently prayed that the kids were safe. He accelerated, followed by Cesar, seeing him in his rearview.

He turned off onto the gravel road. The checkpoint up ahead would be the first test. If the guards were there, then this would be a bust. He slowed his speed on the last corner. Here goes nothing, he thought as he took the corner. When he came up to the checkpoint, no one was there. He put his truck in park and got out. Cesar and Laz did the same.

"What do you think?" Cesar asked, looking around.

"It's a good sign." Jordy rocked back on his heels as he looked around. There was only the long, swaying grass in the field beyond the fence.

"Well, let's find out." Laz ducked down under the bar, blocking the road and opened the gate so they could drive through.

Jordy drove slowly through the checkpoint and started down the slope into the compound. There were two guards weaving and stumbling in the driveway like they were drunk. Sleep, he heard a faint voice in his head; the guards collapsed to the ground motionless. Jordy parked the truck in front of Evander's house and got out. Cesar and Laz did the same.

"So, now what?" Cesar asked, looking around apprehensively.

"We go inside and have a look around," Jordy said.

As they started up the steps, they saw a wide-eyed Brooke Porter tied to one of the porch rails with zip ties. There was a dog's color around her neck with a leash. "My God, she's alive," Laz said, handing Cesar the shotgun to rush over to her.

Brooke flinched away from him, sobbing. "No, please. No more."

Laz knelt beside her. "It's ok," he said gently. "I'm not here to hurt you. You remember me, right? I'm Laz from town."

She settled down. "Please, help me," she begged.

Laz pulled out his knife and cut the zip ties. "See, I'm going to take you home."

Brooke wrapped her arms tightly around Laz's neck, clinging to him as if he were her lifeline. Laz gently lifted her into his arms and carried her toward the truck. "It's going to be ok," he kept reassuring her.

"You stay with her," Jordy said. "We are going to keep searching."

Laz nodded, holding the terrified girl. "I'll catch up once she calms down." Brooke was clutching Laz as if her life depended on it and was not going to let him go any time soon.

Cesar and Jordy exchanged glances at the door. "Ready?" Jordy asked.

Cesar raised the shotgun. "Ready."

Jordy swung open the door. There was a body in the hall. It was Sheriff Clancy. He was on his back, with his eyes closed. Jordy knelt to see if he was alive. He was clearly unconscious. "Out cold," he whispered.

They walked into the large dining room, and there were people scattered throughout the room. Henry was passed out on the floor by the table. Jordy and Cesar lingered near his body for a moment.

"I could end him right here," Cesar said, aiming the shotgun at his head.

Jordy pushed the shotgun aside. "He's not worth it."

Cesar nodded. "You're right."

They turned their backs on him and kept searching. All the people were in the same condition as the sheriff in the hallway. Alive but unconscious. Jordy was not a doctor, but a coma came to mind. He wondered if they would ever regain consciousness. Somehow, he doubted it.

"I count at least twenty in here." He touched the tip of his boot to Mr. Rolex's arm. "I don't see Evander or his butler, Simon," Jordy said.

"Let's keep looking. I'm done with being in here."

They walked outside and crossed the yard to the barn. "I don't sense anything bad," Jordy said, before opening the door to the barn.

"Good, keep it that way."

Jordy's fingers blindly searched the wall, finding the switch to turn on the lights. There were vehicles parked inside the barn but no people. "Let's search the other outbuildings. Evander said the kids were in one of them."

"Let's go."

They came to the first building. Inside, they found more unconscious guards. All the men were in the same condition. Alive but deeply unconscious. Cesar walked up to a cage in the corner of the room. "What do suppose they kept in here?"

Jordy grimaced. "My guess, would be Brooke."

"Animals."

"Yes, they are." Jordy felt his desperation rising. If they could do this to an innocent girl, there would be no telling what they did to the children.

They went to the second building. There were empty bunks but no people. "I'm guessing this is where some of the men from inside the house stay," Cesar said.

"Let's see what is behind door number three," Jordy said, walking to the third and final building.

They opened the door. This building was different. The front of the building had a makeshift guard station. It was empty. He exchanged glances with Cesar as he walked to the door behind the guard station and listened. He heard children laughing. His heart soared as he opened the door.

Chapter 86

The kids were on the floor playing games with Simon. They were laughing. Food wrappers littered the floor, along with discarded water bottles. Petunia was sitting on Evander's lap as he read to her from her book. When Petunia and Jose spotted Jordy and Cesar, they ran to their fathers with wide open arms.

"Daddy!"

Jordy picked up Petunia and hugged her tight. His eyes glazed as he mouthed thank you to Evander. "Daddy, Uncle Evander has been reading to me," Petunia said, laughing. "I need to tell you a secret."

"What is it?" Jordy said, smiling.

"I think he is tired of the book," she whispered. "He looked like he was in pain when I asked him to read it a billion times." She giggled, looking over her shoulder at Evander.

Evander rose from his chair and walked over to them. Simon kept playing with the kids, making them laugh. "Who knew that these kids have so much energy," Evander said, stretching. "So, is it all clear? We checked a while ago, but there were still two guards roaming around."

"Have you been out here all night with them?" Cesar asked, holding his son.

Evander nodded. "I saw the asteroid and figured sh…stuff was happening. Simon and I grabbed the bottled water and some snacks and headed out here while the party was happening at the house."

Cesar slapped him on the back and laughed. "You are a brave man to do a sleepover with twenty kids."

Evander glanced at Simon and shrugged. "I had no idea how good he is with kids. Who knew?"

"Well, let's get out of here," Jordy said, looking at Petunia. "You want to go home and see your mom?"

Petunia nodded. "Did you take care of Walter?"

"I did, but he misses you."

"Of course, he does, Daddy," she said matter-of-fact.

Jordy laughed. "Let's go." He reluctantly let Petunia down so she could run after Simon and the other kids.

"I thought there would be more here," Cesar said, looking around.

"More?" Evander said, frowning.

Cesar looked skeptical. "You know, more than a bunch of empty outbuildings."

Evander chuckled. "Like what, a crack lab?"

"Maybe," Cesar said defensively. "What exactly does Henry do?"

"Henry is a very dangerous man with many talents," Evander said, pausing inside the barn. "He's a major league smuggler and drug trafficker. His claim to fame is that he can move anything from gun shipments to diamonds and everything in between."

"So, why was it so important to control the town?" Jordy asked. He had sensed that Henry was into very bad stuff, but it always made him wonder why it was necessary to clamp down on the town.

Evander nodded in understanding. "Well, another one of Henry's skills is that he is an enforcer. Henry comes in and takes complete control. These people trust Henry with millions in products. What would it say about a super badass that can't control a small town of farmers?"

"I get it," Jordy said.

"You do?" Cesar asked.

"He has to make it seem that the town is complicit and under his control for cover." Jordy thought about how darkly twisted it was for a man to go to such lengths to satisfy his need for control.

Evander smiled at Jordy. "That sounds about right."

"How did you get mixed up with him?" Jordy asked.

There was a far-off look in Evander's eyes as he watched the children playing tag with Simon around the sleeping guards in the yard. He let out a heavy sigh. "Let's call it guilt by association, but no longer. He did me a favor once. I was repaying the debt by letting him stay here."

Jordy sensed there was more to the story. "In the end, you did the right thing. That is all that counts."

"How are we going to get the kids home?" Cesar said, frowning. "They will never all fit in our trucks."

"I'll take them in the big truck," Evander said. "I'm going to need a place to stay for a while. My house is a crime scene."

"After what you did, you can stay with me," Jordy said, as Petunia ran up to him. "Wouldn't that be nice, Petunia? Evander can read to you whenever you like."

Evander rolled his eyes. "Gee, thanks. But if the offer is there, I'll take it. I'll get a camper and bring it to your house until this gets straightened out."

Jordy laughed as he picked up Petunia to hug her close. "Let's go home."

"Daddy, can I ride with Uncle Evander in the big truck?" Petunia asked with that pout that always melted his heart.

"Me, too," Jose said, begging his father.

Jordy didn't want to let her go, but in the end, he relented. "Yes, you can ride with Uncle Evander."

Evander grinned. "This uncle thing is growing on me."

They walked out of the barn with all the kids waiting in the yard. Evander pulled the big truck out of the barn, and they loaded the kids in the back with Uncle Simon. It was hard to believe the snooty butler was the same man. He sat in the back bed of the truck, surrounded by laughing children, loving every minute of it. Evander drove with Petunia in the cab passenger seat beside him. All the way home, he was blowing the air horn.

Jordy kept looking back at them in the rearview mirror. He saw Cesar following and laughing whenever the horn blew. As they entered town, the crowd gathered. Each tearful parent was pulling their reluctant children from the back of the truck. Children have a way of coping and finding joy in the simple things, Jordy thought. A ride in a big truck or playing games with people who truly care for them seemed to make the world less scary. And then there was Brooke…

Laz carried her into Doc's office for privacy. She was still clinging to him for dear life. She was alive but had a long road to recovery ahead of her. Doc came over to Jordy to watch as people were gathered around Simon and Evander.

"He really came through, didn't he?" Doc asked.

Jordy nodded. "He did. There is a real mess at the compound."

"What am I looking at?" Doc said, as Jack Hadley joined them.

"Maybe thirty unconscious people. Some in the house and others in an outbuilding."

Doc groaned. "I'm calling in for help from Dalton Emergency Services. I'm going with contaminated well water because they would never believe it was divine intervention."

Jordy chuckled. "I don't suppose they would."

"I have bad news for you. We found Pastor Ezra this morning. He's dead, and from the state of the body, he died sometime yesterday morning."

Jordy frowned. "But he was there last night."

Doc shrugged. "Don't ask me to explain the impossible."

"He'll be happy to be with his wife again," Jack said. "I know how much he missed her, but I'm sorry to see him go."

"He will be missed," Jordy said solemnly. "I think he hung on just long enough to get the kids back."

"If you will excuse me, I need to get things rolling at the compound after I take a look at Brooke," Doc said.

"Hold up, Doc, I'll give you a hand," Jack said, slapping Jordy on the back before turning to follow Doc.

Jordy waited for people to start to dissipate with their children before feeling it was time to go home to his anxious wife. "What do you say we go home?" he said to Petunia.

Petunia nodded. "Walter needs me."

"Yes, he does. So does Mom." He playfully chucked her under her chin.

Evander exchanged glances with him and smiled. "I'm going to arrange for the trailer, and I'll meet you home later."

Jordy smiled when Evander called the farm home. The word warmed him, chasing away the last of his anxiety. It was over. Now, life could return to normal. Normal. Such a simple word that holds so much meaning.

He got behind the wheel with Petunia sitting beside him. As he drove, he glanced at her. Petunia was so perfect in every way. He would see her graduate from high school, get married, and one day, she would have her own family. She turned and looked at him, grinning, her hand stretched out the window, catching the air.

When he pulled into the driveway, Amelia and Brian were waiting for them on the porch with Walter. As soon as he parked the truck, Amelia pulled open the passenger side door and took Petunia out, wrapping her arms around her. Tears were falling down her cheeks as she looked up and met Jordy's eyes. The love he saw there brought tears to his eyes. This is what made life so special. The love of family and the bond that comes with it was all he needed.

Chapter 87

Everyone in town stood around the tree set up at the center of town, waiting for the tree lighting ceremony to begin. Jordy stood next to Amelia, with her arm through his. "It's cold tonight," she whispered. "It could snow."

"Maybe," Jordy said, pulling her closer to keep her warm.

Amelia nudged him, gesturing towards Petunia, proudly walking her pig wearing the red ribbon Christmas collar that she had made him. "Her and that pig go everywhere together."

Jordy chuckled. "They are bonded."

Amelia looked up at him. "I was going to tell you this tonight, but it's so pretty here, standing near the tree. How would you feel about having another baby?"

"A baby?" Jordy looked down at her.

"I'm pregnant. Nearly three months." She looked up at him, all the love shining in her eyes.

Jordy picked her up and kissed her. "I love that."

"Me, too," she said, smiling at him.

He gently set her back on the ground, scanning the scene, wondering if everyone here felt as content as he did. Cesar and his family stood nearby, with Esme giving him a knowing smile—no doubt she was aware of Amelia's secret. Laz stood beside Brooke, rarely apart from her, and she seemed happier each day, as if each moment was better than the last.

Phil and Brooke's brother came out of hiding. He was trying to patch things up with Bree, but that was going to take some time. She was still furious with him, but Jordy saw signs the ice was starting to thaw between them. He hoped so for the kid's sake. In the spring, the town was going to gather to do a house raising for all those who lost their homes. Bree's was scheduled to be the first.

Pastor Elma stepped up to the podium. "Welcome Wormwood to our annual tree lighting. Tonight, instead of hearing me blather, I think it was fitting to hand this over to Jordy Hart. He has something he wants to tell you."

Jordy exchanged looks with Amelia before walking to the podium. "Hi everyone. First, I was told by Sheriff Jack Hadley, that the investigation is finally over at the compound. Officials feel that contaminated well water caused irreversible comas to people at the compound. The star of Wormwood was a coincidence and was just an asteroid. But we know better. Don't we? Science can't explain it away. We got our miracle. Henry and his crew will never bother us or anyone ever again." Jordy paused as people clapped. He slipped his hand inside his pocket, pulled out a letter, and opened it. "Shortly before Pastor Ezra left us, he gave me this letter. He wanted me to read it to you…" He paused, taking a shaky breath. "To my children,

I wish I could be there tonight, but God has called me home. My lovely wife has waited long enough, too. So, this is not a goodbye, but more like until I see you again. Wormwood is a special place. It is rare to find a town where people truly love and care for one another. It is a place where faith is strong, resilient, and everlasting. So, my children, take care and be kind to one another. Hold God close to your heart, and know I'll be watching out for you. May God be with you. Love, Pastor Ezra."

The crowd repeated, "May God be with you," turning to shake their neighbor's hand while brushing back tears.

"With that, I'll give this back to Pastor Elma," Jordy said, walking away to join his family.

"Well, it's time to light the tree. Gather round." When everyone was close, Elma flipped the switch, and the tree was lit with hundreds of lights, making the town glow. "Merry Christmas!"

Everyone cheered. There was the sound of jingling bells that drew their attention coming from down the road. Evander drove into town on a tractor wearing a Santa's hat. He was towing a trailer with Simon dressed as an elf, surrounded by at least one hundred gift-wrapped packages. The children ran to Evander, laughing and squealing.

"I'll bet that tractor is brand new," Jed grumbled.

"Likely," Jordy said, smiling. "Rock and roll Santa returns."

"I can't picture him as a farmer," Cesar said, shaking his head.

"I don't know, I think he will do fine." Jordy laughed at Jed's sour expression.

"Sheep, he bought sheep. Q-Tip's with legs." Jed snorted. "If you ask me, he is off to a bad start."

Cesar threw back his head and laughed as they all walked down the sidewalk to watch Evander play Santa. Jordy walked hand and hand with Amelia, laughing at Simon, dressed as an elf, complete with pointed ears, as he called out every child by name to hand out the gifts. In his head, Jordy heard a voice whisper, snow. Big, fluffy flakes floated gently down from the sky. "Perfect," he whispered to Amelia.